PLAYING PATIENCE

Playing Patience

Playing Patience/Tabatha Vargo
Editing services provided by Cassie McCown/Gathering Leaves.
Cover Art by Regina Wamba/Mae I Design and Photography
Formatting by Inkstain Interior Book Designing

ISBN-13: 978-1482768954
ISBN-10: 148276895X

BOOK 1 IN THE *BLOW HOLE BOYS* SERIES

PLAYING PATIENCE

USA TODAY BESTSELLING AUTHOR

TABATHA VARGO

ALSO BY

TABATHA VARGO

THE CHUBBY GIRL CHRONICLES

On the Plus Side

Hot and Heavy-Coming Soon!

THE BLOW HOLE BOYS

Playing Patience (Zeke)

Perfecting Patience 1.5 (Zeke)

Finding Faith (Finn)

Convincing Constance (Tiny)—Coming Soon!

Having Hope (Chet)—Coming Soon!

www.tabathavargo.blogspot.com
www.facebook.com/tabathadvargo
www.twitter.com/tabathavargo

To all the broken ones,
may you find the soul that binds you.

PROLOGUE

THERE'S A PLACE YOU LAND right before you hit rock bottom, a sort of cushion before the blow. It's full of fresh air that fills your deprived lungs and so much light that even in its darkest corners it warms your skin. This place prepares you for your plunge, holds you in its calming presence and rocks you softly. Zeke was that place for me. He was like a rainbow in my black-and-white movie, a soothing touch against jagged scars.

And then I reached the bottom.

As I stood over the lifeless body of a man who didn't deserve the peace that death would bring, I knew I was no longer the girl I used to be. The broken parts of me were on the mend and his soul was the glue that would hold them all together.

ONE
ZEKE

I EXHALED A STREAM OF smoke, and a rib-rattling cough took hold of me. My chest ached and my lungs sizzled. The burn in my throat intensified and then relaxation began to seep into my pores. The smoke-filled space swam before my glazed eyes as I melted into Finn's ripped leather couch. The couch separated the band space from the rest of his junky garage.

"If you don't cough, you don't get off," Finn said as I passed him the joint. "So what happened with Ashley?" He took a hit. The tip of it lit up and crackled. "Did she blow you or what?" His voice was strained as he struggled to hold in the smoke before he finally blew it out and hit it again.

"I don't want her mouth anywhere near my junk. Did you see that nasty blister on her lip last week? She tried, but I wasn't having it."

"Can't blame you there. You need to get laid, dude. It's been two weeks since that freak at The Pit. What was her name again?" He lifted his legs and dropped his heavy, mud-covered boots onto the coffee table in front of his couch.

"I dunno. I didn't ask." I shrugged.

I strummed my guitar as I tried to tune it.

"Lucky son-of-bitch. You always get the ones that disappear. I get stuck with clingy bitches. Remember that one last summer that followed me around for a month? Damn, she was a good lay, though." He took a swig from his beer and shook his head at the memory. "Anyway, I say get a piece of ass before this weekend's gig. You play better when your balls aren't in a bunch."

He passed the joint back to me. The smoke filled my lungs as I hit it hard, held it, and then exhaled.

"Yeah, we'll see."

I wasn't feeling it. Too much shit was going on around me and I was getting burnt out on the same old slutty girls.

Once the rest of the guys got there, we practiced for two hours before everyone split and went home for the night. After throwing my guitar case in the back of my rusted El Camino, I drove around for the next hour. My old man didn't usually pass out until eleven, so I knew better than to go home before then.

After a good amount of time, I rolled my car into my yard and cut the engine. All the lights in our single-wide trailer were out, but I could see the flicker of the TV in the front window. Falling asleep in front of the TV was my dad's thing.

Drizzle splattered against my cracked windshield and streams of dirty rainwater started to run down my windows. My boots sank into the softening dirt when I got out of my car, which meant the yard would be a muddy mess in the morning.

A stray cat ran from underneath the bottom step as I walked across the small stretch of front yard from my car to the front porch. Dad's tow truck was parked sideways in the rocky driveway and the cat disappeared under it.

I crept up the broken, wooden steps and stuck my key in the doorknob. The hollow aluminum door begged for some WD-40 as it creaked when I opened it. The door would be my demise one day since it seemed to love waking my dad. The rotting plywood porch buckled under my weight before I stepped into the smoke-filled space.

The scent of beer, Marlboro Red's, and motor oil filled my nostrils. I slipped through the cluttered living room to the hallway that went to my side of the trailer. Dad was passed out in my mom's old mauve recliner. The lights from the TV screen danced across his greasy face. He still had on his dirty work clothes and the bottle in his hand was bent just enough so the matted shag carpeting was getting sprinkled with beer when he breathed out. The ashtray next to him was full of ashes, cigarette butts, and beer.

I didn't bother turning off the TV. I didn't want to risk waking him. Instead, I skulked through the trailer to my bedroom. I was careful to step over the part of hallway where the floor was weak. There was a leak in the bathroom a few years back that ruined the floor and left the lingering stench of mildew right in front of my bedroom. It made living there ten times worse and did nothing to squash the hate I had for the place.

Peeling off my jacket, I stripped down to my boxers. The heater in our trailer was shit, so my room had a lingering chill that only my mom's tattered wool blanket could cut. I turned my radio on low volume and fell onto my bed.

Outside I could hear our neighbors arguing in Spanish and a baby crying. Far off in the distance there were police sirens and the sounds of breaking glass. The interstate was just on the other side of the fence from my place, so the sound of speeding cars was endless. For many years this had been the place I called home. I had a hard time falling asleep in total silence after years of noise pollution to rock me goodnight.

I was dozing off when I heard the loud thump of my dad closing the recliner with his legs. The trailer shifted under his heavy footfalls as he made his way down the hallway to my room. I braced myself for the attack when he plowed through my bedroom door. A dim light lit the space when he flipped the switch. I silently wished he'd just do it in the dark. That way I didn't have to see his fists coming for me.

"Where the hell you been? Did you take money out of my wallet?" He stared down at me with drunken, red eyes.

I didn't respond. There was no need to deny taking the money. He didn't care whether or not I took it; he just wanted a reason to hit something. I knew the feeling all too well. I curled up and protected my face and stomach. His fists invaded the flesh on my arms and occasionally made it through my shield to my face. There were a few hits to my ribs until, finally, he was satisfied and left. Thankfully, he was drunk. He was weaker and slower with a case of beer under his belt. Usually the beatings were worse, but I never fought back even though I could easily whip his ass.

It wasn't fear that kept me from beating him within an inch of his life. It was a promise I made to my dying mother. Every time I thought about lifting my fist and putting it through his face, I'd hear her soft voice asking me to let it go.

"He's a good man and he loves you. He's just got a lot on his plate right now," she'd say as she iced my face.

There was once a time when she took the beatings, but when the cancer came he transferred his rage to me. I was glad to take it—better me than her.

Bruised ribs or black eyes were such a natural occurrence for me that I hardly even noticed them anymore. It was shitty to think I could get my ass kicked once a week and it was nothing, just another day.

I fell asleep with blood on my pillow from my nose and aching ribs.

The next day at school I sported a black eye. I was always fighting, so no one paid any attention to my shiner. It wasn't that I started fights purposely, but people pissed me off easily. Usually my fights took place after a run-in with my dad. I knew deep down it was my way of fighting him back, except it wasn't him I was fighting; it was a football playing jock, or some shitfaced old guy at The Pit.

"I hope his face looks worse than yours," Chet said. He leaned his head back and made smoke rings as he exhaled.

"Do you doubt me?" I lifted a brow in question.

"No doubt. I've seen you in action, bro. I bet he's unrecognizable. Anybody I know?" He flicked his cigarette at Principal William's parked car.

"Nah, just some asshole from my neighborhood." I stuck my hands in my pockets and leaned against the light pole. "We practicing at Finn's place tonight?" I changed the subject.

"Yeah, Finn's got some new shit he wants us to work on. He said around seven."

Finn, the lead singer of our band, Blow Hole, was older than the rest of us by four years. We all knew him; he'd failed school so much that he was only a year ahead of us before he finally dropped out. He still lived in his mom's house. The junky garage became our hangout and we called it the Blow Hole since you could walk in and score a line of coke at any given moment. The name somehow transferred to our band and that's what we've called ourselves ever since.

Somehow Chet and I had managed to make it to senior year. We were both a year behind where we should be, but we were still there. I wanted to quit, but staying in school was another promise my mom had managed to pull out of me with her dying breaths. So come hell or high water, I was at school every day. Whether or not I went to class was a completely different story.

Later that night, we practiced an extra hour at Finn's house. We were three days away from our gig at The Pit and we'd added a new song to the mix. Mostly, we covered songs to get the crowd going, but every now and again we'd throw in an original track.

My fingers ached from playing the guitar so hard for so long. I had to admit we sounded badass. Chet was on the drums and Tiny could play a bass guitar like his life depended on it, but it was Finn who ran the show. He was one hell of a front man and our name was slowly spreading.

When I finally stumbled into my house that night, Dad was already in bed. I fell into a fitful sleep while the neighbors cussed each other in Spanish and the interstate traffic played its familiar lullaby.

After that, the week flew by in a haze of getting high and playing in Finn's garage. It wasn't long until we were setting up for our Friday night Pit show. The stage was small, but it was our favorite place to play. The crowd was wild and a lot of the people came out just for us.

The Pit couldn't have been named more perfectly. It was a large, concrete, underground space. It looked like a vandalized parking garage with a bar, a stage, and a bathroom. The owner allowed graffiti as long as it didn't look like shit, so the concrete walls were covered in large, colorful pieces of art and jagged words. There was even a special spot on the far wall with our band's name in red and black.

After we set up and the horde came rolling in, we played our asses off. The crowd went wild after my guitar solo as Finn belted out a Chevelle song. Tiny, who was at least three hundred pounds, hit the room hard with his bass playing. I looked back at Chet who was playing the drums. He was so high his eyes were thin slits on his face. He nodded at me with a smile, tossed his drumstick in the air, and then brought it down hard. It was a damn good night.

After an hour of playing, we took a break.

"Watch my strings," I said to Finn as I set down my guitar by his mic.

I drank more when I played and I was going to spill over if I didn't take a piss. I cut across the crowded space as the DJ took over and blasted loud techno music. The place lit up in laser lights while the dance floor crawled with dancers that jumped up and down, wigged out of their minds.

"You sounded good up there, Zeke," some random chick said as I walked by.

She reached out and boldly grabbed my ass. This was a normal thing for me and nothing caught me off guard with the girls at The Pit. I turned and was met by a hot redhead with cleavage spilling out of a too-small top. Most of the redheads I'd had were wildcats under the covers, so I was definitely down if she wanted to play later. I leaned in to make sure she could hear me over the loud music.

"Nice tits." I grinned down at her as I ran a finger across her bulging cleavage. There was a jagged tattoo just under her lacy bra line that I wanted to have a look at. "Meet me beside the stage later."

I wasn't asking. I was telling. My blunt nature was something I was known for and that suited me just fine. Dishonesty wasn't my thing and I was born without a filter around my brain. Anything that crossed my mind came out of my mouth, whether it was hurtful or not. The no-filter thing initiated some pretty bad fights in my life. It also didn't help that I had no idea how to bite my tongue.

I pushed on the black door to the bathroom. There were no men's or women's; there was just this room with stalls lining one wall, urinals on the other, and a single sink with a smudged, cracked mirror. It wasn't a hygienic place, yet there were still times when you'd walk in on some dude wall-banging the shit out of some chick. It was no big deal to take a piss next to a couple going at it.

I zipped up my jeans and went to the sink to rinse my hands. There was never soap in the dispenser so I didn't bother. Using my shirt as a towel, I turned to go. A flash of white stood out against the grimy wall and I stopped in my tracks when I noticed a miniscule blond girl balled up in the corner. She was rocking back and forth with her knees drawn up to her chin. Her platinum locks were plastered to her sweaty face and her glazed, red eyes rolled back in her head.

I knew a geeked-out broad when I saw one. I'd probably find out tomorrow that some chick overdosed in the bathroom. It's happened often, but no one really paid attention, so neither did I when I turned and walked away. The least I could do was stop by the bar and let someone know she was in there before I got back on stage.

Before I could make it to the door, she spoke.

"Please help me." Her voice shivered.

She had a soft voice. Not raspy and deep like most women I knew. They all smoked, and hacking up a lung had changed their voices. Instead, her voice was smooth and as small as she was. I turned back to her and she looked up at me with glistening blue eyes. They weren't rolling back in her head anymore; now they were wide in fear.

It was then that I took in her clothes—khaki pants and a white button-up collared shirt. Definitely not the low-cut jeans and high-cut tops the girls I knew wore. She had clean fingernails and no makeup.

How had I not noticed her there before? She stuck out like a whore in church. Except in this case it was the direct opposite. She stuck out like an angel in hell.

Either way, I wasn't going to be fooled. She was probably some rich bitch that came to The Pit for a fix and hid it from her wealthy friends, but then again, it was the loaded ones that had the best shit. Again, I wondered what she was doing in such a vile place, wrapped in all that innocence.

"Please," she whispered. "Something's wrong with me."

She slid up the ceramic tiles and then used the wall to hold herself up.

The stage and my band were calling me. I didn't have time for this shit. I needed to walk out, let the bartender know some chick was fucked up in the bathroom, and then get back to my guitar. Except, the more I looked down at her, the more I knew I wouldn't be able to just walk away. Something about her seemed legit and part of me knew she wasn't here to score drugs.

It wasn't in my nature to give a shit, so it made me angry that I kind of did. I didn't want to see this chick get hurt and she would, since she was obviously out of her element.

"Shit," I growled as I closed the distance between us.

She flinched like I was going to hurt her when I lifted my hands to her face. Her flinch angered me. I'd never hurt a female, but I imagine I did look scary to this petite, straight-laced girl. Her pale skin got whiter and started to blend with her sandy strands of hair. Her baby-blue eyes took on a whole new fear as I moved in closer and used my fingers to open her eyelids wider.

Upon closer inspection, I could see that her bloodshot eyes were severely dilated. Empty black dots surrounded by a sea of blue swam inside her eye sockets. She was definitely on something.

"What did you take?" I asked roughly.

She looked at me like I was insane. Her silky forehead puckered in confusion.

"I didn't take anything, I swear," she slurred.

"Did anybody give you anything, maybe a piece of candy or something powdery?"

My fingers slid down her face to the side of her neck to check her pulse and she stiffened. As I suspected it would be, her heart was beating too slowly. She was tripping on something and her body wasn't taking kindly to it, either.

"No, no one gave me anything." She was starting to freak out.

"Then I don't know what to tell you." I turned to walk away.

I didn't have time for this and my bullshit limit had been reached.

"Wait." She reached out and grabbed my arm. She jerked her hand back like it was on fire.

"What?" I sighed.

Damn, I was getting aggravated. There were people outside waiting for me to finish a set and here I was fucking around with some little white-haired pixie.

"A guy at the bar gave me a drink." She looked at me with crazed eyes. "I thought he just got it from the bartender. It was really sweet, but it tasted fine. I don't think there was anything it in. I would have tasted it, right?"

"Great, just fucking great." I threw my hands up in aggravation. "You got spiked."

I leaned my head back and ran my hands roughly down my face. This was just what I needed.

She reached out and laid her hand on my arm. I looked down at her fingers. The contrast between my tan, tattooed skin and her perfectly manicured, pale fingers was shocking.

"Am I going to be okay?" she asked in a panic. "Should I go to a hospital? My friend, the one who brought me... I can't find her. She wanted the drummer and now I can't find her. Please don't leave me."

Her chest heaved as she began to hyperventilate. She leaned her head down, allowing her hair to come around her shoulders. It was much longer than it looked from straight on. Reaching up, she pushed her hair from her face. She was on the verge of a major breakdown.

With her hair out of her face, I got a better look at her. My eyes were met with soft, untouched skin and flushed cheeks. She had a tiny nose and slightly slanted eyes. She looked foreign, all pale with naturally platinum hair, not the box-dyed white that chicks liked to use. She reminded me of a tiny snowflake fairy.

Shaking my brain and alleviating the crazy thoughts, the situation at hand came back to me.

"I'll go get you some help," I said as I turned to walk away again.

She reached out once more and grabbed my arm. Her fingers weren't as soft as before. Instead, they dug desperately into my forearm. Her mouth gapped open like she was about so say something and then her eyes rolled back in her head. I had to catch her when she fainted in my arms.

TWO
PATIENCE

I SNUGGLED INTO MY SHEETS and sighed as my tingling muscles finally relaxed. I'd practiced extra hard in hopes that I'd come home, shower, and pass out. The burn in my calves told me I'd overdone it, but it felt good to push myself. Soccer was the only thing I was in control of. In a life as secretly chaotic as mine, that small ounce of power was welcomed.

I rolled onto my side and stuffed my arm under my pillow. My eyes fluttered as I started to fall asleep, but they popped back open at the tiny sound. A door opened down the hallway and then I heard the soft click of it closing. The hairs on my arms stood up like a frightened cat. He was coming to see me. I was exhausted, but there was nothing I could do. All I could do was lie still and pray that it went by fast.

It happened more frequently now that I was older. When I was younger it was maybe once a month, but these days it was quickly becoming our weekly ritual, a sick ritual that I'd gotten to know well over the years.

My bedroom door creaked open and I rolled over onto my back. My full-sized mattress squeaked as his heavy weight joined mine. Cold air rushed over my legs as he casually folded my comforter back. I said nothing and lifted my hips as he pulled my nightshirt up and worked my panties down my legs.

His fingertips brushed the inside of my thighs and tickled my bald private areas. He requested that I always shave my pubic hair. I was probably the only seventeen-year-old girl in school that got waxed weekly.

I opened my legs wider as he positioned himself on top of me. He pushed my hair to the side and leaned down to kiss my cheek as he slowly entered me. I hated the feel of his slimy lips on my face. There was the normal burn of my dry skin against his before my body finally gave in.

It was at that point that I'd mentally zone out. I'd close my eyes and replay the day over in my head. I'd go through any plays I'd missed at practice and check off the list of things I needed to do before practice the next day. I'd think about any upcoming games and the rival teams we were going to play. I'd toss around scores and points and estimate what the points for the next game would be.

Far away, I could hear my headboard bump into the wall in his normal rhythm. In the distance, there was the echo of his hard breathing and faintly I could feel his hot breath against my neck. The music my mattress made under us was a song I'd memorized. It always started out as a slow tune that quickened as the minutes went by until finally he'd sing and the mattress became quiet.

He pulled out of me and cold air filled my emptiness. He ran his hand down my leg as he tugged my nightshirt back down. Then I felt his lips brush my forehead.

"Goodnight, sweetheart," he whispered against my skin.

"Goodnight," I rasped.

I lay there for an hour before sleep finally took me away. Only when I was asleep was I able to really breathe. Only in the unconscious moments of my deep dreams was I able to open myself up and allow relaxation to truly seep into me. Sometimes, I secretly prayed for an eternal sleep—one where there is no pain and *he* didn't exist.

The next morning I got up early enough to take a long shower. The hot water washed away the night before as I scrubbed my body raw. My skin was pink and lined with scratches from my loofah. I could never get clean enough. For years, I'd tried to clean myself, but somehow I was still so dirty. I could remember begging my mom for baths when I was nine. She used to laugh and tell her friends I was the cleanest child she knew. If only she knew how soiled I really was.

I washed my hair twice before finally getting out, brushing my teeth, and then getting dressed for school. I skipped breakfast so I could avoid the kitchen and waited on the front porch for my ride. I had a car, but he bought it for me. I'd rather walk to school than go near the gray, four-door Toyota. Instead, I pretended I was afraid to drive and hitched a ride with my best friend, Megan.

Her white Honda Civic jerked as she pulled into my driveway. Why her parents bought her a stick shift, I'd never know.

"Hey, rock star! Nice goal yesterday," she said as I hopped into the warmth of her car.

"Thanks. We're going to kick ass this weekend," I said proudly.

I set my book bag on the floorboard between my feet and pushed my snowy hair from my face. Megan looked over at me with big, brown, puppy dog eyes and I knew she was going to ask me for something I didn't want to give up. She picked at her short, black pixie hair, and then popped her gum.

"Okay, so I know you don't usually do the party scene, but there's a bangin' party going down this weekend at The Pit. I can get us in since my sister used to sleep with the guy that watches the door. He's like forty or something and Melanie was our age when it happened. We have to go, Pay. Please say you'll go. Blow Hole's playing and you know I got a thing for Chet." She applied lip gloss, and then rubbed her lips together.

A car honked at us when she went into the other lane. She paid attention to everything but the road. I dug my fingers into the dash.

"No, you have a thing for drummers. Why can't we just watch movies at your house this weekend like we planned?" I whined.

"I promise you'll have fun. Just do me a solid and go. I'll owe you big." Her car jerked into the school parking lot, then skidded to an abrupt stop in the closest empty space.

No way was I getting out of going to The Pit with Megan, no matter how hard I tried. I'd never been, but I'd heard horror stories about wild girls with their faces pierced shut who were half naked. In a place like that, I'd be the one to stick out. My white-blond hair would fit in, except mine was natural, while most girls with my hair color got it done at a salon. At least if I went I wouldn't have to see my dad if I stayed out too late. Anything that kept me away from him was a good thing.

I stayed late at practice and joined everything possible at school. I had the schedule of four girls and most nights I fell into bed and passed out. It was my survival plan, the way I made it through life. Outsiders would never know that behind closed doors my life was hell. I was well liked and a soccer star, but I was a broken porcelain doll, cracked beyond repair and tossed in the back of a closet.

All eyes turned to Megan when we walked into Pinewood Prep. She stuck out like a sore thumb with her jacked-up plaid skirt and the addition of a really cute hot pink tie to replace the boring navy blue. In a sea of boring grays and navy, her tiny pops of color were welcomed by my eyes.

I remember when she came to school with her new nose piercing. I thought it was adorable and I envied her freedom, but everyone practically hissed at her as we walked down the hallway. Megan couldn't care less. She walked that hallway like she owned it, with her head held high and a secretive grin on her face. She loved the attention, while I was perfectly fine with blending in. The only place I didn't blend in was on the soccer field. It was my kingdom. Even though I was usually the tiniest girl on the field, I dominated.

I spent the rest of the week tutoring after school and then I followed that up with soccer practice. On the days

I didn't practice, I'd hit the gym and work out until I thought my body would collapse. I'd stumble into the house around nine at night, shower, and stay in the bathroom until eleven, and then when I thought the coast was clear, I'd go to my room.

On Friday, I went straight to Megan's after school and told my parents I was staying the night there. I was sure to pack an overnight bag complete with something to wear to The Pit. I somehow thought that wearing my school uniform wouldn't fly. Although, some sick people get off on the schoolgirl look... I would know.

"Damn, Pay, check you out with your cute little body. Girl, what you been doin'?" Megan said as we got dressed to go out.

"Just soccer and the gym." I shrugged.

"Who knew you had all *that* hiding under that God-awful uniform?" She motioned at my half-naked body. "If I were you, I'd go naked all day." She laughed.

"You'd go naked all day if you weren't me." I snickered.

Megan's low-cut jeans showed her deep, pelvic bones and her top was well above her belly button. Her cute belly button piercing housed a cherry charm that dangled low. Her cropped hairstyle was spiked and picked at wildly and she went the extra step of putting black eyeliner on top of her eyelids. She looked hot and I felt under dressed.

I settled on a pair of semi-tight khaki pants and a white button-up shirt. I left two of the buttons undone so I could at least pretend to not be a tight ass. Megan tried to talk me into some of her wild clothes, but the thought of showing more skin than I already was made me feel nauseated. Men looking at me in general made me nauseated. I was a sick girl mentally and no one knew it.

While Megan had her hair and makeup done, I let my pale hair hang and ran a quick brush through it. I used some lip gloss and that was the extent of my makeup.

"You don't need makeup anyway," Megan said as I slid the gloss on.

We said a quick good-bye to her mom, who was quite possibly the coolest parent alive, and then we made our way to the other side of town. Soon, the large, white houses were behind us and we were surrounded by broken-down buildings and trailer parks. I reached up and locked my door, which earned me an eye roll from Megan.

We pulled into a full parking lot that had no buildings around it.

"We're here," she said as she pulled up her emergency brake.

Looking around in confusion, I lifted a brow at her.

"Um, there's nothing here, just a bunch of abandoned cars."

She laughed loudly. "Follow me, silly girl."

I stayed close to her as I followed her to the edge of the parking lot. A set of concrete stairs went down into the darkness. The Pit was giving a whole new meaning to the words *underground club.*

As we went down the stairs, we slowly became surrounded by a concrete tunnel. The tunnel led us to a large opening where a man with his arms crossed sat on stool in front of the main entrance. The music coming from the other side of the bright-red metal door vibrated the filthy floor beneath my feet and put waves in the bottle of soda sitting next to him.

"Hey, Gerald." Megan gave him a toothy smile. "I assumed there'd be no problems getting me and my girl in?" She motioned to me.

She had him by the balls and he knew it. Either he could let us in or she'd squeal about his sleeping with a minor years before. Megan didn't say those words, but he knew what she meant. He looked me over and then shook his head and sighed. He didn't even bother checking our IDs as he waved us in.

"I should've never touched her," he muttered. "Damn complicated women."

Megan shot him a shit-eating grin as we passed him and went through the door.

The world on the other side of that blood-red door was unlike anything I'd ever seen in person. I'd seen crazy mosh pits and wild concerts on TV before, but up close it was a bit overwhelming. Megan pushed her way through the crowd and I followed close behind. Every now and again I'd get bumped into. It took all the strength I had to stay upright.

The loud rock music from the band pierced my eardrums. It was so loud I couldn't even hear myself think. There were half-naked women dancing on the bar and colorful graffiti covered every square inch of the concrete walls. Every person I passed had a tattoo or a piercing and everyone seemed to be showing either too much skin or they were covered in head-to-toe black.

Like when Megan walked into our school, all eyes were on me. I instantly regretted not wearing her clothes. Had

I known that wearing such boring clothing would have brought more attention to me, I'd be as half-naked as the women that surrounded me. I'd never felt more out of place in my life.

Once we got to the bar, I was able to speak to Megan.

"I don't think I belong here," I yelled over the music.

"You'll be fine. You just need a drink."

She yelled out a drink order to the guy behind the bar, then handed me a cup. I sipped it as we pushed our way back through the crowd toward the stage.

That was when I saw him. His head was down as he dug his fingers into his guitar. Perfect music flowed from him and it was as if all the other instruments in the band disappeared. I zoned in on his solo and watched as he moved his fingers up and down. He was amazing.

His loose-fitting jeans had rips and tears in them and the sleeves in his black T-shirt were rolled up. The tattoos on his elbows melted into the ones that disappeared into the sleeves of his shirt. There were letters placed on his fingers, but his hands were moving so fast I couldn't see what they said. Once his solo was over, he looked back out at the crowd. His long, dark bangs still covered half his face. He shifted his head to the side, tossing them out of his eyes and giving me a peek of the little music note tattooed behind his ear.

He didn't smile. He was as hard as the concrete that surrounded us, but in his eyes you could see he loved what he was doing. There was a natural look of joy in his sultry stare as he bathed the women in the front row with his inattentive gaze. He caught a break for a minute and reached over for his beer. I watched as he brought the bottle to his lips and his silver lip ring caught my full attention. He was covered in color and art; he was a standing statue for freedom, and I was drawn to his careless stature.

"Oh my God, Chet is so hot! Look at him, Pay. Isn't he a rock god?" Megan screamed over the music.

I shook my head yes, but I wasn't looking at Chet. Who the hell was Chet? And why would anyone want to look at him when they could feast their eyes on the tall, tatted god with the guitar?

We stood there "rocking out" for a few songs until our cups were empty. Megan was right. I was already feeling more relaxed with just the one drink down my throat.

Once we were at the bar, Megan handed me some money and told me to get more while she went and said hello to some girl I'd never seen. I spent a few minutes being knocked around while screaming to the bartender, who apparently didn't see nor hear me. I was about to give up and walk away when an older guy stopped me.

He wasn't much taller than me, but was thick in the shoulders, which made him feel consuming. He had a bright, friendly smile and that was welcomed in a room full of blacked out, moody rockers.

"I saw you standing there trying so hard to get a drink, so I thought I'd help you out," he called over the music as he handed me two more of the drinks Megan and I were drinking before.

"Oh my God, thank you so much. Here, let me pay you back." I tried to stuff the money into his hands.

"What kind of gentleman would I be if I let you pay me back? Drink. Enjoy yourself, on me." He smiled politely before disappearing into the crowd.

Apparently, looks were deceiving. He looked like a hood rat from the wrong side of tracks, but he was such a pleasant guy.

After being tossed around some more, I made it back to Megan's side and handed her one of the drinks.

"Yay! Thanks, Pay!" She flashed me a big smile, "See? I told you we'd have a blast."

"Yep, you called it." I pasted a big, fake smile on my lips and stood beside her as she socialized with ease.

I spent the next hour listening to the band play and watching the guitarist as he peered out at the crowd with his steely gaze. It disturbed me that I found him attractive. I never looked at boys; males were disgusting as far as I was concerned. So, while I watched him, I played mental tug-of-war over what it was about him that attracted me.

The conclusion was he was attractive because he was untouchable. At least to a girl like me he was. And if couldn't touch him, then that meant he couldn't touch me. A guy who could never touch me *would* be attractive.

I stood that way for a while before I realized Megan was no longer beside me. I turned quickly to see if she was behind me and the room spun. The concrete floor shifted under my feet and the music turned into a loud buzz in my ears. I was drunk... I think. I'd never been drunk before. I looked down at my empty cup and was amazed at how quickly I'd gotten myself drunk.

Suddenly, everything started to spin, and I realized my limbs seemed to be stuck. My arms felt like there were hundred-pound weights hanging from them. I turned and pushed myself back through the crowd. I looked around for Megan as I felt my panic rising. It was then that I saw the black door to my right and the green neon lights that blinked the word "Bathroom."

As quickly as I could manage with weighty feet and arms, I pushed my way over to the bathroom, hoping I'd find Megan inside and she could take me home. Once inside, the music was muffled. With the loss of the loudness, I could really tell something was wrong. I once got a buzz at my aunt's wedding and it never felt like this. I felt sleepy and weighed down. I bent to look under the stalls to see if Megan's shoes were under there, but when I did, the floor suddenly seem too close and I collapsed into a heap on the nasty bathroom floor.

"Megan!" I screamed out. My voice sounded slurred and altered.

No one responded.

Everything around me started to go blurry and a wall of nausea slammed into me. I fell over and crushed my body into the fetal position. I needed help. I wanted to scream for help, but my mouth wouldn't work anymore. The room started to blink in and out as I began to lose consciousness. My heartbeat felt too slow, even though I was in a full-blown panic. It was definitely too slow. I was afraid it would stop beating at any second.

I tried to call out, but I was so tired. Far away, the music got loud again as the bathroom door opened. It went away once the door closed. I popped my eyes open, praying Megan would be standing there, but all I saw was a pair of black boots and long legs in my vision.

He moved closer. I heard running water and then I saw him turn to leave. I needed whoever it was to stay. I needed help and he might be the last person to come in here before I died on the dirty bathroom floor.

I pushed words past my dry lips. "Please help me."

The words slipped from my mouth like a soft prayer. I worried it wasn't loud enough, but then I saw his legs stop. He turned and made his way over to me and I forced my head back to look up at him. It was the guitar god from the band. He stared down at me with angry brown eyes. He was blurry and every now and again he blinked in and out while I tried to keep my eyes focused. I was embarrassed and scared, but I knew I needed help and I would take that help from anyone at this point.

"Please." I could only whisper. "Something's wrong with me."

With the last ounce of strength my legs had, I pressed my body against the wall and pushed myself up. I continued to use that wall to keep me up.

He took me in with an expressionless face, but then the anger in his eyes stabbed at me.

"Shit," he growled. His voice echoed off of the bathroom walls around me.

Then he was coming closer and putting his hands out to touch me. I went into full alert. I wanted to scream for him not to touch me, but between whatever was happening to me and the absolute fear of his hands on me, I was at a loss for words. He used his fingers to open my eyes and I tried to keep them from bobbling around in my head.

"What did you take?" he asked rudely.

I wasn't one of the slackers running around outside. I didn't do drugs and I was offended that he thought I did, but how else would I feel this way? It had to be the alcohol because I don't remember taking anything.

"I didn't take anything, I swear," I slurred.

"Did anybody give you anything, maybe a piece of candy or something powdery?"

He ran his finger down my face and touched my neck. It scared me at first, until I realized he was checking my pulse. I wasn't freaking dead, but I felt like I was dying.

I could feel my panic increasing and I quickly ran the night's events through my head, trying to remember if anyone gave me anything. No one did.

"No, no one gave me anything." I was freaking out.

He rolled his eyes. "Then I don't know what to tell you." He turned away.

I couldn't let him leave me. I didn't want to die, and if I was dying, I didn't want to die alone.

"Wait," I said as I reached for his arm.

Realizing I'd touched a guy freaked me out even worse and I pulled my arm away like he was on fire.

It was obvious he was aggravated by me. He was shifting on his feet and rolling his eyes. To him, I was just another drugged-out chick at The Pit.

"What?" he asked.

Then suddenly I remembered the nice guy at the bar who'd given me the drinks. Had he put something in my drink like on one of those crazy cop shows?

"A guy at the bar gave me a drink," I said in a rush. "I thought he just got it from the bartender. It was really sweet, but it tasted fine. I don't think there was anything it in. I would have tasted it, right?"

"Great, just fucking great." He sighed again. "You got spiked."

Spiked? What the hell did that mean? Was I dying? That's what I mainly wanted to know.

Without a thought to my severe psychological issues with touching men, I reached out and lightly laid my hand on his arm. If I was going to die, why did it matter who I was touching?

"Am I going to be okay?" I asked. "Should I go to a hospital? My friend, the one who brought me... I can't find her. She wanted the drummer and now I can't find her. Please don't leave me." No matter how much I was breathing, I couldn't get a full breath. I began to breathe faster.

That made the room spin even more and I had the sudden urge to stick my head between my legs. I felt my hair slip around my shoulders and cover my face. Strands of blond were sticking to my sweaty cheeks so I roughly pushed it away.

He stared at me like I was from another planet for a bit, then looked away.

"I'll go get you some help," he said.

Then he was walking away again. All the air in my lungs left in a rush and black dots danced in my vision. I was officially dying. I reached out and grabbed him and the room went black.

THREE

ZEKE

"YOU'VE GOT TO BE FUCKING kidding me," I said with my arms full of petite blonde.

Her mouth was cocked open and her head fell back over my arm as I carried her across the bathroom to the door. She weighed next to nothing, but she had the firm body of an athlete. I adjusted her in my arms as I pulled the bathroom door open and worked myself and her through the opening.

I was welcomed by a burst of loud music, smoke, and Finn.

"Damn, man, I see your killer cock strikes again." Finn joked as he threw his arm around my shoulders.

"I found her in the bathroom. Someone spiked her with something. I couldn't just leave her there," I said as I started to work through the thick crowd.

"Damn, dude, that sucks." He pushed at a couple blocking my path.

Finn stuck by my side and helped me shove through. Thankfully, the lights were turned down for the lasers and no one noticed us. The girls in the club love to hang all over the band and usually I'm cool with that, but not right now, not with what could possibly be a dying chick in my arms.

"Since when do you give a shit about some random chick in the bathroom?" Finn asked when I made it to the bar.

"Just shut up and help me, man."

He pushed her hair from her face, then reached for the pulse in her neck.

"Um, dude, she needs to go the hospital now. She barely has a pulse. Get her out of here! I'll cover the show and take care of your guitar."

I looked down at her pale face. Her cracked lips looked as if they were about to bleed, and there were greenish circles forming under her eyes. She was definitely about to die.

Instead of answering, I nodded to Finn. I spun on my heels and headed for the front door. There was no need to try and ask for help or ask someone to call an ambulance. No one would hear me or care, and I would be hated for calling the police or any form of authorities to The Pit. Half the people there were underage and there were enough drugs floating around the place to put us all in prison.

So I just ran to my car holding the girl in my arms. I pulled open my rusted passenger-side door and set her onto the seat. She slumped in the seat. I ran around my car and jumped in. I'd been drinking so things were a little fuzzy, but fuck it, the chick was dying and for some stupid reason I was lucky enough to give a shit.

I squealed out of the parking lot and made it to the nearest hospital in minutes. With the unconscious girl in my arms, I ran to the counter in the ER. The older lady behind the counter looked at me like I was a monster. I'm sure it didn't look good for me, a tatted-up, pierced guy, to be holding a half-dead khaki queen.

"She needs help. I found her on the side of the road. She was conscious at first and said someone drugged her. She passed out so I brought her here."

There was a flurry of nurses and doctors and then the girl was rushed away on a gurney. Having done my job, I turned to walk away.

"Excuse me, son. We need to you stick around to talk to the police," the older lady behind the counter said.

I could see in her eyes she was disgusted by me.

"No offense, ma'am, but I don't talk to cops. Sorry."

I turned and walked away. I could hear her behind me calling out something and then I saw the cop cars parked outside the ER doors, blue lights shining.

"Great," I muttered to myself as the sliding doors came open and I was met by three police officers.

Needless to say, I was questioned until my eyes were rolling back in my head.

"Why the hell would I drug a chick, then bring her to the hospital? What kind of sense does that make?" I said as I leaned back in the plastic hospital chair and spun my lip ring.

I didn't go to the jail for drugging the girl, but the police couldn't seem to look past the drugs in my car. You'd think they'd turn their heads since I was being all hero-like, but it wasn't in the cards for me.

The springs in the dirty bunk dug into my back as I waited to get bailed out. I could already imagine the beating coming my way from my dad. I guess I was due for one; it *had* been a week since my last. At least this one was for a good cause. I'd heard before I was handcuffed and taken away that the girl was okay. I felt pretty good about the fact that I'd saved her. Finally, I'd done something decent in my life.

Three hours later they released me. I didn't ask any questions. I grabbed my shit and headed for the door.

"Hold up a minute, Tattoo. Someone wants to speak with you before you leave." A young cop caught me before I made my break.

I was ushered into a dim room furnished with nothing but a table and two chairs and left alone. I sat down and stared into the dark glass on the other side of the room, a two-way mirror, no doubt. I wasn't there long when the door opened and a tall, finely dressed man came through the door. He unbuttoned the bottom button on his expensive suit, then sat across from me. His alert brown eyes took me in as he ran his long fingers through his graying hair. His receding hairline topped a wrinkled forehead, but other than that, he looked like a fit man in his early fifties.

"Zeke Mitchell. That's an interesting name. It suits you." He tapped his fingers against the tabletop.

"Thanks. Look, man, I didn't do anything wrong." I immediately went on the defensive. "I was just trying the help the girl out and now I'm going to get my ass handed to me by my dad, and the cops took my stash."

He adjusted his suit once more, then chuckled to himself.

"Do you know who I am?" he asked. His brows puckered in confusion as if he were some famous star and I should be star struck.

"Can't say I do." I leaned my chair back on two legs and crossed my arms.

I matched his pointed stare until he looked away.

"My name's Charles Phillips." He waited for my reaction. When I didn't react, he continued." As in Governor Phillips."

I'd never heard of him, but why the hell would the governor take the time to talk to me.

"I'm in deep shit, aren't I?"

"No. I just wanted to shake the hand of the man who saved my daughter's life." His smile was the smile of a dirty politician, all big, white teeth and no warmth.

So I'd saved a governor's daughter. I should've known she was a white-collar girl, all khaki and white linen. I'd known just by looking at her that she didn't belong on my side of town and I was right. She was probably a silver-spoon baby slumming it to piss off her daddy. It happened. They were usually the best bangs. They tried extra hard to be bad girls and were more willing to experiment.

He reached his hand out to shake mine and for a brief minute I contemplated this was a joke. Here I was the epitome of white trash and the man across from me was wearing a suit that cost more than my trailer and car combined. I reached out and shook his clammy hand.

"It was nothing. Can I go now?"

"Sure. Listen, you seem like a man who's quick and to the point so I'll just put it out there. I'll have all drug charges dropped against you if this doesn't go any farther than this room. The last thing I need is for the papers to find out my daughter was drugged. She's fine, everyone's fine, and I'd prefer to keep it out of the media. Does that sounds like a deal?"

And finally the reason for his visit comes out. Whatever got my ass out of this room and home.

"Sure. I'll keep this to myself, but you may want to keep your daughter on her side of town." I stood and he followed me and shook my hand once more.

"Oh, I think she's learned her lesson. Thanks again." Then he turned and left the room.

I followed behind him and walked out of the police station, unscathed.

Thankfully, when I got home, Dad was asleep and none the wiser about my little spell in jail. Finn had texted my phone until it died, so I stuck it on the charger and texted him back to let him know all was well.

I stripped down, took a quick shower, and then passed out in my boxers.

The next day, I took a ride over to Finn's to pick up my guitar. Everyone was there lounging around the garage, including two new chicks I'd never seen before. One of them passed me a joint and I hit it a few times. These days, my life was becoming one big high. I guess it was easy to not think about how fucked up everything was when I couldn't feel anything.

"So what happened with blondie last night?" Finn asked.

My mind flashed back to platinum hair and blistering, blue eyes. It was weird that I could remember her eyes so easily. It made me uncomfortable.

"She lived. I dropped her off at the hospital and dipped out." I shrugged.

For some reason I left out the part about going to jail and her being the governor's daughter. I'm not sure why I cared, but it felt wrong to tell that part. She'd been through enough already and I was almost positive I'd never see her around this part of town again, so there was no need to disclose that bit of information.

Finn nudged me with his boot. "So, The Pit booked us again for next weekend. There's supposed to be some agents coming around town then too, so we need to look sharp. I got a new song I want to bang out. Let's meet up here tomorrow afternoon. You hear me, Tiny?" He tossed an empty beer can at Tiny, who was making out with some black-haired girl in the corner.

"Yeah, dude, I heard you. Practice. Tomorrow. New song. Got it." He went back to kissing the chick.

Tiny was a big boy, but chicks dug bass players and he was one of the best.

I didn't stay long, just long enough to get high and grab my strings. I stopped for gas on the way home and stuck my last twenty bucks in the tank. Being broke sucked donkey cock and at this point I was strongly considering selling some powder to make some dough. A dealer in my neighborhood had offered me a job, but I wasn't quite that desperate. I'm getting there now, though, and I'd been debating dealing and making enough money to get out of my old man's house.

When I pulled up in my driveway, there was a white car parked on the side of my yard. The passenger-side door opened as I shut my door and grabbed my guitar case out of the back of my car. I was close to turning away from the car and rudely walking into my trailer when the sun caught the sandy locks of the girl from the night before.

She shyly smiled over at me as she shut the door and walked toward me.

"Shit," I said out loud to myself.

This was the last thing I needed. Helping some strange chick was out of character for me and all I wanted was to stick last night in the back of my head and forget about it completely. Parts of me wanted to turn and walk away. Maybe if I did she'd take the hint and just leave, but something held me in my spot.

Next door, my neighbor Carlos pulled up in his apple-red Impala. Loud Mexican music blared from his car speakers and the sounds of children laughing spilled outside when he opened the front door to his trailer and called to his girlfriend in Spanish. Across the street two guys started to argue and cuss each other over what I could assume were drugs. And of course, the never-ending sounds of the cars on the interstate filled any quick moments of silence.

The blonde's eyes left my face for a brief moment and skirted the trailer park around her. Her face stayed neutral, though. I could only imagine how disgusted she was. I bet politicians and their families practiced the unbiased face so whenever they went to the shitty neighborhoods they could get the people's votes without seeming like stuck-up assholes. Her impassiveness pissed me off. Parts of me wanted her natural reaction. I wanted to see her lips and nose curl up in repulsion. I hated her composed stance when I bet every nerve in her body screamed for her to run to safety.

I couldn't take it anymore.

"What are *you* doing here?" I asked rudely. I made the face of disgust that I'm sure she wanted to make.

She blinked away her shock at my non-welcome. Then her eyes met mine directly. Her eyes took me in and I felt as if she looked right through me. She nervously picked at her fingernails and bit the inside of her mouth. Finally, she dropped her hands and spoke.

"I just wanted to say thank you for last night. Most people would have left me there to die." She fiddled with ends of her hair.

She had more nervous ticks than any other person I'd ever met in my life. She was like a little fawn on the edge of escape. She looked out of place. Her clean appearance stuck out among the dirty rock road and rusted trailers that surrounded her. Her name brand clothes and expensive purse were begging to be swiped by the nearest hood rat. She had to be smarter than this. Didn't she know she'd walked through the gates of hell for that pitiful thank you? Didn't she sense the danger that was all around her? She needed to leave. She was too fresh for such polluted air.

"You're welcome. Now go back to your side of town," I snapped.

I didn't mean to sound so rude, but it pissed me off that I was once again worried about her. It felt unnatural to me and it was starting to freak me out.

Her cheeks turned pink and a frown pulled on her pouty mouth.

"I shouldn't have come here. I just wanted to say thanks." Her eyes cut me before she turned and walked away.

She made it to the hood of the waiting car that was still running before my conscious peeked out and slapped the shit out of me.

"Hey," I called out to her.

She stopped and faced me again. Instantly, I felt like the biggest dick in the South when I saw her eyes brimming with tears. Someone so sensitive didn't stand a chance around a person like me, but knowing that I'd probably never see her face again made it okay for me to kind of apologize for being myself for some reason.

"I'm rude, but you've seen firsthand what happens to shiny things in a chop shop." I gestured to the world around us. "Your best bet is to stay away from these parts, princess. A pretty thing like you wouldn't last two hours out here. How long were you at The Pit last night before you were dying on the bathroom floor? An hour, tops? Think of my rudeness as a blessing." I adjusted my guitar case in my sweaty palm and turned toward my trailer door.

I looked back to get one final glimpse of her. The contrast between her and the trailer park around her was alarming. Although, with her fair skin, white hair, and pale-blue eyes, I'm sure she stuck out just about anywhere she went. She was unique, a single snowflake with her own icy patterns, and if she stayed in my hell of a neighborhood any longer she'd melt.

"Have a nice trip back to Wonderland, snowflake," I said as I opened my trailer door.

"My name is Patience," she snapped.

Patience... it was as unique as its owner. I liked it, although I'd never admit that out loud. Instead, I shook my head and laughed like she'd told me a joke, walked inside, and shut her out.

FOUR
PATIENCE

"WHAT AN ASSHOLE!" MEGAN SAID once I got back in the car. "He had no right to talk to you like that. All you were doing was saying thank you. Geez, how hard would it have been to say you're welcome and politely walk away? Chet said he was a dick to girls, but damn."

She was right, of course. It took everything I had in me to get out of the car and spit the words "thank you" out. I'm already a naturally shy person, but the fact that he'd seen me in the worst state I'd ever been in made me even more uncomfortable. No matter how shaky my body was or how nervous I was, I knew thanking him was the right thing to do. He had saved my life, after all.

Now, after he so rudely snubbed me and walked away, I was thinking I should have just let sleeping dogs lie.

"What did Chet say his name was again?"

"Zeke Mitchell," she said as she pulled off the bumpy rock road to the main highway. "Even his name screams asshole. The girls love him, though. What is it about girls and cocky assholes? I'll never understand it."

"Says the girl who chases every cocky cock in a ten-mile radius." I laughed.

"Hey, now! A girl has needs. I'm sure one day I'll find a nice boy I can take home to meet my mom, but until then, I'll enjoy getting roughed up by the bad ones." She jokingly purred then growled.

"I'm convinced there's something wrong with you. Anyway, I did what I came here to do. I would've died had he not taken me to the hospital. I thanked him and now I can forget him."

"Yeah, that would probably be best. Listen, Pay, I'm really sorry about last night. I swear I thought you left. I blew your phone up and went searching for you the minute I realized we got separated." She looked over at me and frowned as she made a right turn.

She'd rushed over to my house the minute I was released from the hospital and then she spent the next hour crying on my lap and apologizing. It's not like she drugged me. It happened and it would never happen again. You live, you learn, and you move past it. I'd been through worse and I'd go through worse again.

"You didn't do anything wrong, and up until my arms went numb I was having a good time." I tried to make her feel better. "But I don't know if that's my kind of place."

"I understand. I know it's not really your scene. I'll go alone." She jerked her car into my driveway and slammed on the brakes.

I grabbed the dash to keep my head from being smashed into it at the sudden stop.

"Why in the world would you go back there?" I asked, appalled.

"Well, I didn't say anything because of all the craziness going on, but Chet asked me to come watch him play next weekend. Oh my God, he's so freaking hot. He texted me this morning and called me beautiful. I think I'm in love." She sighed.

"You're always in love." I shook my head. "Promise me you won't go alone. If it comes down to that, I'll go back with you and stuff a bottle of water in my purse for safe drinking. I don't think I want to party as hard as I did last time." I joked.

"I'm totally not laughing at that. You could've died or, had I grabbed your cup instead of mine, I could've died. We have to be more careful from now on."

"Agreed." I smiled back at her.

I looked up at the big, white house that was my home. My eyes met my dad's as he peered down at me from his office window. I'd have to face him at some point, but I'd do just about anything to get out of it.

"You and Chet, huh? What do you think will happen with that?" I asked.

"Well, I know what I hope will happen and it involves a lot of heavy breathing, high-pitched moans, and bad words." She smirked. "He looks like a hair puller. God, I'd let him spank me with his drumsticks." Big laughter spilled from her lips when my face heated up.

"Um, I'm pretty sure that would constitute abuse." I snorted. "Anyway, that's gross. I wouldn't touch his drumsticks, much less any other kind of stick. At least wait a while before you sleep with him." I rolled my eyes and pretended to gag.

"Oh, whatever, I don't sleep with every guy that shows me some attention. Plus, I really like this one, but if it makes you feel better, I promise to make him wait." She playfully nudged my arm with a painted finger.

"Good. Okay, chick, I'll see you in the morning. Try and be here at a decent time. If I'm late one more time, Ms. Marshall's going to give me detention, and if I get detention I'll miss practice."

"I'll try, but I make no promises. This master piece takes time." She motioned at her face and tilted her head back and forth like she was posing for a camera.

"Okay, oh gorgeous one. Just be here." I pushed my door open.

"With bells on," she said with a big cheesy smile.

I climbed out and then watched as her car jerked down the road. Grinding gears sounded until I could no longer see her taillights.

My dad was standing in the marble foyer when I pushed through the front door. His angry eyes devoured me as I took off my coat and hung it in the closet. I felt my stomach turn at the attention.

"Was that your friend Megan?" he asked, as he leaned a hip against the little table by the front door.

"Yes, we were just hanging out." I put my head down, tucked my hair behind my ears, and started to creep around him.

I tensed when I felt him grab my arm in passing. He leaned in toward me; his lips grazed my cheek as he whispered in my ear.

"That girl's bad news. I'm not sure I'm okay with you going out partying God knows where with her. You're meeting the wrong kind of people, Patience, and if I find out you've been doing anything bad with anyone I'm going to be very angry." I didn't miss his meaning. "That boy that helped you last night, I'm assuming that was the first time you met him?"

He was acting like a jealous boyfriend instead of a pissed-off father. It was disgusting. My entire life was a psychology book in the making. Tech students would take tests based on the appalling details of my dysfunctional family one day.

"Last night was the first time I'd ever seen him, and even then I wasn't properly introduced. You know, since I was practically dying and everything." My voice was calm and cool, but my words were sarcastic.

"Don't be a smartass, Patience. Stay away from him. Don't let me find out you were on that side of town again, do you understand?" His fingers started to dig into my arm and I hissed as his pinky nail cut skin.

"Yes," I whispered.

"Yes, what?" He reached up and brushed my hair to the side.

"Yes, sir," I repeated respectfully as I pulled my arm away from his death grip.

"There you are! Where have you been, Pay?" My sister Sydney came bursting into the space.

Dad stepped away from me, and the room instantly felt lighter after seeing her smile. While I was the older, gloomy daughter of depression, Syd was the sunlight in our home. She was twelve and just now coming into herself. I'm pretty sure she wasn't planned since there was such a large age gap between her and me, but instead of being annoyed by my baby sister, like I'm sure most girls my age were, I adored being around her. She made me feel needed and technically she did need me.

I was the one that shielded her from him. I used my body as a distraction so hers could remain untouched, and I'd continue to do that until she was safe and sound and out on her own. She'd never know about what went on behind my door some nights and I'd sure as hell never tell her, but as long as it was my room he visited once a week and not hers, I'd die a happy girl someday. As long as I could protect Sydney, I would be at peace with my lot in life.

"Hey, you." I reached out and tugged playfully at her strawberry-blond hair. "When did you get home?" I asked.

She'd been away for some school trip for the last week, which was a lot like a mini break for me since I only had to protect myself and not her for the week. I actually got a good night's sleep at one point. I hadn't slept well since Sydney and I had gotten our own rooms when I was twelve. I couldn't watch out for her properly when she was in the room next to me, which resulted in a lot of listening out for noises. I'd become the lightest sleeper alive once my parents moved me into my own room. I hated it, but at least there wasn't a chance of Syd waking up and seeing me being manhandled.

"I've been home for an hour. Mom looks good today." She smiled. I instantly felt bad for not visiting my mom before rushing off to the other side of town.

"Does she? I guess I should go up and say hi then, huh? Come with me." I tugged on her arm and dragged her upstairs to our parents' room.

If the space outside their bedroom door smelled like a hospital, then the bedroom itself smelled like the morgue. As much as I loved visiting my mother and seeing her lying in bed, waiting with a smile, I despised visiting at the same time. The room was swarming with death and was a constant reminder that today could be the last day I'd get to see my mother's smile or hear her soft voice.

I was seven when she was first diagnosed with breast cancer. Sydney was only two. Since her diagnoses, she'd been in and out of the hospital. One year she was in remission and things would look brighter, and then she'd go in for one of her six-month checkups and the walls would come tumbling in again once the doctor would let her know her cancer had returned.

I'd seen her in all stages of the disease. I'd held her hair back as she puked after chemo. I'd held her in my arms as she cried for the loss of her breasts after a double mastectomy, and when that wasn't enough, I spoon fed her chicken broth when she was too weak to even lift her arms. That's the stage she was in now, the final stages. My dad was paying a nurse to care for her now since there wasn't much else the doctors could do for her. She'd gotten to the point where she flat-out refused the chemo.

"Three days of being happy and alive are better than five days of being sick and half dead," she'd say when Dad would beg her to go in for treatments.

It was her decision and after seeing her so sick she couldn't move, I understood that decision. Even though selfish parts of me wanted to scream for her to get her ass to the doctor and accept any treatment they offered, the parts of me that understood sickness and pain prayed nightly for her to find peace.

In the future, when my depression gets the best of me, I'll tell my story of the years I spent being molested by one of the very people who was supposed to protect me. I'll tell a high-priced therapist all my dirty secrets and I'll beg for the drugs that will take my memories away. When that day comes, I'll be asked why I never told anyone. The doctor will ask me why I didn't ask for help or run to my mother.

The answer will always been the same. I wanted my mom to live a happy life in her final days. She was dying; everyone in our home knew that, including the live-in nurse that now took care of her. Slowly but surely, she was dying. What kind of person would I be to tell her something so devastating so close to her death? It would take a heartless person to do that.

So instead, I kept it locked in, knowing one day, once Mom is gone and Sydney is safely sent away to college, I'll be able to run away and leave it all behind.

"Hey, Mom," I whispered into the dark room where she lived. "Feel like some company?"

A thin ray of light cut across the musty room and landed on my mom's sunken cheeks. I watched as a tiny smile sucked the energy from her eyes.

"Of course I am. Get your butts in here," she rasped.

Syd and I climbed up in bed with her and snuggled up close. I wrapped my fingers around hers. I didn't miss how thin her skin felt. It was as if the thin barrier that kept her together was slowly dissolving.

I looked over at Syd and she attempted to smile at me. It was a sad smile, one that was for show only. We both knew it could be any time now and moments like this were priceless.

"So, let's talk girl talk," Mom said. Her words were breathless and I appreciated her effort.

She began to softly pet my hand with hers and I closed my eyes and took it in.

Syd and I did most of the talking. At one point we even earned a good laugh from her when Syd proceeded to tell her about some run-in at school with a girl and a fake spider. We stayed and talked until it was clear Mom was exhausted.

That night Sydney slept in my room. When Dad came to my door, he simply said goodnight to us and went back to his room.

I skipped the gym and extracurricular activities that week since our maid, Lynn, was off for the week. I felt fine staying out late with her around since she stayed up so late and her room was next to Syd's. With her being off on vacation, I couldn't take any chances of him going to Syd's room while I wasn't there. Needless to say, I spent more time at home than I wanted to, but it was worth it if it meant protecting my little sister.

Soon it was Friday, and Megan was planning her outfit for our night out at The Pit. I hated that she was so damn hardheaded about going to that stupid place. Her going meant I had to go back. There was no way I could let her go alone. Syd was spending the weekend with a friend so I could afford to get out of the house. After being stuck there after school all week, I needed it. Like I said before, I'd be more careful. I knew what I was getting into this time.

"What do you think of this?" Megan said as she held up a scrap of hot-pink lace.

"What the hell is it?" I asked.

"It's a halter-top. It's going to look freaking hot on me." She held it up to her chest and it looked like it wouldn't even cover one boob, much less two.

"Are you sure it's not too small?"

"Uh, that's kind of the point. Here, you try this one on." She handed me another piece of tiny material, except this one was black.

I help it up to my crotch since it looked like a tiny pair of panties and that earned a laugh from Megan.

"Pay, it's a top. Here, this is how you put it on."

She then began to dress me. She didn't stop at the top. Soon, I was wearing a tight pair of skinny jeans that barely covered my ass and black boots that went up my calves. Usually, I wouldn't be caught dead in anything of the sort, but since I knew I'd stand out less this way, I was all for it. I even allowed her to sit me down and put some makeup on my face and curl my hair.

When I looked in the mirror again I was looking at a different girl. It wasn't me; it was a rocker chick from The Pit, minus the tats and piercings. There was black liner around my blue eyes that made them pop, big hoop earrings in my ears, and my hair hung around my cheeks in a mass of platinum curls.

"Oh my God, Megan. That's... I don't know. I look like a different person." I was shocked.

"No, you don't. You look hot. Not that you aren't always hot, but I just accentuated your hotness."

"Yeah, um... not so much, but thanks. At least now I won't stick out so much. Promise you won't run off with Chet and leave me alone at this place."

"Oh, please! Last time taught me a lesson. I'll be hooked to your side like your sexy conjoined twin." She picked through the makeup on her dresser, throwing random things into her bag.

Gerald, the doorman, said nothing this time as we slipped past him. The Pit, once again, was full of people bouncing off the concrete walls, all dressed in black. Except this time I fit right in. While I was still uncomfortable, it wasn't nearly as bad as the first time. I was completely prepared and I was determined not to lose Megan in the crowd this time.

The band was already playing as we made our way to the bar. We ordered something in a bottle and asked the bartender to give it to us unopened. That got us a stink eye, but we didn't care. This time we were determined to walk out, preferably not drugged and on the verge of death. We hooked pinkies as we made our way close to the stage. Chet winked at Megan once we were close to the front of the group.

I took a quick peek at Zeke and he looked right over me as he scanned the crowd through his dark bangs. I felt a slight twinge when he didn't even notice me, but then I realized I didn't look exactly like the girl he found half dead on the disgusting bathroom floor. When he turned his head away, I took advantage of the time and checked out his tattoos. The one that stuck out the most was the nautical star on the top of his hand that melted onto the side of his wrist. I'm not sure what it was about the tattoo that was so appealing, but that, combined with the flexing of his muscles as he played, was very attractive.

I was beginning to understand Megan's fascination with bad boys, although I'd never admit that to her. Zeke had been a total dick to me both times we spoke, but he wasn't handsy and he didn't make any sexual advances toward me, and in some way I appreciated that about him.

Then again, looking around at all the tattooed, half-naked women in the room, I obviously wasn't his type and just a small part of me wanted to be like the girls around me. I may look the part tonight, but this wasn't me at all and no amount of tiny clothes or makeup could make me like them.

Zeke strummed the chords for his solo and once again I was caught with how untouchable he was for me. He closed his eyes as he played and the light glinted off the piercing on his eyebrow. I found myself jealous of his freedom to be himself. Just like the first time I saw him, he was dripping with moody sexiness. The fact that I could describe him as sexy was a huge step for me, but it was the truth and all the girls pushing toward the stage to get into his line of vision knew it just as much as I did. Zeke Mitchell was sexy. He was a total asshole, but I guess it worked for him.

After a few unopened bottles of beer, and entirely too many stink eyes from the bitchy bartender, I was starting to feel myself relax. The alcohol had made its way through my system and down into my limbs. I was beginning to enjoy myself. I even caught myself swaying to the music every now and again.

An hour after that, I was dancing with Megan and a group of people I didn't know. I was jumping up and down, screaming lyrics I'd just learned, and laughing like I hadn't laughed since I was seven. Like, real laughter, not the fake stuff that I produced around people at school. It was an amazing feeling. I could totally see myself becoming an alcoholic real quick if it meant feeling this way all the time.

And then suddenly the fun was over. The crowd broke and darted in different directions as The Pit filled with police officers. Megan grabbed my hand and pulled me in her direction, but the beer had taken its toll and my reflexes weren't working.

"Come on, Patience! Pick up your feet!" she screamed over the loudness.

The music had stopped and all I could hear were the sounds of the police yelling for everyone to freeze. The lights were flickering and I saw a few people get trampled. Then Megan's hand was ripped from mine and I was thrown back. I lost my balance and fell hard onto the sticky concrete floor. I tried to get up, but some girl stepped on me and I fell back onto my stomach. Then I felt a strong grip on my arms as someone pulled me into the standing position. For a brief moment, I felt relief, but then my arms were pulled behind my back and I was handcuffed.

FIVE

ZEKE

"YOU GOING TO CLASS?" CHET asked, as he passed me a joint.

We were lying in the back of my El Camino, getting high in the school parking lot.

"I doubt it. You?" I took a deep draw and held it.

"Pfft, hell no. I've had enough schooling for the week. Let's go grab something to eat, man. I'm fucking starving my ass off. I'd give my left nut for a burger and a milkshake right now."

We ended up at the McDonald's by Finn's house with half of the dollar menu lying across the dash of my car.

"So, that chick Megan is coming out Friday to watch us play. I hope she wears that tight-ass schoolgirl uniform." He made a growling noise in the back of his throat. "Dude, that shit is fucking hot. Hey, maybe she'll bring your girl with her. You know the blonde. If she can stay sober long enough maybe you'll get lucky," he joked.

"Please. That chick's as straight as they come. *I'd* have to drug her, too, to get her to put out." We laughed.

Later that night, we played at Finn's for two hours before I finally headed home. When I got there, Dad wasn't there, which meant he was out on a call, towing a car for someone. I went inside, heated up two packs of oodles and noodles, then fell onto the couch to watch some TV and eat. I had just finished my noodles when I heard my dad pull up. I threw my bowl in the sink and went to take a shower.

That night he didn't fuck with me. I guess he was too exhausted from work to even bother. I wish they'd work him to death more often. Shit, I wish they'd just work him to death... period. I fell asleep in a pair of boxers with my radio on and dreamt of the blond girl and her strange blue eyes.

By the time Friday rolled around, I'd missed two days of school and was so broke I barely had enough gas money to spit in my gas tank. I'd been to every business in town trying to get a job, but the tattoos and piercings weren't accepted by most. Instead, I found myself on the front porch of Javier, the local dope dealer. Desperate times called for desperate measures, and if I wanted to have gas money and food I needed some cash. Dad worked, but he was the stingiest son of a bitch alive and I was old enough to take care of myself.

I left Javier's place with an ounce of weed. He didn't want to start me out with too much, even though I'd told him I could have that sold in less than thirty minutes at The Pit. I had to start somewhere. An ounce of weed today would be a pound of blow tomorrow. Either way, it was money in my pocket.

I showered, got dressed, and drove over to The Pit. The band was already setting up by the time I got there and there were already at least twenty people at the bar. It wasn't long until we were up on stage playing our asses off for a roomful. I played until my fingers ached and took a swig from my beer every chance I got. It was a good night. I was playing my heart out and later, once everything was settled, I'd sell this weed and get my money.

I scanned the crowd and saw a few familiar faces. A cute brunette in the front caught my attention. She looked up at me with flirty eyes and licked at her bottom lip. She was cute, not sexy, but she'd do. I took note of where she was in the crowd before I moved on. A flash of white hair crossed my vision and my eyes landed on a petite blonde. From behind, the girl reminded me so much of that Patience chick, but this girl was in a tight pair of ass-hugging jeans and the sexiest halter top I'd ever seen.

My eyes traveled down the back of her, past the ends of her long, sandy hair, and landed on her luscious ass. I got so turned on that I played the wrong chord. That earned me a pair of bug eyes from Finn, but no one in the room seemed to notice but my band mates. Her slender shoulders and her back were fully exposed. A tiny mole on her shoulder blade stuck out and for a second I imagined running my finger across it. Her milky shoulders moved up and down as she bounced with the music.

Every dip and curve of her body could be seen through her tight skinny jeans and I knew in that moment there was no way this was the same girl that I found on the bathroom floor. The girl that came to my house and nervously fiddled with everything as she quietly mouthed the words "thank you" would *never* be caught dead wearing such revealing clothes.

Cute brunette in the front row forgotten, I honed in on the sexy, blond girl. I'd never mess with such a straight-laced girl like Patience, but that didn't mean I couldn't dip my stick in a chick that reminded me of her. Then the girl turned and her perfectly shaped nose and shimmering blue eyes came into focus. From up on stage, I watched as Patience danced and laughed with the group of girls around her, including her friend Megan. Instantly, I was pissed off that it was her.

One, she had no business coming back around here. She didn't belong here and her being here was a danger to all of us since she was the governor's daughter. Two, she looked entirely too sexy to be such a sweet, innocent girl. She was headed straight for trouble with those tight jeans and that tiny top. And three, I was pissed because it meant I wasn't going to get some hot, blonde action tonight. Had it been some other cute blonde, then fine, I would have spent my night making her say my name, but not her; I wouldn't put my hands on the khaki, snowflake princess.

I turned my attention away just in time to see the room get flooded with cops. Me and the boys knew the drill and we had unplugged and dipped many times before since we played in some pretty shady places. Just as I was about to unplug and grab my shit, I looked up and saw a flash of blond being pushed around in the crowd. I knew right away it was Patience.

Cussing myself, I set my guitar down and jumped off the stage. She was so tiny and I could see her being trampled to death. I made a plan as I pushed through the crowd toward her. I'd grab her, grab my guitar, and get the hell out through the back.

Just as I was about to grab her, she was pushed to the ground. I watched as she tried to get up but was stepped on. Then, there was a cop scooping her up. I pulled back and ran straight into another cop who threw my arms behind my back and cuffed me. I looked over to see Finn shake his head at me as he grabbed my guitar and ran out the back. At least I knew my guitar was safe.

After the cop cuffed me, he pulled me outside. The cool night air rushed through my hair and gave me a chill. The cop pushed me against the car and I found myself right next to Patience. She looked up at me with frightened eyes and I could only imagine how this felt for her.

"First time being arrested?" I asked casually, like we were at a diner instead of waiting to be thrown in the back of a cop car.

"Yes," she squeaked.

She looked so afraid. For some strange reason this girl played on my conscious and I felt bad for her. I wanted more than anything to unlock her handcuffs and let her scurry home. I wanted to make her feel better, so I said the first thing that came to mind.

"Well, I wouldn't worry about it. Your dad will have you out in no time." I shook my head. "Me, on the other hand, I'll be there for the night."

I didn't miss the sudden change in her expression, except it wasn't an expression of relief. She should have been relieved knowing that her dad would make everything okay for her, but instead, an expression of pure fear filled her eyes. I was about to question that expression, but then I remembered the quarter bag of weed I'd taken out of the ounce and stuffed in my back pocket to sell while I was at The Pit. In that moment, I knew I'd be spending more than one night in jail.

"Shit," I said out loud.

"What?" she asked.

"I just remembered I have some weed on me," I whispered. "Looks like I'll be in jail for a while."

"Drugs are bad for you." She batted big blue eyes up at me.

"So is going to the wrong side of town," I snapped. "But you just can't seem to resist, can you?"

"You don't have to be so mean to me, you know? I'm actually a pretty smart girl. I know coming to this side of town isn't safe for a girl like me, but I also know it's not safe for my friend Megan, either. If she comes, then I come. It's called being a good friend, asshole." She came back at me, then cut her eyes.

A girl had never looked so sexy. She called me on my shit and then threw it back in my face. I had to admit, it was a massive turn-on. The fact that she was in those low-rise, tight jeans and that sexy-ass black top didn't help matters. Then she did something that someone had never done for me before and blew my mind and pissed me off all at the same time.

"Where's the weed?" she asked a little too loudly, making me shush her.

"Shit, why don't just go over there and tell the cops about it instead of yelling it?" I said sarcastically. "It's in my back pocket. I'm sure they'll find it, but on the off chance that they'll find it in their hearts to let us go, let's not mention it."

She turned away from me and toward the officers who were still busy bringing out people from The Pit. Most got away, but there were still the weak ones who were caught. That's what this girl did to me; she made me a weak one. I'd never been caught in a raid before, but stopping to help her got me caught and I was going to go to jail, while her daddy got her off the hook.

"Hey, officer! Can you come here, please?" she yelled across the parking lot.

I couldn't believe it! After all I had done for her; she was going to seriously tell them about the drugs. What a bitch! A young cop stopped what he was doing and worked his way over to us.

"Ma'am, you're going to have to wait until we get everything taken care of here and then we'll let y'all have a seat in the back of the car," the cop said.

"No, I need to confess something!" she said in a rush. She motioned in my direction and rolled her eyes and exaggerated a sigh. "My boyfriend here is trying to play the hero, but he's got my weed in his back pocket and I don't want him to get in trouble for me. I know he loves me and all, but I wouldn't feel right about it, ya know?" She darted her eyes in my direction, then quickly looked away.

I stared openly at her with my mouth hanging open. It was a rarity that someone shocked me, but the little snowflake girl had landed me speechless. No one had ever taken a hit for me. Grown men had refused to fight for me and here she was playing the tiniest hero. I couldn't let it happen, but an unwanted rush of pride ran through my system at her words. Why I'd be proud of a practical stranger, I don't know, but I was.

I said the first words that came to my mind. "I'm *not* her anything and the drugs are mine."

A pink flush rushed up her neck and spread across her cheeks. She looked as if she'd been slapped in the face before she turned her back to me. She had to know I wasn't some punk who would let a woman take my charges.

The cop looked between us and shook his head. "Whatever you say," he said as he started to pat me down. He reached into my back pocket and pulled out the bag of weed and ticked his teeth. "Looks like your little female *friend* got you busted, buddy." Then he opened the door to the police car and lowered my head into the back seat.

Patience joined me in the back, but she wouldn't look at me. I didn't say anything to her. There was nothing to say. I guess technically I could thank her for trying to take up for me, but then again, had she not said anything they may have never found it in the first place.

The drive to the police station was awkward and silent. The cops chatted in the front seat about an underground drug problem and The Pit being the center of it. I wasn't surprised, but it still sucked that we were losing our favorite place to play. These things happened, though, and soon there'd be another place and they'd call us to play. Until then, we'd play in the garage and our groupies would collect there.

The police station was full of Pit people. Tattoos and piercings as far as the eye could see. This wasn't strange in a place like The Pit, but in a police station surrounded by white walls and police, they stood out. They sat Patience and me in a room alone and still she said nothing as she sat across the table from me. The room was the same room they'd put me in when they thought I drugged her. Funny... every time I get mixed up with this girl I end up in a police station.

"You should've just let me take it." She finally spoke.

I shook my head and rolled my eyes. "I'm no bitch, snowflake. I couldn't let a girl take my drug charges, especially the governor's daughter."

"My name's Patience." She smacked the top of the table. "And I don't know how you know I'm the governor's daughter, but that's the main reason why you should've let me take the charges. There's no way my dad would let me sit in jail for long. He'd bail me out as soon as possible, but you'll have to stay."

"It's done. Plus, we wouldn't want to ruin your perfect record. What would Harvard think?" I pretended to be appalled.

"Are you always such a rude ass?" She nervously picked at her nails.

I leaned my chair back in the corner, rested my head against the wall, and closed my eyes. "Always."

The room stayed silent after that. I could hear her anxiously fiddle with the table and the little cup of water she was given. Then I heard the door open. I opened my eyes, but I was tucked away in the corner behind the open door and couldn't see anything. When the door closed, I could see Patience standing before her dad, the governor. His back was to me and I was sure he didn't know I was there.

He towered over her and I watched as she physically cowered in fear. I didn't like to see her react that way. She was supposed to be my tiny savior. She had thrown herself in front of the metaphorical police train for me, yet here she was, cowering in fear in front of the one person in the world who was supposed to protect her. Maybe he was a strict man. Actually, thinking back to how he had acted the first time I met him, I was almost positive he was a strict man.

Then he shocked me when he reached out and pinched her cheeks with his hand. He squished her lips up as his thumb dug into one side of her face and the rest of fingers dug into the other side. She tried to pull away, but it only made his fingers dig deeper. I was on the edge of my seat, ready to pull him off of her, when he spoke.

"This is a new look for you, *daughter*. Who knew you were this wild girl? I wish I had known." His voice was soft and menacing. He leaned in and got closer to her face. She tried to turn her head away, but his grasp was turning her cheeks red. "Is this what you like? Do you like the rough side of things?"

I stood abruptly and her eyes flittered to mine. I'd had about enough of his bullshit and if he didn't take his hand off of her, I was going to remove it for him. He released her quickly and turned to me. Surprise at seeing me there dashed across his expression, but then the calm, cool politician slipped back in place. I suddenly had a deep hate for the man standing in front of me, a fucker who manhandled his daughter and dug into her silky, untouched cheeks. The bastard! I bet he hit her.

Thinking of that and knowing the extent of what it felt like to be beat by your father had my blood boiling. Me, I could take a man's ass beating, but not snowflake. She was delicate and seeing how petite she was and seeing how he towered over her just pissed me off more.

"Ah, our little friend Zeke. I should've known you'd have something to do with *this.*" He motioned to Patience's clothes.

"Dad, he had nothing to do with me being at the club." She came to my defense again, but I wanted to dig into him in any way I could as payback for touching her.

"Of course I had something to do with it. What can I say? I can't stay away from her." I lied.

I heard Patience gasp from beside him as I met his stare. I didn't even think about the effects my little statement would make on her, but I enjoyed the expression that crossed his face. His jaw ticked and I knew I'd hit a nerve, and then an intimidating smile spread across his face.

"She's definitely a special girl. However, I'd prefer it if you stayed away from my daughter." He put a protective arm around her waist and pulled her closer to his side.

It pissed me off even more that he was now pretending to protect her from me. He was the one that was obviously a danger to her, while I had only tried to help her. I could feel the heat of my anger on the back of my neck. I flexed my fists and weighed the charges that would be slammed against me if I knocked this fucker on his ass.

"I'll try, but I can't make any promises. She's pretty addictive and I have one hell of an addictive personality." I hit him with another dig.

Patience stared at me, mouth gapped open in shock.

"Dad, he's fooling around. We barely even know each other," she said with wide eyes as she looked up at her father.

His face had now taken on a deep-red hue.

I put my hand over my chest like I was hurt. "After all we've been through, snowflake. That cuts deep. I'd like to think I know you pretty damn well," I said as I purposely looked up and down her slim figure.

Her face turned as red as her dad's and she threw her hands in the air.

"Stop it, Zeke! He's going to think you're serious!"

Finally, I'd had enough and I was starting to worry that maybe I'd made things worse for her.

"Whatever you say, princess," I said as I fell back into my chair and spread my legs out in front of me.

Crossing my arms, I peered up at both of them through my hair. I bit on my lip ring and watched as she looked up at her Dad. Her eyes were wide with fear and I suddenly felt sick to my stomach thinking about her possibly getting hit when she got home.

"I'm just screwing around," I spit out.

Her dad looked down at her, then grabbed her hand.

"Patience, we're leaving." He then turned back to me. "Son, I think you need to get yourself straight. You're headed nowhere fast."

"I'm not your son," I snapped. "And where I'm headed is none of your business."

He said nothing as he turned to leave the room. Patience looked over her shoulder at me and I didn't miss the worry in her eyes. I didn't like it. I wasn't her concern.

I turned away and heard the door click as it shut behind them.

Three days later, I left the jailhouse with a pretty hefty fine, sixty days worth of community service, and a phone full of text messages from Javier wanting to know where his product was.

SIX
PATIENCE

THE RIDE HOME FROM THE police station was awful. Being alone in the car with my dad was insufferable. Once we made it to our side of town, I could feel the anger radiating from him. The fact that he had been silent for most of the ride scared the shit out of me. I knew once I got home I was in for it. I didn't even want to think about what he was going to do to me.

"I had no idea this was the kind of girl you were." He filled the silent car with his sigh. "I never thought in a million years I'd have to go to the police station and pick up my daughter. Maybe I should treat you like the juvenile delinquent you are. Would you like that, Patience? Do you want me to treat you like you look right now? Huh? Do you want me to treat you like a little whore?" His voice went from calm to vicious as he continued to talk.

I didn't respond. Instead, I stared out the window and watched the big houses go by. I silently prayed that Lynn, our maid, was up and about. I hoped my mom's nurse, Patricia, would be up taking care of Mom. I wished for one that could save me from him, but I knew in the back of my mind that he made sure we'd be alone when we got home. That thought made my stomach turn and I suddenly remembered the time I got sick and threw up on him once he was done with me. I was only nine and he told my mom that I must've had a twenty-four-hour stomach bug.

Once we pulled up to the house, I got out and followed him through the garage and into the house. He threw his keys onto the marble kitchen counter and ran his hands through his hair. I put my head down and started out of the kitchen, but before I got halfway out of the room, I felt his hand come around the top of my arm. My body tensed up as he spun me around to face him. I didn't have time to think as his palm landed hard against my cheek. My ears rang and the metallic taste of blood filled my mouth.

I reached up and covered my cheek as I looked up at him in shock. He was abusive, but not this kind of abusive. He had never hit me and now, as he looked down at me with a strange expression on his face, I knew he was taken aback by his reaction as well. His realization seemed to piss him off even more as he grabbed the tops of my arms and pushed me up against the wall.

"See what you made me do?" he said angrily. Spittle flew from his mouth and landed on my burning cheek.

I'd never been more afraid of him and the fear on my face fueled him. I didn't even see his back hand coming as he hit me again. This time I cried out loudly. I cussed myself for making the noise. The last thing I wanted was for my mom to hear me and become alarmed. I covered my mouth with my hand and waited for him to hit me again. My cheek felt swollen and hot, so hot I expected the single tear that slid down it to sizzle. He slid his thumb under my eye so hard it hurt as he tried to rub my thick eyeliner away.

"I can't even look at you," he hissed out.

And then I was moving as he slung me around so I stood in front of the kitchen table and faced away from him. He smacked me in the shoulder blades as he roughly pushed me over the table and pulled my left arm hard behind my back. My face hurt as he pressed it into the table. I had an idea of where this was going, but since he only ever touched me in my bedroom once everyone was asleep, I didn't really know what to expect. I cried into my hand as he started to rip my pants down. My stomach dug into the side of the kitchen table and I thought for sure if he pushed down on me any harder he'd break my ribs.

Once my pants and panties were down, I pushed myself away into the place I went we he came into my room. The tears stopped and my eyes felt sticky and dry as I stared out the kitchen window into the backyard. The pool looked extra bright and the stars seemed to reach forever. I closed my eyes and wished I was one of those stars—far away, burning in the night sky where no one could reach me.

In the distance, I could hear the table shaking and skidding across the expensive tile floor. A candle holder fell over and cracked in front of my eyes. The arm that he held behind my back got pulled harder and I thought for sure he'd pull it off of my shoulder, but I didn't cry. I didn't feel any pain anymore. Instead, my hand slowly fell from my mouth and I lay there still and silent while I prayed I was dead. If it weren't for Sydney and my mom, I'd welcome death with a smile, but as long as they were here, I'd be here.

My short-term memory had been altered. As I stood under the blazing, hot shower water I couldn't remember how I got there. I couldn't remember the moment he left me or the trip up the stairs to the bathroom, and that scared me. I'd always known I was broken, but it was obvious he was smashing the small pieces of me into even smaller fragments. Soon, I'd be dust in the wind. Maybe then I could float away and stay in my happy place.

After my shower, I stared in the mirror at my cheek. The bruising was getting worse by the minute and I knew I'd have to come up with a damn good excuse for Mom and Syd. My cell phone was going nuts since Megan had no idea where I was. Finally, I texted her back and told her I was fine and that I was going to bed.

When I slipped under the covers, my entire body hurt. I couldn't sleep, so I lay there and stared up at the ceiling. I thanked God Sydney was at a friend's house and my mother would never know what was happening under her roof. If I could just make it a few more years, then I'd never have to see his face again if I didn't want to... just a few more years. I'd already lived through this for almost ten. What's a few more?

I watched as the dark ceiling became gray, then finally bright orange as the morning sun peeked into my room. My eyes felt as if I hadn't blinked the entire night and I was almost positive I hadn't. My body felt stiff and my ribs ached. The injured side of my face felt bigger than the other and I was dreading looking in the mirror and seeing what I had to deal with Monday at school. I hoped it wasn't very bad and if it was, I hoped the two days I had before going back to school was enough for it to heal.

As soon as I got up and got dressed, I called Megan to come and get me. No matter how badly I wanted to be out of this house, I couldn't bring myself to drive that gray Toyota in the garage.

"I'll be there in thirty minutes," Megan said through the phone. We decided to catch a movie, grab some lunch, and catch up on some much-needed shopping.

I spent ten minutes trying to powder away the ugly, swollen bruise on my cheek, and then I peeked in and checked on my mom. The room was dark and she was asleep. I watched her stomach move up and down as she breathed deep. As long as her stomach was moving then she was still with us. Afraid that I'd wake her, I softly closed the door then went downstairs to wait on the front porch for Megan.

"What the hell happened to your face?" she asked with big eyes when I got into her car. "Oh my God, did that happen last night? I was freaking out when I saw you handcuffed. Did your dad freak out on you?" We jerked down the road and worked our way to the movie theater.

I jumped all over her first question. I didn't even think to say it had happened at The Pit the night before.

"Yeah, some bitch stepped on me and I hit my face on the concrete floor. It looks awful, I know. It hurts like a bitch, too. I still can't believe I got arrested." I looked out the window. "I told you going back there was a bad idea. My dad was so pissed." I quickly changed the subject. "What happened with you?"

"Chet pulled me out." She tried not to smile. "I ended up going back to Finn's garage with them. They said Zeke got arrested, too. Did you see him?"

We pulled into the theater parking lot and she slammed her parking brake into place.

"Yeah, I saw him." And I left it at that.

There was no need to go any deeper into that situation.

I was still pissed off about him baiting my dad. Part of me wanted to blame him for my painful table ride, but I knew I couldn't do that. He had no idea how sick my father was. He had no way of knowing that by pushing my dad's buttons he was typing in the combination to release a night of terror on me. I was almost positive, had he known what he was setting me up for, he wouldn't have said those things. Zeke wasn't a nice guy, but he was a good guy. Only a good guy would rush a strange girl to the hospital and only a good guy would save me from being trampled to death by a herd of Pit People.

I barely paid attention during the movie. My mind kept going back to Zeke. I kept wondering if he got out of jail. I hoped he didn't get into too much trouble. If he did, he had no one to blame but himself for carrying drugs around, but still, I did kind of tell on him. Even if I was trying to help, in the end I just made things worse for him. The poor guy had only been trying to help me and I thanked him by getting him drug charges. I hated the idea of him sitting in jail while I was free to go to a movie all because of who my dad was.

At school on Monday, I found out that Zeke was released from jail. Megan and Chet had graduated to texting and I'd dropped a little bird in her ear to find out if he was okay. Apparently, he had to pay a big fine and had two months of community service to get through. Maybe I'd find out what kind of service he had to do and volunteer since, technically, I should have community service too.

After school, I went to the Clerk of Court and paid his fine out of my savings account. It was the least I could do and I'd seen Zeke's home. He probably didn't have money for gas, much less almost five hundred dollars to pay a fine.

I ended up getting to soccer practice late, which earned me ten laps around the field. I didn't mind it. I used that time to zone out and go to my happy place. It seemed I was living in that imaginary world more than the real world these days.

After my laps, I practiced hard and then jogged home from practice. I wanted to be so exhausted that I couldn't stand up straight when I got home.

Once I walked in the door I was bombarded by Sydney.

"What happened to your face?" she asked with wide eyes.

I rubbed my cheek. I'd heard that question so many times that day and different people got different answers. I was becoming the queen of lies.

"Oh, it happened at practice last Friday. I didn't see you before you left to go to your friend's house for the weekend. No worries, Syd. It's healing nicely. So, what did you guys do this weekend? Lots of prank calls and junk food?" I asked as I scooted by her and went into the kitchen for something to drink.

My cheek forgotten, she started talking about all the fun stuff she and her friend Ashley had gotten into over the weekend. I loved hearing about her having a good time. I was happy to know my sister was growing up with happy childhood memories.

"And then her dad took us to that ice cream place down the road and we got sundaes. Hey, did you know Ashley's brother goes to school with you? His name's Jacob and he's super cute. Maybe you guys could go on a date or something?" She poked my side and I jerked. She thought she was tickling me, but really my ribs were still sore.

"I don't think I know anyone named Jacob, but I'm way too busy to date right now, Syd. Maybe once I graduate." I tugged a strand of her hair as I walked by and went upstairs for a shower.

Once I was settled in for bed, my phone went off with a text message from Megan.

Megan: FYI Zeke's serving his community service at that Boy's Club place on North Rhett Avenue.

Me: OK. Why are you telling me this?

Megan: OMG don't even act like you're not into him.

Me: I'm not.

Megan: Whatever. I'm not buying it. You should volunteer. Just saying.

Me: Maybe I will.

Megan: Good. OK, see you in the AM, Zeke Lover.

Me: OMG whatever! Goodnight, slut puppy. LOL

Megan: Hey, I kind of like the sound of that. LOL Goodnight!

THE NEXT DAY AFTER SOCCER practice, I had Megan take me to the Boy's Club so I could volunteer. The Boy's Club was a place for young, troubled boys to go after school. It would be hard dealing with a bunch of badass young boys, but if Zeke had to do it, it was only fair I did too. I walked into a huge gymnasium full of boys running around with basketballs. The sound of squeaking rubber echoed off the walls and mixed with loud laughter and joking, making for a very loud space.

There were older boys and girls wearing bright-blue T-shirts scattered throughout the room. On the backs of the shirts were either the words "Big Brother" or "Big Sister." It was kind of cool they had a place for troubled kids to run to other than the streets.

A few boys caught my attention as they stared at me and snickered to themselves. A brave one stepped away from the group and came up to me. He was no more than thirteen with a dirty white shirt and holey sneakers.

"My friend over there thinks you look good," he said with a big smile as he pointed to another boy in the group.

"Oh, well, tell your friend I said thank you," I said as I started to turn and walk away.

I turned and face-planted right into Zeke's chest. I pulled back and he peered down at me through dark bangs. He shifted his head to the side, throwing his bangs out of his face, and then he sighed.

"You again," he said as he crossed his arms and bit down on his lip ring. "Guess that means I'm going to jail today."

I suddenly got a big case of nerves. "Why would you go to jail?" I fiddled with my hair.

"Every time I see you I end up behind bars. What happened to your face?" he blurted out.

I laughed like it was nothing, and then I threw out one of the lies I'd been spinning.

"It was a stupid soccer ball to the face yesterday at practice."

He didn't believe me. I could see it in his eyes.

"Why are you here? I mean, other than to flirt with underage boys." The side of his mouth tilted up.

"I wasn't flirting with underage boys and I'm here to volunteer. It's only fair since we were both arrested." I began to fidget.

"How did you know I was here?" he asked. He moved in closer and towered over me. Leaning in, he got in my ear and whispered, "Does your daddy know you're stalking me, snowflake?"

He was too close. I didn't like it when guys got too close, and I suddenly felt like I couldn't breathe. I stepped back like he'd burned me.

"My. Name. Is. Patience!" I said too loudly.

My voice bounced off the walls and echoed throughout the gym. Everyone around us stopped and looked at me like I was crazy. Embarrassment set in and I felt my entire body turn red. My cheeks were on fire and I wanted to shrivel up and disappear.

Above me, Zeke let out a throaty chuckle.

"Careful, *snowflake*, if your face gets too hot, you might melt."

SEVEN
ZEKE

SPENDING MY AFTERNOONS HANGING OUT with a bunch of badass brats didn't sound very appealing, but once the judge threw down his gavel there wasn't shit I could say. It was better than thirty days in jail. So after zoning out in class all day Tuesday, I hopped in my car and headed for the Boy's Club to clock in.

I was assaulted by the smell of old gym shoes as soon as I walked into the gym full of young boys. Every noise in the room echoed and made my headache ten times worse. I was approached by a young woman with bouncy black hair and she smiled up at me innocently.

"Are you Zeke?" she asked with a smile.

"That's me," I said with less exuberance.

"Great! You're early." She beamed. "My name's Lindy! Let's get you in a Big Brother shirt and I'll show you to your group."

The idea of changing my clothes sucked, but again, judge's orders are judge's orders.

I followed her through the gym to a little office tucked into the corner. I told her my size, then sat as she went to the back to find a shirt for me. I peeked out of the little window into the gym and watched as the kids played without a care. It was actually kind of nice to have a place for troubled kids to go. I wish I'd had a place like that when I was growing up. Maybe I could've been saved. Maybe I wouldn't be so fucked up.

The sun peeked into the gym as the front door opened and a girl surrounded by a sunny halo entered. Once the door closed, the bright light surrounding her disappeared and I could see it was none other than Patience, my little icy bad luck charm. I sighed out loud.

Why couldn't I get away from this girl? She was everywhere I was and it seemed like every time I saw her, something bad happened to me. I was starting to think she was a gift from the devil himself. She was a pretty box of temptation wrapped in a force field of police officers waiting to arrest me, or a box of sweets with a big-ass invisible mousetrap sitting on the cover.

I watched as she walked into the gym and stood there staring around like she was lost. She had on gym shorts and a tank top with her hair piled on top of her head in a messy ponytail. A pair of knee-high black socks fit against her well-shaped calves. She'd definitely just finished practicing some sport. Soccer, maybe? I'd never found sporty girls attractive, but something about the way she blew a wayward piece of hair from her face and flexed her firm arms at her sides was kind of hot. It made me wonder if she was athletic in bed. I bet she was.

"Here you go." Lindy came around the corner with a bright-blue shirt in her arms.

I felt like telling her blue wasn't my color, but whatever got me out of this shit as soon as possible.

She pointed across the gym to some kids standing right next to Patience.

"That group of boys over there is your group. Since today's your first day, just spend the hour getting to know them and we'll work on activities tomorrow."

I nodded my understanding, then got up and walked out. I watched Patience as I walked up behind her. She was beginning to fidget again and it struck me how cute she was. I heard the boys from my group laughing and joking, and then I watched as the bravest of the group walked up to her and started to flirt. I didn't hear her response, but suddenly she turned and ran right into me.

She smelled like freshly cut grass and female. It was a weird combination since the feminine smell usually wasn't associated with anything outdoorsy, but I liked it. It belonged to her and somehow, even though she was delicate looking and entirely too sweet, it fit her. She looked up at me and suddenly I felt sick to my stomach. A faint black bruise worked its way up her cheek and under her eye. I knew my bruises and this was definitely a backhand to the face. It was at least three days old, which let me know it happened once she left the police station.

The urge to reach up and run my finger softly across her bruise was strong. I'd never wanted to soothe something so bad in my life. I didn't like feeling that way. As a matter of fact, I fucking hated it. I wanted to lash out at her, but more than anything, I wanted to beat the shit out of her dad for laying a hand on such a defenseless person. Then again, I should kick my own ass since I was positive me being a smartass contributed to the problem.

It must have been obvious that I was staring down at her bruise because she swiped at it anxiously with her hand and turned her head away a bit. She told me with her eyes what I already knew. That bruise was my fault.

"You again," I said as I bit down on my lip ring. "Guess that means I'm going to jail today."

She looked as if she was physically shaking and I wondered for a moment if she was afraid of me. "Why would you go to jail?" she asked. She reached up and grabbed at the ends of her ponytail.

Every time I saw her, she got prettier and prettier and after our last run-in at the jail with her asshole of a dad, I looked at her differently. Before, I thought her life was perfect, but after seeing her fucked-up relationship with her dad, I knew not everything was as it seemed.

"Every time I see you I end up behind bars. What happened to your face?" I blurted out.

I shouldn't give a shit what happened to her face, but I did.

She shrugged and attempted to laugh it off. "It was a stupid soccer ball to the face yesterday at practice."

She was lying, but I didn't push it. I knew what it was like to make up excuses for a busted lip or a black eye.

Quickly, I changed the subject.

"Why are you here? I mean, other than to flirt with underage boys." I smirked down at her.

She was so much shorter than me. I liked that. It made me feel powerful somehow... manly.

"I wasn't flirting with underage boys, and I'm here to volunteer. It's only fair since we were both arrested." She shrugged.

I guess being the governor's daughter had its perks, like being able to find out personal information on people's community service, but then again, why would her dad tell her how to find me when he so obviously didn't want us to be around each other? Not that I could blame him after my smartass attitude toward him the last time we were together.

"How did you know I was here?" I asked. I didn't want the kids behind her to hear us so I moved in closer. "Does your *daddy* know you're stalking me, snowflake?"

Her eyes filled with panic and it pissed me off that she was afraid of him. Then she stepped back so quickly she almost tripped over her sneakers. She glared up at me with a pinched mouth. She was pissed off about something.

"My. Name. Is. Patience!" she yelled at me.

I had to admit, I liked it when she yelled at me. Mostly because it let me know she wasn't as weak and defenseless as she looked, but also because I'm a fucked-up individual and occasionally I get off on being jerked around.

Her voice reached every wall of the gym and everyone turned to look at us. I watched as a pretty red blush crept up her neck and filled her cheeks. Her eyes started to water and become bloodshot and she looked like she was about to blow up from embarrassment. The poor thing, she looked like she was about to pass out, but it was funny to see her so pissed off and embarrassed. I kind of enjoyed ruffling her feathers.

I laughed softly to myself, earning another evil glower and I couldn't help but poke the bear one more time.

"Careful, snowflake, if your face gets too hot, you might melt."

She pressed at my chest with tiny palms and actually growled at me as she pushed me out of her way. I fucking loved it. I turned in just enough time to see her fly into the girl's bathroom.

The group of boys started to laugh. I turned and glared down at them. They all stopped laughing and looked around like they weren't being a bunch of nosey asses.

"So, I guess I'm lucky enough to get stuck with you guys," I said as I walked over to the group.

There were three of them and none of them looked old enough to be in any kind of trouble. They couldn't have been much older than thirteen, but then again, when I was thirteen I was smoking weed and getting hand jobs from fifteen-year-old girls behind my trailer.

"Sweet! What's your name?" one of the boys asked.

He was the smallest and still his clothes looked too small. The kid had on two different socks and a torn-up shirt, but he had the biggest, happiest smile on his face and it made you forget about the fact that he was probably miserable at home.

I grabbed one of the little plastic school chairs, turned it around, and straddled it with my arms resting on the back.

"The name's Zeke. What's yours?"

The smallest one bounced the basketball between his legs and switched his feet around like he was a basketball star. “My name’s Keaton. The tall boy there is Riley and the quiet kid over here is Alex.”

My attention went to the quiet kid in the corner named Alex. He looked pissed off and as unhappy about being there as I was.

After introductions, I told the boys to go play some ball and hang out, and then I sat in my chair and watched from afar as I played on my phone. After a few minutes, I felt someone come up behind me. The smell of fresh grass filled my nose.

“I see you decided to come back out to play,” I said without looking up from my phone.

“I wouldn’t think of this as playing. This is just as much punishment for me as it is for you,” she said as she sat in the chair next to me.

I wanted to tell her she’d been punished enough by her dad. I could tell that by her face, but even with my blunt nature I couldn’t bring myself to say it.

“Then why do it?” I asked.

“Because it’s what’s right.” She looked at me like I was dumb.

“Do you always do what’s right?”

“I try to, but sometimes people like *you* make it hard.” She shot me with a sexy glare that I’m sure she thought looked mean.

“Oh, come on. You know you like it when I tease you.” I grinned.

“You call this teasing? Isn’t teasing supposed to be fun? Nothing that comes out of your mouth is fun. You’re an asshole every time I talk to you.” She leaned back in her chair and crossed her arms.

She wanted teasing? Then teasing was what she was going to get.

"Nothing that comes out of my mouth is fun? I resent those words. My tongue comes out of my mouth and I've been told multiple times that it's fun."

Her eyes got large and she started to blush again. Damn, I liked making her blush.

"I should probably go talk to the director and find out what they need me to do. It was nice talking to you again, but we should definitely stay away from each other, I think." She stood and her chair screeched across the gym floor.

"Definitely." I jokingly agreed.

I watched her ass in her tiny gym shorts as she walked away. To be so petite, she had the most beautiful thighs and calves and I was starting to wonder what it would feel like with them wrapped around me. As much as I tried to fight it, she was starting to grow on me, which meant staying away from her was my best bet. A girl from her side of town had no business messing with a guy like me. On the off chance she decided she wanted to take a ride on the Zeke Express, I needed to make it clear she wasn't welcomed around me. I knew myself and if she ever offered, I would jump all over that.

Of course, that plan was shot to hell when she finished talking to the director of the Boy's Club.

"Looks like I'm stuck with you," she said as she plopped into the seat beside me.

She blew at the piece of hair that kept escaping her ponytail and rolled her eyes.

"Well, I was here first. Plus, I have to be here, while you're only here so you can flirt with young boys." I didn't look up from my phone.

"I'm not here to... You know what? I'm not even responding to that. It's too late. I said I would volunteer for a month, so I will, but once the month's up I'm out of here." She blew at the piece of hair again and my fingers itched to push it behind her ear.

Then she got up and walked over to the young boys and started talking with them.

"You guys like playing basketball?" she asked as she tried to dribble a ball. It bounced away from her and the smallest boy chased it down.

"Yeah, basketball's our favorite sport. What's your favorite sport?" the one named Riley asked.

"I play soccer. You guys know anything about soccer?"

I watched from afar as she very patiently kicked the ball around with the boys. She was teaching them how to softly kick the ball with the inside of their foot. She would clap and get excited when they did well and pat them on the back and tell them to keep trying when they didn't. It was kind of amazing to watch. She was so caring, sweet, and patient with the boys. Again, I was struck with how perfect her name was for her.

"Are you the goalie?" the smallest boy asked as he wiped at his sweaty forehead with the back of his hand.

"No, I'm the girl who kicks the goals. I'm the striker." She smiled proudly.

I bet she looked so hot all sweaty in those little, gym shorts. I shook my head, trying to shake out the image of

Patience pulling off that tank top and having a sexy little sports bra underneath.

When our hour was up, I pushed up from my chair and stretched. Sitting for almost an hour in that tiny chair had my ass numb and my legs stiff.

"Okay, boys, I guess I'll see y'all tomorrow." I yawned.

"Yeah, he doesn't want to miss the chance for a nice hour-long nap," Patience joked with the boys.

They all laughed. She looked over at me and the smile on her face was so bright and happy that I caught myself smiling back at her. As soon as I realized it, I turned and walked away. I didn't even tell her good-bye. I stopped by the bathroom to take a piss before I left and then I pushed on the heavy blue doors of the gymnasium and walked into a shadowed evening. It was close to dark and parents who'd just got off from work were showing up to collect their kids. I threw on my black hoodie and started toward my car.

My door creaked as I opened it and jumped inside. I cranked up my loud engine and turned on my headlights. They shined directly on Patience who was sitting on the curb out front. I sat a minute and debated leaving her there, but the thought of her being stuck in the dark alone bothered me. I pulled up next to her and she looked up and rolled her eyes.

"Don't you have car, rich girl?"

I knew it was an asshole thing to say, but I said it anyway.

"Yes, I have a car." She looked back down at her phone and dismissed me.

"Then why are you sitting out here instead of driving it home?"

I knew I should just pull off and be done with it, but this wasn't the greatest place for a pretty girl like Patience to be sitting in the dark alone.

"I don't drive. I'm waiting for my friend Megan to pick me up. She's supposed to be here. I'm sure she's on the way." She bit the inside of her mouth.

"But you haven't heard from her and she isn't here?" I sighed and flexed my hand around my steering wheel.

"She'll be here. I'll be fine."

I pushed my head back into the headrest in aggravation and sighed. "Just let me drive you home. Text your friend and tell her you have a ride."

"Thanks, but I'd rather just wait."

I looked down at her and rolled my eyes.

"Are you scared I'll take advantage of you once you're in my car? Because if that's the case, trust me when I say *you* have nothing to worry about."

And she didn't. Not because I didn't think she was attractive, because I did. I wanted to peel off every piece of clothing she wore, except those hot knee-high soccer socks, and have my way with her. The reason she had nothing to worry about was because I knew better than to jump the rich man's fence. Plus, she was probably a virgin and virgins tend to be clingy and annoying afterward.

"While it's nice to know you think I'm a dog, I'd still rather just wait for Megan. Thanks anyway." She gave me a quick, sarcastic smile.

At that exact moment, her phone dinged. She looked down and sighed. Then she shook her head and looked back up at me.

"Offer still stands," I said as I let off the brake and inched up like I was about to ride off without her.

"Fine." She stood and swiped at the dirt on the back of her shorts.

She walked around the front of my car and my headlights illuminated her thick thighs as she cut a path in front of me. I reached over and unlocked the passenger-side door and pushed it open. She slipped in next to me, shut the door, and then reached over for the seatbelt that no longer existed.

"No seatbelt, but if you're worried you'll fly out of the car, you can slide over and I'll hold you in." I grinned over at her as we drove off.

She fiddled with her hands in her lap as I pulled out of the parking lot. All that did was draw my attention to her legs. I followed her thighs down to her knees and back up. I wanted to reach over, slide my hand over her thigh, and rest my fingers in the warmth between her legs. I looked up and saw her watching me as I stared at her legs. She looked away quickly like she didn't catch me checking her out, and I chuckled softly to myself.

"So, what's the deal with you? Do you, like, kick puppies during your free time and stuff?" she asked as she worked the lever 'round and 'round to roll the window down.

I was shocked that she even knew how to use it, since I'm sure every car she'd ever been in had automatic windows and air-conditioning.

"I don't kick puppies, just people." I looked over and watched as the headlights from oncoming cars dashed across her face. The light reflected in her eyes when she looked over at me.

"Something pretty bad must've happened to you when you were younger to make you so angry," she said casually.

"Why do you say that?" I couldn't help but ask.

She was silent for a few seconds before she finally responded.

"I know broken people when I see them." She looked away and focused on the passing trees.

I assumed this was the part where she was going to try to psychoanalyze and then fix me. A lot of women had tried, but none ever succeeded. Some of those women were hardcore and understood what it was to have nothing and live a shitty life. The princess in the passenger seat knew nothing of those things.

"Pfft. You know nothing about being broken," I snapped.

"Yeah, I guess not." She looked down and shook her head.

Suddenly, the memory of the way her dad treated her and the fact that she had an old, healing bruise across her cheek popped into my head. I felt like shit the minute I thought about it. Who's to say this girl didn't get her ass kicked once a week like me?

I knew right away when we made it to her side of town. The trees, broken-down buildings, and trailers were replaced with medium-sized brick houses and then massive houses surrounded by iron fences and perfectly manicured lawns.

She directed me where to go and I turned left or right when she told me to. That was the extent of the conversation for the rest of the ride. When I pulled up to her house, I was taken aback by how huge it was. Why did these people need such big-ass houses? It was a huge, white, two-story house with big columns and about twenty-five windows just on the front. There was a Jaguar parked in the driveway and a plush, green lawn. The sprinklers popped up and water began to squirt all over.

My car looked like a heap of trash sitting in the front of her house and part of me wanted to ram my big rust bucket into that expensive-ass Jag.

She turned toward me and the side of her mouth tilted into a tiny half smile.

"Thanks for the ride. I guess I'll see you tomorrow?"

"Maybe." I didn't smile back.

She continued to sit there like she was waiting for something.

"Are you waiting for a goodnight kiss, snowflake? Because you're not going to get one." I leaned over her and popped open the door.

Her scent invaded my senses and I felt her warm breath against the side of my face as I leaned across her. For a brief moment, I contemplated a tiny kiss. Mostly because I hadn't kissed a girl since I was fourteen—kissing was too personal—but also because her lips looked so sweet and juicy that they made me wonder what it would feel like to kiss her.

She cut her eyes at me and sighed and then she jumped out of my car like it was on fire while she muttered something that sounded like "asshole." I laughed as she slammed my door and turned toward her house. I waited for a few seconds and then sped off. The quicker I got back to my stomping grounds, the better.

EIGHT
PATIENCE

I CURSED MEGAN'S CAR THE entire ride to my house. Go figure her alternator would go out the minute I needed her to get me. And go figure I'd get stuck riding with someone who very obviously despised me for some unknown reason.

I suffered through another uncomfortable ride as I called out directions. When he pulled up to my house, the first thing I noticed was my dad standing in his office window, looking down at me. I knew in that moment I was going to have a bad night and I contemplated having him drive off and drop me off at Megan's house. Had it not been for the fact that my baby sister was stuck in that house, I would have.

I looked over at him and attempted to smile through my fear. His eyes looked even darker in the night. His piercings kept catching the light and drawing my attention to his mouth and eyes. I thought of a way to kill time. I never thought I'd ever feel this way, but the last thing I wanted to do was get out of Zeke's old, ragged-out car. He wasn't safe, but he was safer than what waited for me inside that huge house full of lies and death.

"Thanks for the ride. I guess I'll see you tomorrow," I said.

I was hoping he would say something about the Boy's Club or his community service. I was hoping he'd say anything to start some kind of conversation. I'd even settle for a sarcastic asshole response. Instead, he barely responded.

"Maybe," he said with a straight face.

He wanted me to get out of his car. I could tell he wanted to be rid of me and out of this fancy smancy neighborhood. I couldn't blame him. I wanted the same thing.

"Are you waiting for a goodnight kiss, snowflake? Because you're not going to get one," he said.

He leaned into my lap and my entire body tensed up. I thought for sure he was about to do something crazy, but instead, he popped open my door and leaned back. His warm breath caught the side of my cheek on his way up. It was minty, which was surprising to me. I expected him to smell like weed or something equally appalling.

I knew my time was up and I had to face the music. My dad had seen me pull up in Zeke's hunk of junk and he would know the car didn't belong to anyone he was okay with me spending time with. A swarm of irrational anger rang through me and I jumped out of the car. Why couldn't he just be social for once? I just needed a reason to *not* go inside. Was that too much to ask?

"Asshole," I muttered as I slammed his door.

I heard his laughter as he drove away.

Once inside, I was met with Sydney who was making herself a bowl of ice cream in the kitchen.

"Hey, you. How was practice?" she asked around a spoonful of cookie dough ice cream.

"Good. We have a game Saturday against Fort Dorchester. I'm going to go get a shower. I'll come tuck you in, okay?" I called out as I made my way to the stairs.

The quicker I got my shower, the quicker I could go see my mom and the quicker I could go to bed.

I stood under the steaming water and let the heat take the tension out of my tight muscles. I'm not sure how long I stood that way until finally my skin started to feel numb. After I dried off, I cleared the foggy mirror and checked my bruise. It was looking much better, but I was sure Zeke knew how I'd gotten it. It was strange that someone who knew nothing about me knew more about the inner workings of my home life than my best friend. I guess it was a good thing Zeke was so uninvolved with other people. Otherwise, he might be tempted to tell everyone the governor was an abusive asshole.

I'd rather him think I got slapped around. I'd never want anyone to know the kind of actual abuse I went through. It was embarrassing for me and I understood how disgusting my situation was.

When I got to my mom's room, she looked well. For once she had some color to her cheeks and her smile was an actual smile, versus the fake thing she gave Syd and me so we wouldn't worry. I crawled up in bed with her and she brushed my wet hair while I told her about my day. I left out the fact that I'd spent an hour of my afternoon at a shitty gymnasium full of juvenile delinquents and one certifiable asshole.

"I wish I could make it to your soccer games," she said sadly after I told her about practice.

"You're there, Mom." I smiled back at her and her eyes filled with tears before she continued to detangle my mass of hair.

It wasn't long until we were joined by Sydney. We sat and watched TV until both Mom and Sydney fell asleep. I didn't bother waking Syd. If she was sleeping next to Mom, then she was safe for the night and I could attempt to get some sleep. I had yet to see my dad and I knew as I crept down the hallway on padded feet it wouldn't be much longer before he came and said his peace or did something else.

I passed my mom's nurse, Patricia, on the way to my room and she smiled at me and mentioned how Mom had a great day. Once I saw her disappear into Mom's dark room, I knew I was on my own.

I closed my bedroom door behind me and slid under my blanket. I rolled over onto my side and stuck my arm under my pillow for support. It was then that I saw my dad sitting in the chair by my window, looking back at me. What kind of crazy person sat in a dark room and waited? A predator, that's what kind.

"Who dropped you off?" he asked calmly.

I knew the minute I said Zeke's name that calm exterior would crack.

I swallowed hard and sat up on my elbow. "Zeke Mitchell."

I could have lied, but somehow I knew he already knew the answer to his question. Lying would have made it worse, so instead, I was honest.

It was dark in the room so I couldn't see his reaction, but I'm sure it wasn't good.

"Why do you constantly ignore my rules, Patience? Where did your mother and I go wrong?"

He sighed into the dark room when I didn't answer his question. I knew it was a rhetorical question. Anything I said at this point was going to piss him off even worse.

"You used to be such a good girl, but not so much anymore. I'm not very happy with this change." He stood and adjusted his robe.

I waited with bated breath for him to untie his robe and come to my bed, but instead, he walked across my room and opened my bedroom door. The light from the hallway spilled into my room and landed on his face. I could see his flushed cheeks and bloodshot eyes and I knew then he'd been drinking his expensive scotch. I loved that damn bottle of scotch. Whenever he drank he got tired, and once he fell asleep he was out for the night. It was beginning to look like I definitely would be getting some rest tonight.

He turned to leave my room, but suddenly turned back toward me.

"Stay away from that boy, Patience. I mean it. Stay away from him *and* that girl Megan. You have a car. I suggest you use it. I better not catch you around them again. Do you understand?"

He didn't even wait for my answer. My room went dark again as he shut my door. I heard his footsteps go down the hall to his office and then I heard his office door open and close. The office couch was where he slept most nights, so I knew I wouldn't have to worry about him again. I closed my eyes and fell into a peaceful sleep.

The next day I rode the bus to school. That was something I hadn't done... ever, now that I think about it. Megan's car was being worked on anyway, and I'd walk before I drove my car or asked my dad for a ride.

The school day went by pretty fast and before I knew it, I was on the field practicing. I was sidetracked and missed a few goals, prompting my coach to lay into me about the importance of practicing and getting a good night's sleep. I thought that was funny considering the night before I actually slept pretty damn good.

I hitched a ride with my teammate, Casey, and had her drop me off at the Boy's Club for my hour of volunteering. I knew I'd have to call my dad to get me and I remembered I wasn't supposed to go around Zeke, but I'd made a commitment and I meant to follow through. If I had to jog all the way home I would.

Casey drove like an eighty-year-old woman and by the time I made it the Boy's Club I was already twenty minutes late. When I walked in, I was met once again with the loud echoes of the boys wilding out around the gym. I narrowly missed a basketball to the face as I made my way across the gym to my group and Zeke.

My group wasn't where they were supposed to be and I scanned the room until I found them. Tucked away in the corner behind the bleachers, Zeke was sitting in one of the small plastic chairs with his back to me. He was playing a guitar as the three boys sat with their eyes glued to him. The closer I got, the clearer I could hear what he played. It sounded pure, untainted by the rest of his band. I stopped in my tracks and listened as he played a song that sounded familiar. I couldn't put my finger on it, but I knew I'd heard it before. Afraid to interrupt, I stood there and listened. It was beautiful.

It wasn't the guitar that I'd seen him play before and I wondered where it came from. It was plain, beige, and looked too small for him, but he still played it perfectly.

"Can you teach me how to play?" the quiet boy, Alex, asked.

I'd never heard him talk until now. His eyes were lit up and he looked so involved in Zeke's playing. It was such a special moment, but I knew Zeke would snap the kids head off and ruin it. Instead, he stopped playing and shocked me.

"Well, that song is kind of hard, but how about I show you how to play something easier. If you like it, I'll teach something harder. Deal?"

Alex practically clapped his hands like an excited schoolgirl, then quieted down as Zeke started to pick an easy tune for the boys to listen to. It was a slow rendition of "Smoke on the Water" as he picked each chord slowly for the boy to learn. He was saying what each chord was and showing the boy how to place his fingers on the guitar. Then he handed Alex the guitar.

"Okay, you hold it like this," he said as he positioned the boy's hands properly.

Then I watched as he very patiently helped Alex pick each part of the chorus. When he was done, he looked up at Zeke like he was a god. It was so adorable.

"Good job, kid," Zeke said as he ruffled Alex's hair. "Now, see if you can do it by yourself."

He praised Alex when he hit the right chords, then softly chuckled and helped him when he didn't. It was like watching a completely different person and somehow I knew I was seeing the real Zeke.

I reached down to scratch my leg and it brought attention to me. Right in front of my face, Zeke turned into the asshole. His back went stiff and his eyes pinched at the corners.

"Okay, that's enough for today. Y'all go play," he said in a stern voice.

Alex smiled up at him, thanked him, and then ran off with the other boys. I heard him say something about being a rock star as he passed me.

"If there's a guitar in a five-mile radius you find it, huh?" I asked as I sat beside him.

"Yeah, I guess so." He didn't look up at me as he picked at it and tuned it.

"Where'd you get that one?"

"Some kid brought it in and left it on the bleachers," he answered.

"You're really good with that thing." I pointed at the guitar.

He grinned up at me. "I'm really good with a lot of things."

Somehow I knew the flirty, sexual innuendo side of Zeke was a front. I'm not sure how I knew it, but I just did.

"You don't have to do that with me, you know?" I wasn't sure if I was headed in the right direction, but I felt like I should make it clear that I wasn't judgmental.

"Do what?" His brows turned down in confusion.

"Pretend. I saw you with Alex. You're a nice guy, Zeke. I don't know why you insist on playing the asshole."

"I don't pretend anything. What you see is what you get." He glared at me.

"If you say so." I smiled at him and shook my head. There was no way in hell I'd let him intimidate me with those deep eyes.

It was too late. I'd been given a peek into an alternate Zeke universe, and nothing he could tell me would convince me otherwise. He was nice guy who played the part of the asshole.

I took the guitar from him and ran my thumb across the strings. It made an awful noise and I cringed.

"Well, I suck at the guitar." I giggled.

He didn't laugh. He just stared back at me like he was pissed off about something. Then out of nowhere he came over and adjusted the guitar in my arms.

"You're holding it wrong," he said.

I jerked when he touched my hand to move it down in the right position. I wasn't sure if he noticed how uncomfortable it made me to be touched, but if he did, he didn't mention it.

"There. Does that feel more comfortable?" he asked.

It did and I looked up at him and nodded. He slung his head to the side and shifted his overly long bangs out of his face. I loved when he did that.

"Put your finger here," he instructed.

Again, he reached down and touched my fingers as he put them in position. His hands were rough and warm. And even though I'd had the initial jerk, the more he touched my fingers, the less uncomfortable it became. This was a revelation for me, since from the time my dad started coming in my room, I'd rarely let anyone but my mom and Sydney touch me.

"Now, strum it," he said.

I did and it sounded so much better.

He reached down again and rearranged my fingers against the strings. I felt a soft pull in my lower stomach as he softly moved my index finger and pressed it down.

"Again." He was closer now and still I wasn't bothered by his closeness.

I ran my thumb across the strings again, and again it sounded good. This continued, him moving my fingers and telling me to strum the strings until finally I could hear the song I was playing. It was the same song he'd been playing when I walked in. Except my version was a slower, crappier version.

"I know this song," I said. "What is it?"

Finally, he grinned down at me and shifted his bangs again. His lip piercing captured my attention and I had to stop myself from looking at his mouth. He must have caught me looking because his grin got bigger. He leaned in closer; his breath shifted the hair around my ear.

"Patience." The way he said my name sent a wave of heat down my spine. "By Guns and Roses... It's your anthem."

I felt my cheeks heat up.

"You were playing it when I came in," I said as I fiddled with the guitar again. Anything I could do to keep my eyes away from his.

It was starting to make me uncomfortable how *comfortable* I was with him. He was a stranger for crying out loud and a mean one at that. I should be deathly afraid of this dude, but instead, I felt safe around him. Maybe it had something to do with the fact that he'd saved me twice now or maybe we had some freaky cosmic connection. All I knew was being around him was nice. I didn't have to put up any fronts or play the governor's daughter. I didn't have to pretend to give a shit about fashion or be the best soccer player on the field. I could just sit and be me. I didn't have to pretend to be the Patience that everyone else thought I was because he didn't give a shit either way.

"I was." His eyes were darker.

He really knew how to pull off that dark and dangerous look.

"Do you like playing that song?" I asked casually as I handed him the guitar.

He picked at the strings a bit and then shrugged. "Not really."

"Then why were you?" I adjusted my tank top and sat back in my chair.

He played a little tune and shot me with another sexy grin.

"It reminds me of you."

NINE
ZEKE

THE MINUTE THE WORDS CAME out of my mouth I regretted them. The sweet, pink blush that covered her cheeks was the main reason. The other reason was because it sounded like something a pussy whipped punk would say. I completely ignored the fact that it was true. I was playing that song while waiting for her to show up. No one needed to know I was actually kind of looking forward to our little words war. It was fun teasing her and getting under her skin. It kept me from thinking about the fact that I wanted to get under her panties even more.

Thankfully, she didn't respond or make me explain. Because of that, I instantly liked her more. Most women would have questioned and beat that confession to death, not Patience. She was much too good for that. Instead, she smiled back at me and then jumped up and went to play ball with the boys. Again, I enjoyed the gym shorts view for the rest of my hour.

Afterward, when I saw her sitting on the sidewalk, I just pulled up and she opened the passenger-side door and got in. I didn't have to ask and she didn't pretend like she didn't need a ride. I'm not sure why I did it. My gas hand was low and I didn't have two dimes to rub together, but it just felt like the right thing to do.

The drive to her house was a quiet one and again, I appreciated the fact that she was so different from most girls. Most girls couldn't sit and enjoy a peaceful ride with just the radio on low. Most girls felt the need to pollute the silence with overdramatic nonsense. Not Patience. She stared out the window and every now and again I'd catch her nodding her head to the music and smile. She had a beautiful smile, one chock-full of honesty and genuine sweetness. I liked to see her smile.

Once we got closer to her house, that smile slipped from her lips.

"You can let me out here," she said as she leaned up like she was ready to dart from my car.

"I can take you all the way. I don't mind." I continued to drive.

"No, please just stop the car here." She suddenly seemed tense and annoyed.

I pulled over onto the side of the road and turned toward her.

"What's the deal?" I asked.

Better question, why did I care? If she wanted to get out of my car, then by all means, get the fuck out, but something wasn't right. Something was off. She went from peaceful and smiley to tense and worried in a matter of seconds.

"Nothing, I just feel like jogging from here." She turned to get out and sent me a big fake smile.

I reached out and grabbed her arm. A quick moment of terror rushed through her expression and then melted away just as quickly. She'd done the same thing earlier when I touched her hand to show her how to play the guitar. It was brief, but I didn't miss it.

"Cut the shit, snowflake. What's going on?" I asked.

She sat back, looked up at the ceiling of my car, and sighed.

"My dad told me to stay away from you."

I took a minute to celebrate the fact that she didn't try to correct me on her name. I liked snowflake. It fit her so well.

"Gotcha. You should definitely listen to what Daddy says." I grinned over at her.

"Yeah, it's just easier I guess." She shrugged.

"Although..." I leaned over closer to her. Her unique smell swarmed around me. "What's the fun in that?"

She looked up at me through her long lashes and took a deep breath. I liked that I affected her. It was only fair since she affected me. I wanted to move in closer. I wanted to touch her. Mostly because she was so damn untouchable and I had a rebellious streak in me that was ten miles long, but also because I was starting to wonder stupid shit. Shit like what her hair felt like and if her cheek was as soft as it looked.

I needed a swift kick in the ass. What would my boys think if they could hear my thoughts?

Then she caught me off guard by reaching up and running her finger across my lip ring. Her fingertip felt soft against my lip and some strange part of me that I didn't know wanted to kiss her fingertip. It was the most out of character thing ever... for me, and I think for her, too. Nothing shocked me anymore and it was strange that something so innocent managed to.

She pulled her hand back like my mouth was full of snakes and then looked away from me. She reached up and tucked a strand of hair behind her ear, but it was as defiant as I felt and it slipped back out. I reached up and captured it in my fingers. Her hair was indeed as soft as it looked. I didn't miss the odd expression on her face as I tucked the piece of hair behind her ear again. I should have stopped there, but instead, I ran my finger down her baby-soft cheek.

"What is this?" Her voice cracked.

The question brought me back to myself and I snatched my hand away. I did the first thing I could think of that would make the moment disappear. I leaned back and grabbed the crotch of my pants.

"What this? Come here. I'll show you."

The glazed look in her eyes vanished and she glared over at me. Without saying another word, she popped open my door and jumped out. I watched as she started to jog toward her house. I waited until she was in her yard before I pulled away.

Ten minutes later, I was stranded on the side of the road out of gas and waiting for Finn to bring me some. An hour and about ten text messages and phone calls later, I finally gave up on Finn and called my dad. He wasn't too happy about having to bring me gas. When he got there, he said nothing to me. He pulled up, rolled his window down, and pushed a red can of gas out the window at me. I took it from him and watched as he pulled away.

When I finally made it home for the night, all I wanted to do was grab a shower and go to bed. But the minute I walked in the door, I was hit with the raunchy smell of beer and Marlboros and I knew I was in for a rough night.

I barely made it through my bedroom door before he was on my back and punching me. Only a bitch hit a man from behind. I wanted to tell him what a bitch I thought he was, but instead, I stood my ground as he went in on me. He threw a few upper cuts to my ribs and I fell back against the paper-thin trailer wall. I messed up and moved my hands away from my face and he took the opportunity to land a hard punch straight to my right eye. An explosion of pain rang through my head and I dropped. When I woke up, it was two in the morning, the trailer door was wide open, and my dad was passed out in my mom's chair.

I skipped school the next day since my right eye was blood red and surrounded by a mean-ass bruise. Instead of school, I went over to Finn's so I could kick his ass for not showing up.

"Sorry, bro. I got stuck with a one-nighter who wouldn't leave. I finally got her out around ten this morning," he said as he crashed onto his couch and sighed.

"You know how to get a one-night stand to leave, right?" I said as I picked up the rolling papers and started to roll a joint.

"No. Please enlighten me, oh great one." He waved his hands around like he was summoning someone. I kicked him, making him laugh.

"If you want a one night stand to leave, all you have to do is pull out your wallet and ask how much you owe her."

Finn burst into laughter. "Damn, that's fucked up, dude. Leave it to you to come up with some shit like that."

Once I was done rolling up some green, I lit the joint and took a long, hard hit. I strained to hold it in as long as possible as I passed it to Finn.

"So, what happened to the eye?" he asked as he blew out his hit.

I tried to come up with a damn good excuse, but my head felt all fogged out. Not that I was making it any better by smoking weed and getting high. When I didn't respond quick enough, Finn started in on me.

"I hope you at least kicked their ass."

I didn't say anything. Instead, I cut my eyes at him and gave him a look that said I did.

Who knew? Maybe next time would be the straw that broke the camel's back. Maybe next time I'd get tired of being his punching bag and I'd haul off and beat my dad to death. Sometimes, that's what I felt like doing when he went off on me. The thought of spending the rest of my life in jail wasn't very appealing and I was already planning on leaving Dad's house very soon. I could take his shit for just a few months more. I'd done it for years. What's a few more months?

If I had the choice, I would've skipped community service, too, but again, the jail time thing wasn't something I wanted to do. So, after spending the day with Finn and smoking entirely too much weed, I drove over to the Boy's Club. Patience met me at the door. She had a light glistening of sweat over her face and her eyes were unusually bright. Guess what they say is true—exercise is good for you. She looked vibrant and full of energy, while

I felt like finding the nearest bed and taking an all-night nap.

She popped out her ear buds and rolled them around her phone. I leaned in to open the gymnasium door for her and she stopped me.

"What in the hell is that smell?" she asked. Her cute mouth curled up in disgust. "Did you just leave a house fire or something?"

Shit! I didn't even think to run home and change my clothes and now I was about to walk into a place full of juvenile delinquents smelling like weed. She thought I smelled like a house fire, which was hilarious. Leave it to Patience to be the only seventeen-year-old alive to not know what weed smelled like. I bet she'd never even been near the stuff, with the exception of The Pit. I knew for a fact it rotated around the room there.

"No house fire," I said as I pulled my shirt over my head.

I walked back to my car and threw it in the front seat. When I walked back to the door she was still standing there waiting on me. Her eyes looked like big blue pools of shimmer as she openly stared at my chest. I loved the way she looked at me—like I was the only guy she'd ever seen with his shirt off.

I watched as her eyes landed on each of the tattoos on my chest and arms and then moved down my stomach. Her eyes were taking me in and for some reason it was a massive turn-on. It was as if she touched me every place she looked. I started getting hard. I'd never had a girl get me hard just by looking at me. More than likely it had more to do with that fact that I hadn't had sex in weeks, but still, I really fucking liked it.

"You're going to go in there like that?" She motioned at my naked chest.

I chucked to myself. "No, I was going to see if you would run inside and get me that stupid Big Brother shirt."

"Oh." Her eyes flicked over my chest once more. "Sure, be right back."

She pulled open the door and slipped inside. A few minutes later she came back out holding the god-awful blue shirt. I pulled it over my head and shifted my hair out of my face. She watched openly so I smiled down at her as I pulled open the gym door and held it open for her.

"After you." I motioned for her to go inside.

I wasn't usually the gentlemen type, but she had gotten a good view of me. It was only fair that I get to watch her tight little ass in those gym shorts I loved so much. She didn't disappoint as she shifted her hips. Unlike most girls, she wasn't doing it on purpose. She had a natural sway that had me practically bobbing my head from side to side. Her ponytail bounced with the beat of her walk. I was so involved with watching her ass and thighs that I slammed into her when she stopped abruptly to miss a wild basketball.

I wrapped my arm around her waist to keep her from tumbling over. Her hips and ass melded into me and I'd never felt something so fucking amazing. It turned me into a caveman. I wanted to grab her by the back of her hair and bend her over the nearest anything. Tonight, I'd fall asleep thinking about doing her from behind.

I didn't let go of her immediately. Instead, I held her close to me and enjoyed the feel of her ass against my now rock-hard cock. Women say men think with their penis and in that moment, my penis was the only thing thinking. It took me minute to realize that her entire body had gone tense in my arms. I didn't feel her nails as they dug into my arm. I didn't hear her begging me to let her go.

"Let me go, let me go, let me go," she was saying over and over again as she slapped at my arm.

I released her immediately and she turned and faced me. Her pupils were dilated and there was more fear on her pale face than I'd ever seen a person display. She was hyperventilating and shaking so badly I thought she'd pass out. Instead, she took off and ran out the gym door. The sun poured in and then the door snapped shut, leaving me in the shaded gymnasium. It was like she'd left the darkness of hell and walked into a heavenly room full of light. It was a perfect metaphor for my current situation. She belonged in the light and I was right where I was meant to be—stuck in a dark, dank gymnasium, surrounded delinquents.

I wanted to chase after her, but that was something I'd never do. Chasing after women was for bitch boys and I was determined I wasn't going to let this chick change me. As it was, she already had me thinking crazy thoughts. I had more control over my actions than I did my thoughts. So, instead of going after her and making sure she was okay, I went to my group and sat in my trusty chair to wait the hour out.

She never came back and the hour was the longest one I spent at the Boy's Club yet. It dragged since I didn't have her to tease and talk to. The boys did their own thing, which made me feel like nothing more than a glorified babysitter. Every now and again, one of the boys would come up and ask where Patience was. I just shrugged and said I didn't know.

Once my hour was up, I walked out into the cool evening air and made my way to my car. I checked the parking lot to make sure she wasn't there waiting for a ride, and then I pulled out and headed home. I stopped at the first red light I got to and my headlights lit up the park across the street. Sitting alone on a swing with her head down was Patience. My headlights practically reflected off her platinum locks. I turned my blinker off and instead of turning at the light, I drove straight into the park parking lot when the light turned green.

My loud car caught her attention and she looked up. I cut the engine and got out. She was writing in the sand beneath her with her shoe as I walked over to the swings. Sitting in the swing next to her, I pushed over and softly bumped her knee with mine.

"The boys were asking about you. I think Keaton has a serious crush on you."

The side of her mouth tilted up, but she continued to stare at her feet. We sat in silence after that until finally she leaned her head back and sighed.

"I'm sorry for that back there," she said without looking at me. "I don't usually claw the hell out of people who are trying to keep me from falling."

Sure, I had originally wrapped my arm around her to keep from falling, but I kept it there for much different reasons.

"Don't worry about it. I was feeling you up after a certain point. So we're even." I grinned at her when she looked at me with wide eyes.

"Really? Well, in that case, serves you right." She smirked back at me and let me know she was teasing me. "Is that what happened to your eye? Did some chick punch you for being too touchy feely?" she laughed.

I had forgotten about my eye.

"Yeah, something like that." I nodded.

She leaned back and pushed off with her feet. I held on to the two chains holding the swing up and watched as she went back and forth beside me.

"So, what's your deal, snowflake?" I asked.

She looked over at me. A strand of blond stuck to her face.

"What do you mean?" she slowed.

Again, she didn't correct me when I called her snowflake. I'd won that battle.

"What do you do when you're not being the governor's daughter, the soccer star, the Good Samaritan, or a wannabe rocker chick at The Pit?"

Her brows puckered as she thought for a minute.

"I don't really do much else, I guess. Just school and stuff."

"You go to the prep school, right?"

She sighed and rolled her eyes. "Yep."

Chet had told me about the sexy schoolgirl uniforms they wore there, and I pictured her in it. Damn.

"I'd like to see you in your sexy schoolgirl uniform," I said.

Her cheeks turned bright pink and she shook her head. "Are you always so blunt?"

"Always," I said as I leaned back in the swing.

"I suppose I like that about you," she said softly, like she was confessing something huge. "It's refreshing. Even if you do say some pretty vile things." She reached out and playfully pushed my arm. "What about you? What's your deal?"

"I don't really have a deal. My dad's no governor, I've never played any sports, but I've played the guitar since I was seven, I don't help people, and I could never pull off the rocker chick look." I swiped at my bangs like a girl would.

She laughed at the last part and it made me smile. She had an amazing laugh.

"Well, that's pretty cut and dry, except you're wrong about one thing."

"What's that?" I asked.

She looked over at me and her ponytail rested against the side of her face. "You helped me."

She had me there. I still didn't know what made me help her in the bathroom that night at The Pit. It was a question I'd asked myself a few times. I was changing some and I wasn't sure I was okay with going soft since I needed my hard shell to keep myself alive.

"Only because I was hoping to get laid." I lied.

"If you say so," she said as she pushed off on the swing once more. "So you live with your dad?" she asked.

I didn't want to answer, but since I'd initiated the questions, I felt like I had to.

"Yes."

"Do you ever see your mom?" She stopped swinging and pulled her hair out of her ponytail. I got caught up in her movements as she ran her fingers through it.

"No, I don't see my mom. And unless I straighten my ass up so I can go to heaven when I die, I probably never will. She died a few years back." The words burned my throat as I said them.

I rarely talked about my mom. Mostly because it caused this strange pressure in my chest that I didn't like, but also because I didn't think it was anyone's damn business. It was different with Patience. She wasn't being a nosey bitch. She was just making conversation.

"I'm sorry," she whispered. She looked over at me with a wounded look in her eyes. "My mom's dying."

I didn't say anything. There's not really much you can say to something like that and even if there was, I wasn't the kind of guy who'd say it. Instead, I looked away.

"I don't know why I said that," she mumbled. "It's actually the first time I've said it out loud. I'm sorry."

When I looked back up at her, her bottom lip trembled and the strange pressure that I hated so much when I talked about my mom seeped into my chest.

"Don't apologize," I said as I stood up. I needed to move. I needed to do anything that would make the pressure in my chest go away. She stood up next to me and looked back at me with those big blue eyes. "Come on, let's get you home."

I reached out and tucked a stray piece of hair behind her ear. She jerked at the contact and then her body relaxed.

"Thanks," she said as she started to walk next to me to my car.

"No worries, you'll owe me one," I grinned over at her.

TEN
PATIENCE

I'M NOT SURE WHAT MADE me tell Zeke my mom was dying. Even saying the words made me feel sick, but we were having an honest moment and I wanted him to know I sort of understood his pain. I'd seen the look in his eyes when he said his mom was dead and it had been like a punch to the ribs to see such a hard, carefree guy show so much pain in that brief moment.

Being around Zeke was like watching a movie on a broken TV and having the screen blink on and off. Every now and again, I got to see brief flickers of the real him and I had to admit, I really liked those brief moments. More than I should.

We didn't say much on the drive to my house and he even stopped and pulled over before getting to my house without me saying so. I appreciated him doing that.

"Well, I guess I'll see you tomorrow afternoon?" I said, before I got out of the car.

"It's a date." He grinned over at me.

I popped open the car door and got out. I shut the heavy door and turned to walk away.

"Hey, snowflake," he called out. I turned back around and leaned into the car window. I was starting to like my nickname, although I'd never admit it to him.

"Yeah?"

"I'm sorry about your mom. I'm an asshole, but even I wouldn't wish that kind of pain on someone." He looked uncomfortable with his confession.

I nodded my understanding and stepped away from the car. I stood there as he drove off. His car stood out in the upscale neighborhood. It wasn't often a car with a mismatched hood and smoking tailpipe drove through here, but truth be told, I was even starting to like his car. It suited him somehow.

Once he was out of sight, I turned and jogged the rest of the way home. After my shower and visit with my mom, Syd and I watched a movie in my bed. She fell asleep halfway through and I didn't wake her. I turned off the TV, got under my comforter with her, and then got another amazing night of sleep.

Thankfully, Megan's car was back on the road and she was able to pick me up for school the next morning. I was told to stay away from her, but Dad was already gone before she got there. I'd have to make arrangements for her to pick me up at the stop sign near my house. She'd question it, but I'd cross that bridge when I got to it.

I was never so happy to see her jerk into my driveway. I hated riding the bus full of staring freshmen and sticky seats with gum on them. It was disgusting and I prayed I'd never have to do it again. Still, it was better than riding with my dad or driving the car that was supposed to be mine.

"I've missed you, chick. Anything new going on? How's the voluntary community service going?" She laughed.

I immediately thought of Zeke and how glad I was that I'd decided to volunteer. I couldn't deny the fact that I was starting to like him. Nothing could ever come from it because I was a total mental head case, but still, it was nice to think I was capable of liking a guy. It gave me a tiny spark of hope and I wanted to latch on to that hope and water it and load it down with sunlight so it could grow.

"What is *that* look about?" she asked with wide eyes.

"What look?"

"Oh my God, don't even try to play me! I've seen that look before, just never on *you*." She giggled. "So, spill it, woman! Who's the guy?"

I tried to school my face, but no matter how hard I tried, I couldn't get the smile to go down. I tried to smooth the sides of my mouth down with my fingers, but still the goofy smile remained.

"I have no idea what you're talking about." I looked out the window since I couldn't keep a straight face.

"Oh come on, Pay. As women it's our job to talk about boys. Tell me about him. Anyone I know?" She tapped her fingernails on the steering wheel.

"Okay, so you have to swear not to say anything." I sighed.

Her eyes lit up at the prospect of some juicy gossip.

"I swear I won't." She turned into the school parking lot and barely missed another car. They blew their horn at us and Megan flipped them off.

After I unlatched my hand from the dash, I ran my fingers through my hair and took a deep breath. This was the first time I'd ever confessed being in *like* with someone.

"So, you know I've spent the last few days at the Boy's Club with Zeke," I started.

"Oh my God, did you and Zeke make pre-babies?" Her eyes were so big I was afraid they were going to pop out of her head.

"Did me and Zeke what?" I'd never heard anything of the sort.

"You know! Did you guys bump uglies? As in, did you have sex?" She was motioning with her hands for me to hurry up and tell her.

"God, no! Geez, Megan. What I was going to say, before I was so rudely interrupted, is he's been taking me home afterward and I don't know... I guess I kind of like him." My face felt like it was about to combust.

"Well, of course you like him, Pay. He's hotter than hell. Plus, it doesn't hurt that he's amazing with a guitar, which has to mean he's good with his fingers, but you know me. I have a thing for tattoos and rock stars. I didn't think you did, though. I've never even heard you say a guy was cute before. Honestly, I was starting to think you were into girls." She shrugged.

"I am *not* into girls."

"Hey, no hate over here. You know I don't care about shit like that." She held up her hands palms out. "But I just figured..."

"Yeah, well, you figured wrong." I jumped out of the car and started toward the school. Within seconds, Megan was right beside me.

"So, Zeke, like, talks to you? Because Chet says he's not much of a talker."

I laughed thinking about all the stuff that came out of his mouth.

"Yeah, he talks some. He'd never admit it, but he's not a bad guy."

"Tell that to all the girls he's left behind. Although, it's not like they didn't know any better. Chet says Zeke is pretty upfront about only wanting one-night stands." She waved at some guy as we walked by.

"Yeah, that sounds about right. I don't know. We've only talked a little. I'm not, like, in love with him or anything. I was just saying I like him." I instantly started to worry that Megan would tell Chet and then Chet would tell Zeke.

Oh my God, he'd never let me live that one down. This whole talking about boys thing was new for me and I didn't know if I could trust Megan to keep her trap shut.

"Listen, Megan, please don't say anything to Chet, okay?"

"Cross my heart, hope to die!" she shouted across the hallway to me.

We parted ways as she went to her homeroom and I went to mine.

After a long, exhausting day of school, I went to practice and sweated my ass off. We played a scrimmage to get ready for Saturday's game and I left practice with twelve goals. Damn, I loved playing soccer.

Since Megan was spending more and more time with Chet, I had Casey take me to the Boy's Club after practice again. It worked since it was on the way to her house. When I went inside the gym, I was met with Zeke showing Alex how to play the guitar again, but this time it was a bigger guitar they practiced on. It had to be Zeke's and I thought it was sweet he would let some kid touch his guitar.

"Sounds good, Alex," I said as I walked up and ruffled his hair.

He smiled up at me as he picked slowly at the guitar.

I sat across from them and Zeke looked up at me. I smiled at him, but he didn't smile back.

Great! We were going to pretend we didn't have a nice talk the day before.

He shifted his hair out of his eyes and looked away as he helped Alex. I took the time to take a good look at him. He was tall. At least six-one, and even though he said he'd never played any sports, he had an excellent body. I remembered the day he took his shirt off because he smelled like smoke. His chest and arms were so beautiful and his tattoos were amazing. I even had a little shock at seeing one of his nipples was pierced. I didn't even know men did that and I liked it, but those tattoos were like living art on his skin. I'd give just about anything to take his shirt off and get a good look at them again.

Without realizing I was staring at him, he bit down on his lip ring and then licked his bottom lip. I didn't know much about being turned on by a guy. I only knew what Megan and other girls said, but I was almost positive that's what was happening. I couldn't look away from him, his dark hair that hung into his face and those full lips he was constantly biting and licking. Everything about him was dark, yet there was a tiny light inside of him that flashed on occasionally, and as sad as it sounded, I was willing to sit in the darkness and wait for that brief bright moment.

They were playing a different song today and I sat and listened as Zeke patiently showed Alex the right chords. Finally, he sent Alex to go play ball with the other boys and I watched as he played. His guitar was nothing like the little beige one that kid had brought to the gym. His was much bigger and it was a darker wood. There was writing on it that I couldn't make out so I leaned in to get a better look. He looked up at me and stopped playing.

"Wanna give it another try?" He turned his guitar toward me.

"Sure." I smiled.

He handed me the guitar and it wasn't as heavy as it looked, but it was way bigger than the other and was hard to hold. I strained to hold it up and he laughed softly.

"Whatever you do, please don't drop it." He flashed me a genuine smile.

I liked it when he smiled at me.

"I won't. This doesn't look like the one you play on stage."

"It's not. That one's an acoustic. It was my first one. The one I play with the band is more expensive and a different kind, but it's nice to know you pay such close attention to me when I'm on stage."

I didn't respond to that. I just fiddled with his guitar. Except, instead of trying to play anything, I turned it over so I could read what was written on it.

"What are you doing?" he asked.

"I noticed the writing and I want to see what it says," I said as I leaned down and tried to read it.

I'd taken my hair down, so it slipped in my face while I was looking down. I looked up when I felt his fingers sifting through my hair as he tucked it behind my ear. He met my stare before quickly looking away. It was then I realized that I didn't turn away from his touch. I didn't even jerk. It was a revelation for me.

He ran his finger across the guitar.

"All these are quotes my mother wrote on my guitar when she was sick. Things that she thought were insightful. See right here..." He pointed to a different spot. "That's her signature."

There was softness in his voice that I'd never heard before. Not that we were together all the time or anything, but Zeke was just naturally a hard guy. Hearing him speak so softly was kind of strange. Somehow, I knew I was getting another rare glimpse and I soaked it up.

"So this guitar means a lot to you, then? I mean, more than the one you play with the band?" I asked.

"This guitar is my most prized possession," he said as he ran his finger down the length of it. He shook off his emotional moment. "So if you break it, I might have to kill you," he joked.

"Thanks for the warning." I laughed.

"I always give fair warning to my females." He winked.

"*Your* females? I'm not your female."

"No, but you want to be." He lifted a challenging brow.

In the back of my head I feared Megan had already opened her big mouth. I didn't respond. Instead, I placed my fingers on the strings and strummed it. Again, it sounded awful, and again, he touched my fingers to position them. This time I didn't freak out inside. This time I didn't want to run away. Instead, I enjoyed the feel of another person's hands on mine. It was nice to be touched by someone other than my mom or Syd.

I liked it when he touched me and I didn't want him to stop. The strangest part was I felt guilty for liking it. It was like I was dishonoring the broken parts of myself for enjoying being touched when, after so many years of my life, being touched by a male was a bad thing. There were still alarms going off in different parts of my body, but Zeke made me ignore those alarms. No, Zeke made me run through and smash all the alarms with a baseball bat.

After our hour was up, we left the gym and walked into the evening breeze. I stopped at the edge of the curb and he continued to walk to his car. When he realized I wasn't walking with him, he turned around with a confused look on his face and came back over to me.

"Aren't you coming?" he asked.

"Oh, no. Megan's car is back on the road and she should be here any minute to pick me up."

His expression seemed to drop a bit and I relished in the fact that he might want me in his car as bad as I wanted to be there.

"Are you sure? I'm already here and I don't mind. Just text Megan and tell her I got you."

"Are *you* sure? It's way out of your way," I asked as I pulled my phone out of my pocket.

I hoped he was sure. I wanted him to take me home so badly. I enjoyed that twenty minutes of being alone with him.

"How else am I going to get you alone?" He grinned.

"Do you want to get me alone?" The minute the words left my mouth, I wished I could reel them back in.

Was I flirting? It surely sounded like flirting when I played it back in my head, but I didn't flirt... like, ever.

"I most definitely want to get you alone," he said as he reached up and ran a finger down my cheek.

I knew in the back of my head I shouldn't put much stock into his words. I'd heard the stories about the kind of guy Zeke was, but it was so hard not melt when he seemed so convincing.

"Then let's go." I shyly smiled back at him.

I texted Megan as I walked behind him to his car. Once we were in, he started the loud engine and pulled out of the parking lot.

"So, how about we go somewhere fun?" he asked.

It was unexpected and since I didn't want to go straight home, I was ecstatic when he said those words.

"Um... hold that thought." I pulled out my phone again.

I sent Syd a text making sure she wasn't alone. Once she texted back and confirmed that Lynn and Patricia were still around, I felt better about staying out later than usual. I knew there'd be hell to pay when I got home, but there was always hell to pay. I might as well enjoy myself while I was free.

"Okay, I'm all yours." I smiled up at him.

"I like the sound of that," he said. The side of his mouth tilted up in a sexy grin.

I didn't mean it that way, but I didn't feel like correcting him.

"So, where are we going?" I asked.

"I thought you could come hang out with me at Finn's house for a bit."

It was then that I remembered I was in sweaty practice clothes.

"But look at me. I can't go around people like this." I motioned to my clothes and hair.

"What's wrong with how you look?" he asked.

"Um... I have on sweaty clothes and I look like ass."

He laughed.

"You should know, I think those cute little, gym shorts you run around in are sexy as fuck." He looked over at me and lifted a brow.

I could feel the heat in my cheeks and instead of responding, I looked out the window to hide my blush.

When we pulled up to Finn's house, I was surprised by the amount of people there on a weeknight. Didn't these people have jobs or go to school? They were lounging around his garage and the inside of the place smelled like it was on fire. It wasn't until I saw the guy across the room smoking a joint that I realized what the smell was.

"Patience? What the hell are you doing here?" Megan ran up to me with a big smile.

"Um... I'm with Zeke. What are you doing here?"

She flashed me a big, goofy grin and pointed across the garage to Chet. He threw up a hand and I waved back.

Megan's eyes got large as she looked behind me, and then I felt arms come around me. I stiffened and was about to claw the arms like a wildcat until I heard Zeke speak. Just that fast, I felt calm. If anything alarmed me, it was the fact that I was okay with him touching me after a short amount of time. You'd think that after almost ten years of abuse, it would take me forever to become comfortable with someone, especially a guy.

"Do you play cards?" he whispered in my ear.

My entire body lit up with goose bumps and I shivered. His throaty chuckle sent his breath across my cheek.

"Sure."

He nodded at Megan and she had a big grin on her face as she backed away and walked back over to Chet. Zeke reached down, grabbed my hand, and then tugged me over to a small card table.

"Spades?" he asked as he straddled a chair next to the table.

I noticed the beer in this hand.

"Okay." I sat across from him.

He won the first hand, and then I won the second.

"So, snowflake, let me ask you something," he said as he flipped a card over and took a book. "Do you have a boyfriend?"

I stared open-mouthed at him for a bit until I could figure out how to answer his question.

"No, I'm not seeing anyone. I've never had a boyfriend." I mentally kicked myself for confessing the last part.

What was it about him that made me confess everything so easily? It was like when I got around him, I just opened my mouth and words fell out.

"Never?" His brows puckered.

I knew right away where he was going with this. No boyfriend meant no sex. No sex was supposed to mean I was a virgin, but my case was much different and I really didn't want to go there.

"Never."

"Oooh." His eyes got big like he was just realizing something. "I get it. You're into chicks."

Did I have the word "lesbian" written across my forehead or something today?

"No," I said adamantly.

"No, that's cool." His smile was too big. "I don't discriminate. Trust me. I like chicks, too. You know what? We should like them together, like at the same time." He leaned in and ran his thumb across his bottom lip before he softly tugged on his lip ring.

My eyes shot to his mouth and he smirked at the attention. I rolled my eyes.

"I don't like chicks, and if I *did* I certainly wouldn't share with *you*." I flipped my card over and picked up the book.

"Okay, so you're not a lesbian. Then what are you?"

Aggravated by his question, I sighed loudly and answered honestly.

"You want to know what I am? I'm shattered, that's what I am. There are tiny pieces of Patience scattered all over."

"I'd like a piece of Patience." He reached across the table and ran a finger across my hand.

This time I did tense up, but for entirely different reasons. My heartbeat sped up like I was on the verge of a panic attack, but instead, a rush of euphoria filled me.

"I don't know if I can give you a piece." I heard myself flirt back.

This earned me another sexy grin. Damn him for being so freaking sexy.

"Why not?

"Because I don't know where they are." I felt myself frown at those words.

What started out as innocent flirting had just that quickly become a sad truth. I was a shattered girl and I had no idea where my pieces were or how to put myself back together if I did find them.

"I bet I could find your pieces." He leaned in and bathed my cheek with heated breath.

I didn't miss his hidden meaning, but I chose to ignore it. "Good luck. I've been trying to find them for years."

I shrugged off my shiver and started to deal the cards again.

"Challenge accepted," he said as he leaned back in his chair and took a swig from his beer.

His dark-brown eyes never left my face and a part of me was afraid he'd secretly already found a few pieces of me. The room around us suddenly felt too hot and too small.

How did he do that? How did he evaporate all the cold air surrounding me with just a look? Did he know what he was doing with those eyes and those lips that were starting to drive me wild, but scared the shit out of me at the same time? I wanted to run away from him, yet being close to him somehow made everything feel okay. He was driving me insane and not in good way. I'd never felt so torn over my emotions before.

Physically, I wanted everything his eyes and lips promised. I wanted to feel his skin against mine, his fingertips, his mouth, but mentally, I wanted to hop on the next plane to anywhere far away and never look back. I couldn't understand or handle the thoughts my body sent to my brain. I was turned on by them, yet sickened by them. I was freaking Jekyll and Hyde with boobs and girl parts.

"I didn't issue any challenge. I was just making a statement." I swallowed hard.

"Yes, you did. You just begged me to find you. Consider it done."

ELEVEN

ZEKE

I WAS GETTING LAID TONIGHT. End of story. It had been too long, and if I didn't bust a nut in the near future, people were going to start getting randomly punched in the face. I was due for some serious stress relief and I didn't think putting my fist through the face of some random dude was going to do the trick. I needed female attention and I wanted that female to be the snowflake princess.

As I flirted with Patience, I knew I wanted her. She'd been driving me fucking crazy with those tiny gym shorts. There was even a point when she shifted her legs and I got a glimpse of purple panties. I'd never loved the color purple so much in my life. I went home that night and dreamt of being wrapped in purple warmth and woke up with a throbbing hard on.

Usually, I steered clear of girls like her since there was always a chance of an inexperienced female sprouting feelings, but something told me she wasn't a virgin. A virgin wouldn't switch her hips the way she did when she walked across the gym.

She said she never had a boyfriend. I wasn't sure how that was even possible with a girl like her. If I were prone to relationships, Patience would be right up my alley. Thankfully, I wasn't, but some guys were. Maybe she wasn't the boyfriend type. Maybe she was high maintenance and no dude would dare try. Either way, it didn't matter to me. I could no longer take being around her and not tasting her. I wasn't accustomed to spending so much time with a girl and not getting at least a taste.

I felt confident that I could get what I wanted. She was flirting with me and I'd seen the way she looked at me. I knew that look. I'd probably given her the same look. She wanted me just as badly as I wanted her. I also enjoyed the fact that she didn't jerk away from me every time I touched her anymore. That had to be a good sign, but still, I had to move slow and ease her into it.

I didn't usually work at all to get with a girl, but I wanted to do this right. Also, I was thinking Patience was the kind of girl I could remain friends with afterward. I'd never had a friend with benefits before since I was a hit-it-and-quit-it kind of dude, but I really liked her... as a friend, of course. I hoped things didn't get weird afterward and we'd just fall into the friend role.

After a few beers and eight hands of spades, it was getting late and I knew if I wanted some alone time with Patience before taking her home, I needed to snap to it. She picked up the cards and stuffed them back in the box. I kept my eyes on her the entire time, and I could tell from the pink blush that ran up her neck and landed on her cheeks that she knew I was watching her. I leaned in and breathed her in.

"I want to be alone with you," I said honestly.

Honesty was the best policy when it came to women. Sometimes they didn't like what you had to say, but they could never say you didn't warn them.

Her eyes met mine and I saw her visibly swallow.

"You do?" she looked up at me through her lashes.

I didn't answer. Instead, I reached out and linked our fingers together. I wasn't the hand holding type, but whatever I needed to do to touch her.

I celebrated the fact that she didn't jerk away from me. I set my beer on the tabletop and held her hand as I walked her out of Finn's garage and to my car. I nodded to Finn and the guys as I left and I didn't miss the big goofy smile on her friend Megan's face. They knew what we were going to do and I didn't care.

I let go of her hand as I made my way to the driver's seat. She popped open the passenger-side door and slid in. Once we were in and settled, I cranked up the car and turned to her. She looked so fucking hot, my little timid temptress. She had to know what she was doing. Maybe playing the shy sweetheart was her thing, but something told me she was a freak in bed.

I let my eyes wander up her black soccer socks to the tiny peek of creamy leg between her socks and gym shorts. It was chilly out, so she had on that damn hoodie, but I knew what was under it. I wanted to see her naked. I wanted to see if all of her was a soft as her hands and cheeks.

Once we left Finn's house, I headed in the direction of hers, but I knew I wasn't even close to taking her home yet. I looked down at the exposed part of her legs once more and I couldn't take it anymore. Her skin called to me and I needed to touch her. She was looking out the window at the passing scenery, so she didn't see me reach across the car, but when I laid my hand on the skin above her knee, she gasped and looked over at me.

There was a brief moment of panic in her eyes before she lowered her lashes and took a shaky breath. I felt the tension leave her leg under my palm so without looking over at her, I molded my hand to her inner thigh and pushed my fingers down to the space between her knees. Her skin was so warm and soft. All I could think about was moving my hand up and reaching inside her panties. I swear if that happened and my fingers met moisture, I'd jerk my car to the side of the road and fuck her right there on my front seat.

I kept my hand still but began moving my fingers softly back and forth inside her knee. I felt goose bumps rise on her leg beneath my palm and heard her breath get deeper. She was affected already and I was just getting started. Her tiny responses fueled my confidence, so I moved my hand up higher on her leg. I thought for sure she'd slam her legs together and move my hand, but she shocked me. Instead, she leaned her head back against the seat and her legs opened an inch more. That little movement was like a big green light for me.

I looked over at her to find her looking back at me. The headlights from approaching cars danced across her face and I realized she was more than just some hot chick. She was beautiful. The wind from her window pushed strands of her hair across her face and she swiped at them. She looked at me with trusting eyes and a nervous smile, and it was like a splash of cold water. She wasn't like the other girls I'd been screwing around with and I knew that from the start. I was letting my hormones cloud my decisions. Patience was a beautiful girl and I wanted nothing more than to feel her all over me, but she was untainted and I didn't want to be the one to contaminate her.

I let my hand slip back down to the safe zone and then I softly patted her knee. As hard as it was, I lifted my hand from her skin and wrapped it around the steering wheel. At the next light I came to, I put on my blinker and headed straight for her house. The trip to her house felt like an eternity. I'd never denied myself a woman when I wanted her and being shut up in this cramped car with her was hell. I didn't think I'd ever get her out of my car.

When I pulled up to the curb around the corner from her house, I put the car in park and turned to her.

"Tonight was fun. It's been a while since I got to kick some ass at spades." I chuckled.

"Um... you're delusional. I totally won all but three games. Also, you should know, I let you win those three." She grinned at me.

I laughed out loud at that one. "You *let* me win, huh?"

Her smile dropped and she looked away. "I let you do a lot of things."

"You do? Like what?"

She reached her hand across the seat to mine. I let her slip her fingers in between mine and then I tightened my fingers around hers. She held my hand and rubbed circles on my palm with her thumb.

"Like this." She looked up at me and the side of her mouth tilted up.

"Okay, you let me hold your hand? What's the big deal with holding hands?" My brows puckered in confusion.

"I don't let anyone touch me." She looked away. "Ever."

Her words had some deeper meaning behind them. It was such a small moment, but I could sense the fact that her confession was huge. Suddenly, I felt privileged. Something as small as holding a girl's hand felt enormous.

"Why not?" I asked.

I had a feeling I knew the answer. I'd seen the bruise on her eye and I was positive her dad hit her occasionally. Maybe it had something to do with that.

"I just don't like it. It makes me uncomfortable."

"But you're okay with me touching you? That doesn't make any sense."

"Why not? You're a nice guy, Zeke. I'm not sure what it is about you, but I trust you. I feel comfortable with you and I know you'd never do anything to make me uncomfortable." She shrugged.

"You're the worst judge of character, snowflake. You'd never make it where I come from." I shook my head.

"Are you saying I'm wrong about you being a good guy?"

"I'm saying that the entire time we were at Finn's place all I could think about was getting you alone and having sex with you. Does that sound like something a nice guy thinks about?"

"All guys think about sex, but you didn't really try anything. Instead, you brought me straight home. What does that say about you? I think it says you're a nice, respectable guy."

She was wrong. I wasn't a nice guy. I was me and I wasn't good enough to be around her, much less inside of her. I knew that and I think she knew that, but there was no way in hell I'd admit that to her. Instead, I cocked my head back and laughed it off like I did when I got uncomfortable with a conversation.

"Whatever helps you sleep at night, baby."

Then she was there, right beside me, staring me in my face, and the car felt too small. She reached up and pushed my long bangs out of my face with her finger. She ran that finger down the side of my face and it felt like I was being touched in the pit of my stomach. I bit down on my lip ring and she traced my bottom lip with her finger once I released it. It was too much. I'd never had a girl explore me this way and I wasn't sure if I hated it or loved it. Then she looked me in my eyes and smiled.

"You can hide in there all you want, but I can still see you."

I didn't say anything as she scooted back over to the car door, popped it open, and then jumped out to jog home.

It wasn't until I was almost home that I realized she was right. I hid myself a lot, but only because I was secretly afraid to get close to anyone. Getting close to people was dangerous. People died and the ones that didn't die hurt you.

The next day at Boy's Club we didn't talk much. I stayed to myself and played on my phone while she took the time to show the boys some soccer drills. When it was time to leave, she said she already had a ride and I didn't try and persuade her to ride with me. I was broke as a joke anyway and I didn't really have the gas. I'd made arrangements with Javier to work off the weed that was taken by the police and I was hoping to make some money this weekend.

After Boy's Club, I went over to Finn's and finally got a chance to practice. Finn got us booked at some new underground club a town over on the following Saturday. I'd missed so much practice because of my community service and spending too much damn time with Patience. My guitar was starting to feel foreign against my fingers and that was no good.

By the time Saturday came around, I'd barely seen my dad and I'd barely talked to Patience. Dad was easy to avoid when I crashed on Finn's couch, and I think Patience was avoiding me as much as I avoided her. I drove to Mount Pleasant, the town over, with the radio on, my guitar in the middle, and Tiny in the passenger seat butchering the shit out of a Smashing Pumpkins song. There was a reason he played the bass and didn't sing.

The club we were playing at was called The Icehouse and it made me think of snowflakes, which made me think of Patience. This thinking about a girl shit was really starting to piss me off, but no matter what I did to occupy my time, something always brought me back to her.

"Megan's coming to the show tonight," Chet said as he helped me run some wires while we set up.

"What's the deal with her? You getting some of that or what?" I asked.

"Pfft, man, she's the best sex I've ever had. That girl's a major freak. I'm talking about the biting, growling kind. I think I'm going to keep her. No, scratch that, I'm definitely going to keep her. At least until I get bored." He laughed.

At least one of us was getting laid. Then I realized something. Patience had said before that she wouldn't let Megan go to an underground club alone. Did that mean she was going to be there, too? I wanted to ask Chet, but I couldn't bring myself to do it. If I asked it would look like I gave a shit if she was there or not, and I didn't. I really didn't.

So when we started to play and I saw her walk in with Megan, it wasn't excitement I felt. It was annoyance. Mostly because she was there and she came knowing I'd be there too, but also because she looked so fucking hot I couldn't take my eyes off of her. The prep-school Patience was gone, and in her stead was a sexy little vixen with a low-cut top and the tightest pair of jeans I'd ever seen a female wear.

I tried to keep my eyes away from her as I played, but every now and again they moved over her against my will, and I'd get the sudden rush of heat that ran down my spine, wrapped around my pelvic bones, and landed in the crotch of my pants. It was like nothing I'd ever experienced before. I wanted this girl more than I'd ever wanted a girl in my life, but I couldn't and I wouldn't touch her. No matter how badly my body begged me to, I refused.

An hour later, she had some drinks in her system and was dancing on the floor with Megan. It was nice to see her smiling and happy even though I knew I'd have to take her home. Megan was obviously drunk out of her mind and there was no way in hell Chet was going to let her drive home, which was fine by me, considering there was no way in hell I'd let Patience ride home with her. I'd had a few beers, but I didn't even have a buzz and once I saw the two girls partying hard, I started sipping my beer instead of drinking it.

I took my attention away from Patience for a bit and scanned the crowd. It was a full room and everyone was having a good time. I turned and looked at Chet and he threw his drumstick in the air. Show off. When I turned back around, I saw Patience talking with some guy. She had my attention from that point on. I openly watched as she flirted with the guy she stood next to. I suddenly felt tense all over. My arms felt stiff and my eyes were starting to burn from staring so hard.

The guy reached up and picked something from her hair and I saw red at the thought of his hands touching her. It took everything I had in me to stay on the stage and keep playing. She leaned forward to say something to him and bits of her cleavage became visible. Patience wasn't the kind of girl to do something like that on purpose, although I knew girls who did. I'd been around women enough to know when they were obviously bending over just right to show some tit, but not Patience. She was smiling innocently back at him and had no idea the fucker was ogling her bare skin. He took her in with greedy eyes and slyly smiled down at her.

She looked up at him with big blue eyes and smiled and then he touched her again as he put a hand on her back. I saw her smile become uncomfortable for a second and then she seemed to relax. I didn't. Instead, I missed a chord and then another right after that, which prompted Tiny to poke me with his guitar and question me with his eyes. He was silently asking me if I was okay. I wasn't, but I nodded and continued to play.

The more time passed, the more I could tell Patience wasn't herself. I couldn't take my eyes off her and she was definitely acting strange. The playful flirting, the cleavage, and those painted-on jeans... none of it was her. Then she picked up a shot glass and slammed the liquid down like she'd been drinking her entire life. They say liquor takes away all inhibitions and she was making sure to melt all her insecurities away.

By the time our set was over, I was fuming. I couldn't get off the stage fast enough. I set my guitar next to Finn and then jumped down from the stage. I made my way across the room to the bar where they were standing and talking. I took flirty boy in as I grabbed her arm and pulled her away from him. He attempted to say something, but I turned back toward him and eyed him hard. He must have seen the anger in my eyes because he shut up and turned away.

"What are you doing, Zeke? Let me go," she slurred.

I didn't respond as I dragged her across the room to the bathroom. She was more clumsy than usual, which did nothing but piss me off even more since I knew it was because she was drinking. I pulled her into the bathroom and let the door slam behind us. Finally, I let her arm go as I made sure there was no one else in the bathroom with us.

"Are you going to tell me what this is about?" She crossed her arms, which pushed her tits up even more.

"Yeah, what the hell do you think you're doing?" I motioned to her body.

She looked down at herself, then back at me like she was confused.

"Megan dressed me. It's no big deal. I blend in better this way."

"The hell you do! I suggest you not let her dress you again. Those guys out there were practically waiting to rape you."

"First of all, there were no "guys." There was a guy, as in one, and he was actually kind of nice. Secondly, I can wear whatever the hell I want."

"Of course he was being nice. He was too busy enjoying the fucking show to be a dick."

"What show?"

"That show!" I pointed to her cleavage.

She sighed and sucked her teeth.

"Every girl in there is showing cleavage. I stick out more when I don't. I'm fine. Don't worry about me, okay?"

"I'm not worried, but I'm taking you home." I swiped my bangs out of my eyes and bit my lip ring in aggravation.

"I'm here with Megan. I have to ride home with her." She glared at me with glazed-over eyes.

"Have you stopped to look at your friend lately? She's drunk as fuck. Chet's taking her home and I'll take you."

"Why are you suddenly talking to me? You ignored me for the last few days."

"I didn't ignore you and I'm talking to you because you're about to do something stupid. Stick close to the stage and then I'll take you home after the show. Just listen to me. I know the kind of guys that hang out around places like this, snowflake, and trust me when I say you're way out of your league." I turned and started to walk out.

"You mean guys like you?" she asked from behind me. "Do you think you're out of my *league*, Zeke?" Her voice sounded sleepy and slurred.

I turned back to her. She was using the bathroom wall to hold herself up and the sadness in her eyes angered me.

"No, you're out of mine." I turned, left the bathroom, and didn't look back.

TWELVE
PATIENCE

ZEKE ENDED UP BEING RIGHT about the jerk at the club. No sooner than I got back to the bar with Megan, he was trying to get me to go outside with him and give him a blow job. Sick bastard. I spent the rest of the show next to the stage, but not because Zeke told me to. I did it because I couldn't peel Megan's drunken ass away from Chet for five minutes.

Once the show was done, the guys packed up the stuff and we all walked out to the cars. Like Zeke had said she would, Megan literally fell into Chet's car so I told her goodnight and went to stand next to Zeke's car. I wasn't happy about Megan getting too drunk to drive. I was planning on staying at her house since my sister was staying at her friend's house for the night.

Now I was going to have to go home, and I could only hope I wouldn't be bothered tonight. Chances were, since Sydney wasn't home, my dad would come to my room tonight. Just thinking about it made my stomach turn.

When Zeke came over to his car, he said nothing to me as he pulled open the driver's side door and jumped in. Once he cranked up his loud engine, I pulled open the car door and got in too. He sat and talked to Finn a minute about something I didn't understand. It was almost as if they were talking in code. They were talking about selling the loud and getting the green. I assumed they were talking about music and making money playing. I never did understand the different kind of slang that bounced around.

Once we were on the way out of Mount Pleasant, he leaned down and turned on the radio. I watched the mile markers on the interstate as we passed them and counted down the time I had before I was back home in hell. I didn't want to go home. I'd go anywhere. I didn't care where it was if it meant staying away from home tonight. My dad would come to my room. He'd smell the alcohol on my breath, see the makeup on my face, and I wasn't afraid to admit to myself that I was scared of him. He was changing. It was never innocent, what he was doing to me, but ever since I got arrested, he'd been vicious about it.

"You look deep in thought. What's on your mind?" Zeke asked from across the car.

I couldn't tell him what I was thinking, even though I wanted to. I knew in the back of my head I could trust Zeke. I knew I could tell him my secrets. He thought I was a privileged rich girl and while I did come from a rich family, my life had been just as hard as the people in his world. I wanted to tell him that. For some reason it meant a lot to me that he know I was never more myself than when I was with him. I needed him to know that Patience, the soccer playing governor's daughter, was just an act, but the girl I was when I was just hanging out with him... that was the real me.

But as much as I wanted to spill my guts and free myself, I knew I couldn't. Not just because of what Zeke might think, but because I had my mother and sister to worry about. If Zeke did spill the beans and tell, it wouldn't be long until rumors about the governor started to circulate and make its way back to my house, to my mom.

"Nothing much. I'm just thinking about stuff." I turned in my seat toward him. "Let's go somewhere, anywhere. I don't care where you take me. I just don't want to go home yet."

He looked over at me with his signature grin. His eyes filled with laughter.

"It's after midnight. I'm pretty sure your dad's already going to kill you," he said as he switched hands on the steering wheel.

"Then I guess I better enjoy my last few hours alive, shouldn't I?"

Maybe it was the alcohol or maybe it was how comfortable I felt with Zeke, but I was actually flirting. The words even sounded flirty when they came out. He looked over at me with a serious look on his face and then he shook his head.

"Don't do that, snowflake."

"Do what?" I asked.

"You're flirting with me. I'm sure it's the alcohol talking, but I'm no different from the guys at the bar. If anything, I'm worse."

"What if I think you're different?"

"Then you're more naïve than I originally thought."

We were rapidly approaching my house and I was running out of time to convince him to take me somewhere else, but I couldn't think of a place for him to take me or a reason why I didn't want to go home that sounded legit.

When we pulled into my neighborhood and I saw we were passing huge houses, I started to freak out. It wasn't going to be good and I kept remembering what it felt like to be slung against the kitchen table and treated like less than nothing. I couldn't do it. I wouldn't do it. If I had to sleep next to the pool in my backyard I would, but I wasn't going in my house with these clothes on and alcohol on my breath. I couldn't wait any longer. I had to say something.

"Please," I said as calmly as possible. "Please don't take me home, Zeke. I'll go anywhere, anywhere but there."

He looked over at me with a strange expression on his face, and then he pulled his car over on to the side of the road.

"What's the deal? Why are you so afraid to go home? You can tell me anything, you know."

I suddenly felt uncomfortable with the conversation and all I wanted was to get out of his car and away from my house.

"Just forget it. I'll find somewhere to go." I popped the door open and turned to get out.

His warm hand wrapped around my arm as he stopped me.

"Get back in here. You can crash at my place as long as you promise to be quiet. My dad will shit a brick if he sees me bring a girl home and I promise you my dad makes your dad look like a saint."

He turned the car around and headed toward his house. If only he knew. My dad was definitely not a saint, and I'd face anybody or anything in his trailer park if it meant staying away from home for the night.

Twenty minutes later, we pulled into his yard. The lights in his trailer were out and I was finding it hard to maneuver my way to the trailer door. He reached out and grabbed my hand as we crept up the rickety steps. He put a finger to his lips, telling me to be quiet, as he softly popped open his trailer door. The smell that welcomed me could only be described as foul and the small space felt suffocating.

The light above the stove in the kitchen lit a small area through the living room and made it possible for me to see there was no one in the living room anywhere. Zeke closed the door behind us, locked it, and then ushered me down a long, dark hallway.

"Be careful of the floor right here," he whispered into the dark.

He pulled me through a doorway and then he shut the door behind us and flicked on a dim light. His room was small, but organized. There was a small twin-size bed, a weight bench, and a dresser that looked like the only thing holding it up was the clothes in the drawers. He went to his closet and pulled out a blanket and started laying it on the floor. I sat on his bed and unzipped my boots. Once I pulled them off, I stuck them in the corner and crawled onto the pallet that he made on the floor.

"No. I'll sleep down there. You sleep in the bed," he said.

Then he pulled his shirt over his head and threw it in the corner. He filled the small space to begin with, but once his chest was naked he somehow felt bigger. I took in his tattoos and wondered to myself what he would do if I got a closer look. I watched from the floor as he unbuckled his belt and pulled it off. He did this as he kicked off his boots. His eyes never left mine.

I didn't think he would, but he pulled his jeans down, revealing a pair of black boxers with guitars all over them. I couldn't help the smile that spread across my face.

"More guitars?" I asked.

"Yes, more guitars." He mocked me. "Do you want a T-shirt and some shorts?

The thought of sleeping in Zeke's clothes warmed me and I shook my head yes.

He went over to his dresser, pulled out a black T-shirt and a pair of gray boxers, and then tossed them to me.

"I won't peek," he said as he dropped to the pallet of blankets on the floor and attempted to get comfortable on his back.

"Why can't I just go in the bathroom?"

"You might wake up my dad."

"Oh, okay. You promise you won't peek?"

I didn't really mind the idea of him seeing me naked and that freaked me out a little.

"If I wanted to see you naked, then I'd just get you naked." He yawned and threw his arm across his eyes.

There was no way I could respond to that. It bothered me that he didn't want to see me naked, but at the same time, I didn't want him to try and get me naked. I could say all day that he wouldn't be able to get me out of my clothes, but something told me I'd eat those words if he ever tried.

I turned my back to him and peeled off my top. I thanked every god I could think of that I'd worn a bra even though Megan swore I didn't need one. I snatched up the shirt and pulled it over my head. I peeked behind me to see his arm still over his eyes, so I unbuttoned my jeans and pushed them down. They were tight, so tight I couldn't get them off as fast I wanted. Once they were down around my ankles, I bent over and pulled them off. Zeke's boxers slid over my panties as I threw them on like I was dressing for a fire.

The shirt almost reached my knees when I tugged on it. I turned quickly to turn off the light and ran right into Zeke. Staring at his naked chest, I sucked in a deep breath. When I exhaled, I could feel my heated breath against my cheeks as it reflected off of his skin. I was so close, too close. My usual reaction would have been to jerk away immediately, but my palms landed on his hard pecks and they stayed there as if they'd melted into his hot flesh—not because I was feeling him up, but because I was so shocked by being this close to a naked man and it not being a tragedy.

I should've been appalled. I should've been thoroughly disgusted given my history with the opposite sex, but I was none of those things. Just like in his car when he touched my leg, my body buzzed and hummed and physically I wanted to mold myself to him and swim in his warmth. However, the mentally disturbed parts of me were still present and making themselves known in the back of my mind.

I felt his heartbeat racing beneath my palm. Looking up at him through my lashes, I was struck once again by how handsome he was. He peered down at me with his steely gaze that I was now accustomed to and the air around us crackled and popped. I knew I needed to say something or do something, but my legs felt boneless and I couldn't seem to find my voice. When I finally did, I said the first thing that popped in my head.

"You promised." It was barely a whisper.

My body tensed against my will when I felt his hands slide up my sides. The corner of his mouth tilted up and his small smile tugged at his lip ring. His dark eyes could see inside me. I was almost positive of that and it freaked me out more than him touching me.

I held my breath as he leaned his face closer to mine. Technically, I'd never been kissed and secretly I was hoping Zeke would be my first kiss, but instead of pressing his lips to mine, he brought his mouth to my ear.

"I told you I was a bad guy. You can't trust guys like me." His deep voice worked its way down the back of my neck, leaving goose bumps along the way.

He told me before that I shouldn't trust him, but the funny part was that I did. I don't know why I did; I just did.

"I trust you." My voice sounded foreign to me, like I had something stuck in the back of my throat.

"If you knew what I was thinking you wouldn't. My mind is filthy. I'm not sure you could handle it."

He was right. I probably couldn't handle it, but that didn't mean I didn't want to know what the hell he was thinking.

"I can." My voice shook like a scared little girl's.

"Is that so?" he asked as he nuzzled my neck.

I started to get jittery. My insides were shaking so hard and I couldn't decide if it was from fear or excitement.

"Remember the other day in my car, when you told me you'd let me do things?" His tongue flicked over my ear lobe and I let a soft hiss slip through my teeth.

"Uh-huh." It sounded childish, but it was all I was capable of saying.

The room suddenly felt smaller and hotter. A rush of warmth spread throughout my body and I could feel my pulse in my temples my heart was beating so fast and hard. I breathed in through my nose and took in the scent of his heated skin. He smelled amazing, like men's cologne and fresh laundry.

He surprised me with a soft kiss to the side of my neck and I split right down the center. The top half of me wanted to run out into the cool night air and jog home, but the bottom half of me wanted to fade into him and become one.

"You let me hold your hand. What else will you let me do, snowflake?"

I used to hate it when he called me snowflake, but now I was beginning to think she was who I really was. There was Patience, the governor's daughter, and then there was Snowflake, the girl who was starting to melt in Zeke's very capable hands. Given the choice of who I'd want to be for the rest of my days, I'd choose Snowflake every time.

A soft noise pushed past my moist lips and I felt him smile against the side of my neck. His breath shifted the hair that hung against my cheek and it made me shiver even more. Everything in me trembled as my insides began to push at my seams. The healthy girl deep within me wanted to be free. She wanted to explore all the dark corners of Zeke, but the scarred me, the one who'd been broken down beyond belief was still holding her back.

"Will you let me do this?" he asked as he slipped his hands down my sides and brought them around my backside.

I stiffened for just a second as a tiny hint of panic seeped in, but the minute he started drawing lazy circles on the back of my thighs with a single finger, I squashed that panic and let pleasure take its place. A tiny murmur came from deep within me and he softly growled his approval against my ear.

"And what about this? Will you let me do this?" he asked as he brought his hands up and slipped them into the back of my boxer shorts. He filled his large hands with my ass and gave it a soft squeeze.

Only my thin pair of cotton panties kept his hands from touching my heated skin. My breathing increased and my heartbeat sped up.

His hands moved down, taking the boxer shorts with them, and I didn't stop the shorts when they slid down my legs and around my ankles. He brought his hands around to my stomach and ran his finger along the top of my panty line and pelvic bone.

"What do you want me to do? Do you want me to move my hand lower?" I felt his breath against my cheek as he moved his head down and kissed my collar bone.

I didn't respond. Instead, my body took over and I pressed my pelvic area against his hand.

"Yeah, you want me to move my hand down. You want me to touch you here, don't you?" His hand left my body for a brief second, and then I felt a fiery finger trace a path over the top of my panties right over the most sensitive parts of me.

My body jerked on its own accord, and I couldn't stop the noises that slipped over my tongue. I'd never experienced anything like this. In my life, when someone touched your personal areas, it was disturbing and sick, but when Zeke touched me, it was soft and life-altering in a whole new way.

"Tell me what you want, Patience," he said sweetly against my cheek.

And just like that, I no longer hated the sound of my name. The way he said it was so personal. After being called a nickname by a person so much, when they finally called you by your actual name, it had an emotional feel to it. It held a strange sense of finality, as if he'd somehow just given in to me.

His eyes connected with mine as he dipped the tip of his finger under the band of my panties and ran it back and forth across my pelvic bones. He worked a new finger inside my panties, until finally his hand was cupping me. He wasn't moving his fingers, but just the pressure from the heel of his hand was almost enough for me.

I tilted my head back, my eyes closed, and my mouth opened on a wordless sigh.

"Please tell me what you want, baby." His words were all around me.

My body got another rush of chills and my shoulders began to shake. When I finally spoke, my voice trembled with my body. "I don't know."

He was asking me what I wanted, but I didn't know. I wasn't like most girls who read about sex or even experimented with it. To me, it had always been a despicable act of injustice upon me, but this wasn't like that. He was feeling me out before he touched me. He was making sure I was comfortable with his hands before he moved them. It was as if he knew my fear and understood it, and because of his understanding, I was able to enjoy touch for the first time in my life.

He took a deep breath and his chest trembled, letting me know he wasn't as unaffected as he looked. "Can I touch you?" he asked.

There was more? I thought for sure this was the height of my sexual peak, but I guess I was wrong.

"You're already touching me." My voice sounded deeper, more seductive, and I celebrated that. Maybe I was changing before his eyes, because I felt as if I were. I was experiencing a mental transformation and I was almost certain that transformation was reflected on my outside as well.

"No, can I *touch* you?" With his question, he let a single finger press up against a part of me that had never been touched. My body came alive and the sensitive nub that had never been so sensitive before started to throb against his finger.

I swallowed loudly and I lost control of myself. All the strength in my body went away and I was worried that my knees would buckle and I'd topple to the floor. I gave in and collapsed against his chest. Little puffs of air blew back into my face as I began to softly pant against his skin. His chest rose and fell with a rhythm that I understood well. Coincidently, it was close to the same rhythm his finger was beginning to use as he pressed harder against my hot spot and began a circular motion.

I was going to pass out. Except this time it wasn't from fear; it was from raw pleasure. My breathing became erratic and I was now digging my fingers into his shoulders. My body was so tight it felt as if it about to snap, and something, although I had no idea what it was, was just beyond the horizon. It was there, waiting to consume my body and ready to erase every dark memory I stored.

The slide of his finger against my body was so erotic. I had no idea my body was even capable of getting wet, but he'd somehow made it happen. Every one of my five senses were heightened and I found myself participating in a ritual as old as time as my hips started to move with his rhythm.

There was an ache, much sweeter than the one that had been sitting on my chest for the last ten years of my life, and I was positive this new ache I was experiencing would help soothe the old one just a little. My body seemed to be ascending in some manner. I was rising, yet my feet were still planted firmly on the floor.

"Please, Zeke," I croaked.

I didn't know what I was asking him, but I knew he had the answer.

"That's it, baby. You're almost there," I heard him say in the distance.

I leaned my head back farther and I felt him nuzzle my chin. I heard someone whispering his name over and over again, but I couldn't have been me. No way would I do such a thing, but he confirmed it.

"I love it when you say my name. You're whispering it now, but that's about to change."

I felt the bed against my back as he laid me down. That should've been the part where I started to freak out, but I didn't. Whatever he was offering, I wanted it. Anything to make the ache in my lower stomach go away. It started to spread all over and my body felt like it was being reborn. He was the cure for my ache. He knew it and now I knew it.

His finger stopped its movement and it was on the tip of my tongue to beg him to keep going. He fit his body between my legs and rested on his forearm. He was hovering above me and his face was so close to mine, yet he never kissed me. I wanted him to kiss me. I needed to feel his mouth against mine. Our bodies were practically connected in every other place. It made sense for us to kiss.

I was about to lean up and kiss him, but he buried his head in the space between my shoulder and my neck. His breathing matched my own and it made me feel good knowing he was as affected as me. And then he thrust his hips and I felt his hardness press against the outside of my panties. The warm ache suddenly turned cold and everything in me froze. Shards of my internal ice poked me everywhere and made my skin feel prickly. The room felt too small, his body too heavy, and I couldn't breathe. No matter how hard I tried to suck in a breath, my lungs had seized their movement.

I was a sick girl, sicker than I ever really understood. I was psychologically destroyed. How could a person go from being so into something to scared to death of the one person who made her feel safe in a matter of seconds? It was possible; I was proof it was possible. My body went from being in a hazy, pleasurable state to tense and anxious. My fight-or-flight reflexes kicked in against my will and I wanted to run.

He was breathing hard, thrusting against me, and whispering something, but all I heard was the rhythm of my headboard at home. That damn beat would stay with me forever. I didn't know I was crying until I felt my warm tears rush into the hairline at my temples.

He must've felt the change in me because he looked up into my face. Everything stopped and he stared down at me in confusion. He reached up and ran his thumb beneath my eye as if to see if my tears were real, and then he opened his mouth to say something, but a loud door shutting on the other side of his trailer stopped his words. I'd never seen a guy move so fast. He jumped up and went for the light switch. He flicked it, turning the light off and leaving me in darkness. I wanted to crawl into a shadowed corner and disappear forever.

He stuffed the boxers I was wearing into my hand.

"Put these back on and be very quiet," he whispered into the room.

I pulled his boxers on over my panties and sat back down. I assumed the reason he wanted me quiet was so his dad didn't know he had a girl in his room. Zeke was older, but maybe it was one of his dad's rules or something. Either way, I silently said a thank you to Zeke's dad for interrupting what was about to be a very uncomfortable moment. I didn't want to answer any questions. I didn't want to explain my sudden mood change. There really was only one explanation for it and there was no way I could've made up a lie that quick.

We sat in dark silence as his dad moved around. We heard water running and cabinets closing until finally the front door opened and closed. Zeke remained silent until his dad's loud truck cranked up outside and pulled away.

Once his dad was gone, we sat in silence next to each other on the bed for another minute before he stood up. He looked down at me, a streetlight from outside his window cutting a path across his face. His expression was stern and he looked angry. I felt bad for leading him on, but it wasn't like I did it on purpose.

"Goodnight," he said as he turned away and got on the floor.

I peeled back the covers on his bed and climbed in.

"Goodnight," I responded.

I was the queen of silent crying and I cried myself to sleep.

THIRTEEN
ZEKE

WITH WIDE EYES, I LISTENED to her quietly cry above me on my bed. I didn't know what happened, but it scared the shit out me. I didn't mean for it to go that far. I hadn't meant to do more than look at her when I lied and told her she'd wake my dad if she changed in the bathroom. I couldn't even believe she fell for that and I was really shocked when she turned and started to undress. She seemed too shy even for that.

I watched from beneath my arm as she peeled off her clothes and I was done. Her white, lacey bra and panties had nearly done me in. I'm not sure what possessed me to stand and go to her, but it was a force I couldn't fight. As I stood behind her and she adjusted her clothes, her scent filled my room. Except this time it wasn't the scent of freshly cut grass. This time it was a soft feminine smell, a light baby powder mixed with her natural scent.

When she pulled her hair out of the collar of the shirt, I wanted to reach out and run my fingers through it. I'd never seen a female look so sexy in my entire life. She looked amazing in my clothes and it gave me an odd satisfaction, as if my clothes being against her skin made her mine in some way. She could never be mine, and even if that's what I wanted her to be, I'd never do that to her. I'd run until I couldn't run anymore before I tarnished her life by making myself a part of it. She deserved better than I could ever be for her.

When she turned and looked at me, I felt myself give in to her completely. No one's ever had that kind of control over me and while I should've fucking hated it, it felt right. For the first time in my life, being with a woman didn't feel like a dirty, erotic sin. It felt real. The way she felt against my skin, the way her body felt beneath my fingers, it was right.

It was more than just trying to get laid. It was more than seeing a hot chick naked. For the most part, I hadn't even cared about making myself feel good. Just touching her and pulling those natural reactions from her was enough for me. I'd never looked down at a woman and thought about her beauty, but Patience was so beautiful. The way she moved, the sounds that came from her perfect mouth, they were too much for me. Kissing wasn't my thing. In fact, I never kissed girls, but I'd almost kissed her. As it was, I'd already done more with her than any other girl in the kissing department. I wasn't the kind of guy who planted soft kisses on a female, but I couldn't keep my mouth away from her. It was like I was a completely different guy when it came to her.

When she froze beneath me and I saw that look of pure fear on her face, it had been like a shock from an electrical outlet. It looked like she was crying, but I wasn't positive until I ran my thumb beneath her eye and felt the moisture.

Why had she let me go that far if it wasn't what she wanted? Why had she been so responsive to my touches if it made her sad? It was the most confusing moment of my entire life and in that brief moment of reflection, I let old Zeke take center stage again. I was about to say something hurtful and rude when I heard my dad getting up for work. Then the real fear set in.

The chances of him coming in my room before work were slim, but it would've been my luck that he would. I didn't want Patience to see that side of my life. I didn't want anyone to know the embarrassing details of me getting my ass kicked. I didn't feel relief until I heard his truck pull away.

Instead of sleeping, I lay there and forced myself to stay put until I heard her breathing even out. It was getting ridiculous. All the back and forth with Patience was making my head spin, and to top it off, I felt like my balls were about to explode.

I got up, grabbed something to eat, and then took a hot shower. I was sure to soap up and use my hand to get some relief. Hopefully getting off one good time would help with my crazed Patience hormones. I had to find a girl from my world to have sex with. That's all it boiled down to.

When I got out of the shower, I dried off, threw on some clothes, and then went back into my room to check on Patience. She was still sleeping peacefully, and had I not heard her crying the night before, I still would've known from the puffiness around her eyes. She turned onto her back and the covers shifted and revealed a soft leg and my gray boxers. They were big on her and had shifted throughout the night so her white panties were showing.

I reached over to pull the cover back over and her eyes popped open. She leaned up on her elbows, looked around the room, and then seemed to remember the night before.

"Good morning, sunshine," I said blandly, as I searched through my sock drawer. "It's about time you woke up. You want to grab a shower before I take you home?"

She sat up with sleepy eyes and disheveled hair. She looked amazing and all I wanted to do was climb under the warm covers with her.

"I'll just grab one when I get home. Let me get my clothes on and rinse my mouth out."

She went into the bathroom and came out minutes later wearing her clothes from the night before. I grabbed my guitar and we left. The ride to her house was a quiet one and when I stopped a few houses down from hers, she opened the door and got out. Before I could pull away, she leaned down into the window.

"Thanks," she said with a tiny smile.

It was a single word, but it sounded so final that my stomach ached.

"No worries."

I watched as she walked away from my car, and then I pulled off and didn't look back.

I spent the entire day Sunday at Finn's house, but when a joint was passed my way, I turned it down. The appeal of getting high just wasn't there. Every now and again, I'd think to myself that weed could never get me as high as Patience did in my bed, but as soon as the thought would enter my mind, I'd squash it.

"Dude, what the fuck is wrong with you?" Finn asked after I played the wrong chord for the tenth time. "We've been playing for years and I've never heard you screw up like this. You did it the other night at The Icehouse, too. You're not snorting that shit, are you?"

"Nah, man, I want to slow down, not speed up. I just have a lot on my mind I guess."

Thankfully, the guys let it drop, but I was seriously having a hard time concentrating since Chet decided to bring Megan to practice. Every time she lifted her phone to text, I wondered if it was my snowflake on the other end.

I stumbled into my house at close to midnight, drunk out of my mind. My old man was waiting at the door when I got there. I was too drunk to remember most of the beating, but the next morning when I woke up for school, my lip was swollen and there was blood smeared all over my face. Apparently, I didn't block too well when wasted.

Patience didn't come to community service for the entire week, and though I swore it had nothing to do with the fact that she wasn't there, the week was the worst I'd had in a while. When Friday night practice rolled around, I gave in and asked Megan about her. I tried to play it off like I was glad she wasn't around aggravating me, but really I was worried. It didn't seem like her to disappear from the face of the Earth.

"Where's your girl Patience? Why isn't she around getting in the way?" I asked Megan as I tuned my guitar.

"What's wrong, Zeke? You pissed you didn't get in them panties?" Tiny laughed.

I glared over at him. "She's not my type."

"Whatever, dude. Your type is female and she was *all* female," Chet said, earning a pissed-off look from Megan.

"She's been sick. The flu I think. She missed school all week too. I haven't seen her since that night at The Icehouse and she's hasn't really texted me either." She shrugged. "It's weird. Patience never gets sick, but I think she's okay."

None of it sat well with me. Patience missing school and Boy's Club didn't seem like her. Maybe she really was sick, but my gut instinct that came around at the wrong times told me she wasn't. I tried to push it out of my mind.

I didn't go home that night. Instead, I crashed on Finn's couch.

We found out Saturday morning that The Pit was open again and by Saturday afternoon, we were booked to play there that night. I'd never been so happy to see those concrete walls. All the graffiti had been painted over, but there were some guys with spray paint working on something new on a far wall. We set up and started playing once the room began to fill.

Two hours later, I was drenched in sweat and had a hell of a buzz. I played my ass off and the crowd seemed to be feeding off our energy. A redhead that I'd seen before kept giving me flirty eyes from the front row and I decided halfway through the set I was taking her back to Finn's and getting some. A couple times I leaned down while I was playing and took in her overflowing cleavage.

After the set was over, we packed up our stuff and headed to the cars. The inside of the club was still jumping and we could've stayed and partied the rest of the night away, but I had a willing redhead named Stephanie on my arm and hard-on that was aching against my jeans.

"Hey, Chet, we'll catch y'all at Finn's place later," I called over my shoulder as I grabbed the redhead around the waist and pulled her to me.

I knew her name, but it wasn't necessary. Redhead was a good enough name for me. I'd been upfront and honest about what the night was about and she seemed perfectly fine with being a quick one-night fuck.

When I turned back around to leave, I almost walked into Patience. Her blue eyes met mine and then landed on my hand, which was holding Stephanie close to me. She took in the girl next to me and her eyes drifted up and then down. Her face was expressionless when she looked back at me, but I saw the tiny crack in her armor when a brief second of pain filled her eyes.

"Hey, stranger! Long time no see," I slurred.

Her lips bent into a fake smile.

"Yeah, I've been kind of busy this week." She shrugged.

I couldn't tell if she was lying or not, but I wanted to know what was so important that she missed Boy's Club and school.

"I'll be right back, baby. I'm going to run to the bathroom before we leave," Stephanie said as she tilted her head up and kissed me on the neck.

It was obvious she was marking her territory for the night, but Patience didn't seem to catch on. Once Stephanie was gone, the room disappeared around me and my attention honed in on Patience. She was wearing another pair of tight jeans and a light-blue top that made her hair and eyes pop.

"What's that about?" she said as she motioned to Stephanie, who was easing her way through the crowd toward the bathroom.

"A man has needs, snowflake." I grinned down at her.

Her throat worked up and down as she swallowed hard.

"The same needs I couldn't fulfill." Her eyes flicked down as if she were ashamed of herself.

The pain in her eyes made the pressure on my chest feel heavier. I wanted to tell her she had nothing to be ashamed of. I wanted to tell her that being with her, even without the sex, had been wonderful, but I didn't respond. I just shrugged my shoulders and shook my head like I was aggravated by her. Really, I was aggravated with myself because I wanted Patience to fulfill my needs. I wanted to take her somewhere quiet and do anything she wanted. I'd even cuddle if it meant being close to her, but it would never happen because I'd never let it happen.

"It is what it is," I finally said.

She didn't respond. Instead, her eyes filled with tears that never fell and she nodded her head like she understood. Damn her for always being so understanding. Damn her for not bursting out of her skin the way I would've had I seen her with another guy. I was pissed that she'd just step aside so easily. We weren't in a relationship or anything and we never would be, but I'd never give up on her that easy. Though, technically, wasn't that what I was doing? I was giving up on her, but I was doing it *for* her. I could never be what she needed in her life and she could never be what I needed in mine. Whatever it was we had going on needed to end. It was already practically nonexistent anyway.

It was then that Stephanie returned from the bathroom. She put her arm around mine and shot Patience an evil grin. Patience smiled sweetly at her, then looked at me. Something in her eyes burned me. Maybe it was the resolution I saw in them, the fact that she was perfectly okay with just walking away and letting me leave with Stephanie. For some reason it hurt in my chest and stomach, and that hurt did nothing but piss me off even more.

"Have fun tonight," she said with a big fake smile.

"I will." The minute the words came out of my mouth I wanted to shove them back in and swallow them down.

She looked down and took a deep breath, and then she turned and walked away. I stood there stuck to my spot until I felt Stephanie tug my arm.

"Are we going to do this or not?" she asked impatiently.

I nodded my head and we left.

I ended up dropping Stephanie off at her house and pulling away without even touching her. Needless to say, she was a total bitch about it. After seeing Patience, I couldn't have gotten it up if I wanted to and suddenly I had no desire to fuck the loose redhead anymore.

I didn't want to go home. It was after midnight and I didn't want to deal with my dad. I went to Finn's house instead. The party had relocated to his place and the garage was full of people who were at the club. As soon as I walked in, I slammed two straight shots of vodka. I knew in the back of my head that my drinking was getting out of hand, but it seemed like the only thing that brought me peace lately was Patience and she was something I wasn't willing to indulge in anymore.

"Damn, man, I think you just broke a world record for the fastest fuck." Finn laughed as he threw his arm around my shoulder.

I didn't tell him nothing happened. What would they think if they knew I dropped off a wet-and-ready female without even touching her? They'd think I lost my fucking mind, and I was starting to think the same damn thing. Finn started talking about something that had to do with The Pit, but once I saw Megan's spiked haircut, my eyes started to search the garage for those platinum locks I'd come to love so much.

She was sitting in the corner, drinking something from a red Solo cup. She looked over at me as soon as I spotted her and I didn't miss the relief that showed on her face. Without even saying anything to Finn, I walked away and started straight toward her.

FOURTEEN
PATIENCE

I COULDN'T DECIDE WHAT WAS worse—what my dad put me through when Zeke dropped me off Sunday morning or seeing him with the slutty redhead. The abuse my dad handed me kept me out of commission for the rest of the week, but seeing Zeke with the half-naked skank was going to keep me down much longer. I knew that the minute I felt like running to the bathroom and puking up the little bit of food I'd managed to eat that day.

I'd spent the week hiding in my room while I pretended to go to school and practice. The table ride my dad took me on when I got home from Zeke's house had left me with a set of fractured ribs. So I spent the week in bed, barely able to breathe. It was the longest week of my life and not until Saturday morning did I even feel close to normal.

Things were definitely getting out of hand and needed to change. I was getting desperate and having crazy thoughts. I was starting to plan my getaway. The plan was to pack the dreaded gray Toyota full of everything I could, kidnap Sydney, and drive until I couldn't drive anymore. It's what I really wanted to do, but with my mom hanging on to dear life, literally, I couldn't bring myself to leave her.

It seemed like the only time I felt alive anymore was when I was with Zeke. He was slowly becoming my freedom. So when Megan texted me and told me Blow Hole was playing at The Pit, I jumped at the chance to see him. Had I known I'd leave The Pit with fractured ribs *and* a fractured heart, I would've stayed my stupid ass in bed.

I wanted to leave right then and go home, but that wasn't a possibility. I wasn't sure I'd survive another attack from my dad so soon after the last time I came in late looking like, what he called, a slutty heathen. So I spent the rest of the night playing the third wheel to Megan and Chet. I even followed them back to Finn's garage and took an already opened drink from some dude I didn't know. Self-destruction was kind of my thing now apparently.

I camouflaged myself in a corner with my red cup full of God knows what and watched as the people around me laughed, got high, and lived free lives. My ribs were still hurting like a bitch, but I didn't care. And then I looked across the garage and saw Zeke staring back at me and everything changed. The room disappeared, including everyone in it. I felt my nerves go into hyper drive when he started to creep across the room toward me. His eyes never left my face and he had on his signature pissed-off expression.

"I see you're the original party girl now," he pointed to my cup.

"I see you took the trash out and dumped her somewhere," I said, referring to the redhead.

He grinned at me and shifted his bangs out of his eyes. "Do you want me to get you a napkin? There's a little bit of jealousy on your chin."

I glared back at him. He was right. I was totally jealous, but at the same time, it was wrong of me to want him for myself when I could never be his. Not in the biblical sense anyway. No guy I knew would ever be okay with never having sex and sex wasn't an option for me. I didn't think it ever would be.

"I have nothing to be jealous of."

I wished I could've had a better comeback than that, mostly because it was a big, fat lie, but also because he was so snappy with the comebacks and I wanted to burn his ass with a good one.

His face suddenly got serious. "You're right. You have nothing to be jealous of."

I wanted to ask him what that was supposed to mean, but it seemed useless. Instead, I tilted up my cup and took a big swig of the mystery drink. When I brought my cup down, I blurted out the one thing that was eating at me.

"Did you sleep with her?" I asked.

His face was stone-like, dark skin over steel. His eyes cut into mine and I knew I'd gone too far. I sounded like a jealous girlfriend and it was none of my business who he had sex with. I knew that and he knew that.

"You're a nosey one tonight, aren't you?"

I didn't miss the fact that he didn't answer my question.

"Whatever," I said as I pulled away from the wall and started to walk away.

He grabbed me around the wrist and pulled me back.

"No," he said.

That tiny word made everything better and I hated it. Why did I care who he slept with? He was a sexual guy and I was sure he screwed a different girl every chance he got, but somehow seeing it made it real and it sucked.

"Good, there's hope for you yet. I knew there was a decent guy in there somewhere." I attempted to smile at him.

He didn't smile back. Instead, he leaned in and glowered down at me.

"I wouldn't be too hopeful, snowflake. Do yourself a favor and quit deluding yourself into thinking there's anything even remotely decent about me. I make the guy your *daddy* warned you about look like a little bitch. I get high, I drink, and I like to fuck. If you're as smart as I think you are, you'll jog your pretty little ass back to Pleasantville and stay away from me." He licked his thick lips in emphasis before he lifted his beer and downed it like it was water.

"You just proved my point. Only a nice guy would give a girl like me that kind of warning."

There was more to him than just sex, drugs, and music. I'd gotten a glimpse of the decent guy he kept locked inside. He could try and hide from me all he wanted, but I knew the truth. He was good. He could've left me to die, but he didn't. He could've taken full advantage of me in his room that night, but he didn't.

Sometimes when he looked at me, I saw more in his eyes. I wasn't sure what it was, but it was a spark of something that begged to be released. It wasn't the delusions of a girl with a crush. I wasn't seeing things that weren't there.

He moved quickly and pressed me up against the wall. His large hands captured the sides of my waist and gently squeezed. My ribs ached and protested, but I didn't show any pain. Leaning down, he ran his lips up the side of my neck until I could feel his breath against my hairline. He nipped at my earlobe and then planted a soft kiss behind my ear. My legs wobbled and my eyes closed.

"You're doing it again, pretty girl," he whispered. The smell of vodka roamed around me. "You need to understand the nature of the beast. Even a rattlesnake hisses in warning before he attacks."

I swallowed hard and took a deep breath. "You wouldn't attack me."

"You bet your sexy khaki-covered ass I would."

"Then do it." I dared him.

He leaned back and looked down at me with an arrogant smile.

"Nah, you haven't earned it. Plus, I have a thing for redheads." He fingered a strand of my hair.

And just like that I was pissed off. He was so annoying! He thought he was all that with his overconfident ass smothered in sexiness. He thought he was God's gift wrapped in tattoos and piercings. It was like he expected women to drool over him. Well, damn him and damn me for doing exactly what he expected. I could practically feel the drool on the side of my mouth.

Did he think because he was baked in red-hot lust and seasoned with pheromones he could talk to people any way he wanted? Did he think because he could play the guitar all the women around him were just supposed to turn into Zeke groupies?

Sure, I totally wanted to throw my panties at him every time he played, but the point is he didn't know that.

"You're so aggravating. It's like you live to piss me off and I'm over it, all of it. So go get your slutty little redhead. I'm glad she wants you so badly, because I sure as hell don't. I really couldn't give a shit less about what you do with her. I hope you fuck her until her face falls off. " I turned away and flicked my blond hair with the back of my fingers, making sure it whipped him in the face.

He grabbed a fist full of it and gently tugged me against him. His warm body was pressed against my back. His strong heartbeat slammed into my shoulder, reminding me how tall and big he was. His breath tickled my cheek as he pressed his lips to my ear. Goosebumps invaded every inch of my skin and I shivered. He felt my shiver and chuckled softly. It was deep and dark... sexy.

"Spit all the lies you want, snowflake." His hand snaked around me and under my shirt. My abdominal muscles clenched, making my ribs ache as he ran his finger around my belly button. "Your body spoke my language the other night and it said differently. I'm not stupid. I see the way you look at me. It's hot and I fucking love it. I bet you fantasize about me, too. One day you're going to beg me for the things you fantasize about. If you're a good little girl, I might give you some relief when that time comes. So I suggest you play nice." He planted a hot kiss on the side of my neck and then cold air rushed in against my back and replaced him.

I stood there in shock for a bit. For one, I'd never talked like that to another human being in my life. The F-bomb wasn't something I dropped very often and I surprised myself when the world slipped out. Two, my body was super sensitive and I felt like melting into a big pile of Patience right there in the middle of Finn's shitty garage.

He was right. I had responded to him that night at his house. I was responding to him now. I wanted things from him that made my stomach flutter and turn at the same time, but wanting and doing were two different things. I fantasized about the things I could never do and then punished myself for thinking the things that were a direct conflict with my sanity.

The point was Zeke was making me even crazier than I already was, and staying away from him was the best thing I could do, but I couldn't. The messed up part was I loved the way he made me feel. I loved the color he brought to my life. In the moments when life sucked away all my oxygen, he swooped in and helped me breathe. He was practically a stranger, a bad boy from the wrong side of town, but in some bizarre way he helped me survive.

I slammed my empty cup in the trash and headed for the door. Megan was cozy in Chet's lap and I wasn't about to take her away from him just so she could take me home. I had two feet and after being barricaded in the house for a week, I needed the exercise. I couldn't even find it in myself to be afraid of the repercussions of coming in late. With the mood I was in, I'd be more afraid if I were my dad. I could totally see myself breaking his fingers and not giving a shit who in the house knew it.

Finn's neighborhood wasn't the greatest. There were a lot of cars on blocks and sirens. I'm pretty sure I passed a few drug deals, and once, a group of guys whistled at me, but after an hour of walking, the area became cleaner. I walked into a gas station that had bulletproof glass around the registers and bought a pack of gum to get rid of the smell of alcohol. Then an hour after that, I was on my side of town.

My cheeks burned from the cold air as I huddled into my jacket. My lungs hurt from breathing in the cold and my ribs were aching so bad I wanted to cry. Walking this far wasn't my brightest idea, but at that point I was almost home. That was a good thing considering the night was turning gray and I knew the sun would be up soon.

I would've called Megan to come and get me, except my expensive phone couldn't seem to ever hold a freaking charge. A dead phone wasn't very useful to anyone and it crossed my mind several times to just the throw the damn thing in the road and let someone run it over.

Finally—I'm not sure how much longer due to my dead phone and no watch—I walked through the front gates of my neighborhood. I was coming around the corner and could see my house in the distance when I heard squealing tires all around me. I froze as Zeke's beat-up car pulled up and he slammed on the brakes right in front of me.

He jumped out of the driver's side with wild eyes. He pulled his phone out of his pocket, dialed a number, and then waited

"Hey. ... Yeah, I found her. ... Okay, I will," he said into the phone.

He stuffed it back in his pocket, then stared at me with angry eyes.

"Where *is* your phone?" he asked calmly.

Anger was bubbling just below the question and I could tell at any minute he was about to lash out on me. I didn't know why, but he was definitely pissed off at me.

"It's in my pocket. It's dead. Why? What's wrong?"

He pinched the bridge of his nose and took a deep breath.

"Megan's been calling you and texting you all fucking night. Please tell me you didn't walk here all the way from Finn's house."

"Why? Is she okay?" I started to panic.

I shouldn't have left her there alone. A real friend would've stayed.

"She's fine! She's freaking out because you were nowhere to be found. We thought someone ran off with you or some crazy shit like that!" I jerked when he raised his voice at me. "Now, again I ask, did you walk all the way here from Finn's house?"

I was afraid to answer the question.

"Well, I didn't mean to make her worry, but as you can see, I'm perfectly fine." I held my arms out to my sides to show I was fine. "I'm sleepy as hell and I fully plan on going home and passing out, but other than that, I'm fantastic."

I stepped around him and started toward my house, but I didn't get far before he grabbed my wrist and pulled me back to him. His nostrils flared as he stared down at me with pinched lips. His face was turning red and I was afraid I was about to feel the wrath of Zeke.

"Answer the question." His words were a sinister whisper.

I met his stare until I couldn't anymore and I had to look away.

"Yes, but it was fine. See? I'm fine."

He dropped my arm and shook his head at me. Still, his angry eyes burned into my flesh.

"Do us both a favor and stay on your side of the world. Don't come to The Pit. Don't come to Finn's house. Just stay the hell away from all of us."

And then he turned and walked away.

His words hurt. They hurt way more than they should have. I felt them snake around me and squeeze until I couldn't breathe. Just a few hours ago he was melting me, but with those words he did more than melt me. He seared me and then turned me to ash.

His tires squealed once more as he drove away. All that was left of him were two burnt rubber marks on the road in front of me.

FIFTEEN
ZEKE

FEAR WASN'T THE SOUND OF my dad's heavy footfalls as he came down the hallway ready to beat my ass. Fear wasn't waking up from my repeating nightmare of my mother's dead eyes. No, those things knew nothing of fear.

Fear was looking around Finn's house for Patience and not finding her. It was asking her friend Megan where she was and her saying she had no idea. The truth was I never knew what it meant to be afraid until the moment I thought about her trying to walk home from Finn's party and being raped and murdered.

Megan called her phone over and over again and we all went out searching for her. For hours we searched, until finally I saw her walking to her house. The relief I felt when I saw her blond hair in the gray dawn was so extreme, I couldn't put it into words even if I wanted to.

As I drove away from her, I couldn't remember what it was I said to her. I just knew I was pissed off. I was pissed at her for being stupid enough to walk alone in the dark in Finn's neighborhood. I was pissed because she was just casually walking while Megan and I were in a full-blown panic. I was pissed because she was able to put me in a full-blown panic to start with.

Thankfully, I'd set out on my own to find her. The last thing I wanted my friends to see was me flipping out over the fact that I couldn't find some chick. And I *was* flipping out. I'd never felt that kind of anxiety. My fingers still felt stiff and numb from gripping my steering wheel so hard for so many hours.

At one point, I almost ran out of gas, but thankfully I'd finally started making some money from Javier and I was able to fill up and keep looking for her.

Halfway to my house my memory started filling in and I could remember telling her to stay away. Her staying away would be a good thing, but at the same time, the week without seeing her had been hell. I didn't know what was happening to me and I fucking hated all these conflicting issues bouncing around my head.

Then the guilt started to set in—another emotion I'd never experienced until Patience. I felt bad for yelling at her, but I was so mad at her for putting herself in danger I couldn't even see straight. She was the queen of bad decisions and coming near me was one of her worse yet.

I had her cell number in my phone since Megan insisted I program it just in case. Once I made it to my yard, I pulled out my phone and sent her a text.

Me: I yelled at you b/c what you did was stupid.

It wasn't exactly an apology, but it was as close as she was going to get. An hour later I got a response.

Patience: Should I bring you a napkin? You might have some apology on your chin.

I laughed. I liked the fact that she could dish it out. I also liked the fact that she got me. I didn't want to admit it before, but she definitely got me. I didn't have to send her an apology for her to know my text was my way of apologizing.

Me: Smartass.
Patience: Mean ass.
Me: Goodnight, Snowflake.
Patience: Goodnight, Zeke.

I passed out as soon as I got in my bed and didn't wake up until after two that afternoon. Once I was fully awake, I got a shower and headed out. I passed my dad in the living room and, as usual, he said nothing to me. Either he was hitting me or he was ignoring me. I'd made some pretty good money selling drugs for Javier so far so I wouldn't be living here much longer anyway.

When I showed up at Finn's house, I walked in on Chet and Megan making out on the couch.

"Don't y'all have homes of your own?" I said as I set my guitar next to Chet's drums.

"So are you and Patience okay?" Megan asked, as she wiped her mouth and adjusted her top.

"We're fine, but there's no me and Patience," I said as I fell onto the couch.

"Oh, okay. Whatever you say." She grinned at me.

"Seriously, we're just friends."

"I saw you two together last night in that corner." She nodded to corner of the room. "Looked like more than friends to me."

Finn came in and saved me from having to respond, but the truth was I didn't know what the hell Patience was to me anymore. I just knew I didn't do the girlfriend thing and if that's what she was looking for, she was looking in the wrong place.

She quit coming to Boy's Club. I guess she took what I said seriously when I told her to stay away. The week went by slow and it sucked entirely too much ass. We played The Pit on Friday night and I saw Megan, but still no Patience. So when I ran into her at Finn's house party the following night, I'd be lying if I said I wasn't a tiny bit excited. I could see on her face that she was excited too.

"Long time no see, rich girl." I teased her.

She rolled her eyes.

"My name's Snowflake." She grinned.

Damn, she was fun to flirt with.

"So did you miss me?" I nodded at my friend Connor who walked by and said hey.

"I missed you about as much as you missed me."

I couldn't help myself. I had to say something sweet.

"That much, huh? Damn, I must be pretty special." I winked.

Her smile spread and I got a satisfied feeling. I liked making her smile. Something told me she didn't do it often at home.

"Yeah, must be." Her cheeks turned pink. She reached up and tucked her hair behind her ear shyly. "You guys should play. We need some music in here."

She was right. The place was entirely too quiet.

"You just like to watch me play."

"Maybe." She shrugged and looked up at me through her lashes.

I loved it when she did that. She looked so fucking hot when she flirted. There was no more denying anything. I liked Patience, too damn much if you asked me, and I missed her. Damn, it was hard to admit that to myself, but worse things have happened.

We hung out together most of the night and I sneaked in a touch every now and again. Not once did she jerk away from me, and I was glad to see she was becoming comfortable with me. When Megan drank too much and passed out on Finn's couch, I smiled to myself because I knew I'd get to take Patience home.

Once I got her in my car and we weren't surrounded by a bunch of people, I could really turn up the flirting. Usually, I was the big flirt at Finn's parties, but it hadn't even occurred to me that I didn't pay any attention to any of the other girls who were there. At one point, Stephanie, the redhead, even tried to throw herself at me, but I hardly noticed.

"I think she does this to me on purpose," Patience said as she rolled down her window.

"Why would she leave you stranded on purpose?"

"I never get stranded because you always take me home. She only drinks too much when you're around." She peeked over at me.

That could only mean one thing.

"So she drinks too much to get us alone?" I asked.

"Yes."

"Did you tell her you liked being alone with me?"

I really hoped that was the case because I loved being alone with her.

"Not exactly in those words."

"Then what did you tell her?"

My car felt too big. I wanted her to be closer to me. I looked over at her and her eyes connected with mine. It wasn't safe to drive with her in the car. It was hard as hell to keep my attention on the road when she sat just a few feet away.

"It's not important." She shook her head.

"It is to me."

And it was. It was entirely too important. Why the fuck was it so important?

We were getting closer to her house and it seemed like the closer we got, the more nervous she got. Something was definitely going on at her house. I wished to myself that she'd open up and tell me so I could help, but then again, I never talked about my problems at home so I couldn't really expect her to talk about hers.

"Zeke?"

I loved the way she said my name—like an emotional plea, like I was the only thing she ever wanted to hold on to. It made me feel important; it made me feel needed.

"Yeah?"

She twisted the ends of her hair nervously. "Would you take me home?"

"I am taking you home, babe."

I was hoping she'd say something else. I'm not sure what else I wanted to hear, but the way she said my name was so deep and desperate. I felt like there was something else she wanted to say to me.

"No, I mean will you take me to your home. Can I stay with you tonight?"

Just like that, my car shrunk five sizes and she felt so close I could feel her body heat against my side. What was she saying? Did she want to have sex with me? I couldn't deny the fact that I'd been thinking about having sex with her from the word "go," but there was a problem and the problem was I knew my dad would still be awake. I couldn't take her there. I didn't want her to see that.

"I don't think that's a good idea, snowflake."

I watched her face fall and I felt awful. I didn't want her to think I didn't want her because God knew I did, but I just couldn't take that chance.

She put her head down and fiddled with her fingers. "I don't want to go home."

And then I understood. It wasn't that she wanted me; she just didn't want to go home, and if she didn't want to go home, there had to be a damn good reason.

"How about we go to the park for a bit?"

A tiny smile lifted the side of her mouth. "Okay."

So I went to the park close to the Boy's Club and we parked, but instead of making out, like most people did, we talked.

"So how's your mom doing?" I asked.

"She has her good days and her bad days. Cancer's a bitch."

"Agreed."

I didn't have to tell her that my mom died from cancer as well. When she looked over at me and nodded, I knew she knew. And that's how the next hour went. She told me about her sister, Sydney, and how close they were. She told me about her love of soccer and about the game she played earlier that day. As tiny as she was, I would've never known she was such a badass at soccer.

When it was my turn to talk, I told her about how the band got started and about the guys. I made her laugh a few times when I talked about Tiny and the girls that loved him. She asked questions, but nothing too personal and nothing I wasn't willing to answer. She was so respectful of my privacy and I appreciated her for that. Not once did my dad or her dad come up. I was thankful she didn't ask about mine and I knew better than to ask about hers.

"Have you ever had a girlfriend?"

"Nah, just girls I've screwed around with." I shrugged and stretched out my legs.

"Yeah, I heard you have a different woman every night." She laughed, but it sounded forced.

"I used to, but not since I've met you."

Her eyes crashed into mine. I wasn't sure why I confessed that. Maybe it was because we'd been talking for so long and I was comfortable with her. I don't know, but the minute the words left my mouth her eyes lit up. They were fluorescent-blue pools of emotion and I could tell my confession pleased her.

"Really? Why?"

I knew she'd ask me that and the truth was I didn't know why.

"Maybe I'm waiting for you." I looked over at her and grinned.

She took a shaky breath and looked away.

"You shouldn't do that," she said softly. "I don't think I could be like the girls you're used to."

Good. I didn't want her to be anything like the girls I was used to. I wanted her to be Patience, my snowflake, her own unique self. There was no one like her and I wouldn't want her any other way.

"Good," I said.

She shook her head. "No, not good."

I reached over and pulled her closer to me. Her palms landed on my chest and she looked up at me. I didn't miss the nervous expression on her face or the fact that her body shook a little.

"Yes, it's very good." I ran my fingers through her hair. "The first time I saw you I knew you were different. I think you're perfect just the way you are." And I meant that. I really did, but that didn't mean I wanted to say it out loud.

I was already cursing myself for saying something so lame. Why was I sitting in my car sweet-talking this girl when what I should've been doing was trying to get in her panties?

She reached up and pushed my hair out of my face with her finger. She was so close I could feel her warm breath against my mouth. Her eyes glowed in the darkness as she stared up at me.

"I'm far from perfect. Trust me. I'm the most flawed person I know." She turned away.

Cupping her chin, I turned her to face me again. Her lips looked so plump and moist, even being turned down in a frown. I wanted her to smile. I wanted it like I wanted my next breath, and I wanted to kiss her. I'd fought with that one for a while, but I definitely wanted to kiss her.

"Patience." Her name came out on an exhale.

I let my hand slip around to the side of her neck. My fingers twirled in the soft baby hairs behind her ear.

"Yeah?"

We were both breathing so hard my car windows were fogged over. It was the first time in my life I'd fogged windows doing something other than sex.

She reached up and tucked her hair behind her ear and bit at her lip like she knew what I was thinking. She closed her eyes and sighed when I ran my thumb across her bottom lip.

"I think I want to kiss you."

There. I'd said it. It was out there and there was no taking it back. I hadn't kissed a girl since I was fourteen. Mainly because it felt entirely too personal, but with Patience I wanted to be personal. I wanted to taste her in ways I hadn't tasted other women, and kissing was the only way I could do that.

Her eyes widened and her throat bobbed up and down as she swallowed hard. Her breathing accelerated as I gave her a minute to let my words sink it. If she wasn't okay with being kissed good and hard, I was giving her plenty of time to say so. I had a feeling once my mouth connected with hers it would take a lot for me to stop.

"I think I want you to kiss me," she whispered.

I looked down at her sweet mouth and bit at my lip ring. I tilted her head up to meet mine and moved in. I let my lips skim hers and they were every bit as soft as they looked. A tiny noise escaped her mouth and I lost it.

I pressed my lips to hers and experienced a new world. I closed my eyes and took her in. She threw her arms around my neck and melted into me. I felt her fingers in the hair at the back of my neck and then her mouth opened a bit and I took that as an invitation to deepen the kiss.

It was better than sex somehow. I'd had enough sex in my life, but this was deeper. This was different. It was being inside of her on a whole other level. I was letting her breathe me in. I was breathing her in and she was the breath I needed to take for most of my life.

Everything bad went away in that moment. She soothed every scar, took away every bad memory. She made me better. My eyes were closed, but there was so much light around us. At least it felt that way, and it heated my skin. I was absorbing a healing heat and it spread through me like a euphoric fire.

I kissed her until we were out of breath and hanging on to each other. Then I broke the kiss, took a deep breath, and went in for more. I couldn't get enough. She clung to the front of my shirt like I was her savior and I thought that was fitting since, in so many ways, she was mine. She was the sense of peace I'd been searching for in all the wrong places.

She pulled away and took another deep breath and licked at her lips. It drove me wild. She tasted me the same way I tasted her and I liked it. She pressed herself tightly against me. Her body fit to mine like she was made specifically for me, and I was beginning to think she was.

She leaned up and kissed me again and I let her take control. She pressed up into our kiss as she got up on her knees beside me. I reached behind her and hooked my hands to her hips. She was above me, around me, inside me, and then she shocked me when she slipped one leg over me and straddled my thighs.

I broke the kiss and looked up at her. The usual panic wasn't there. Her eyes were wide and full of excitement. They had the same glazed-over look as a girl in the middle of sex. Her hair hung down into my face as she showered my lips and cheeks with her soft, panting breaths. She looked too far gone, but she'd looked similar that night at my house, the night she stopped me with tears on her cheeks. I couldn't go through that again. I'd explode.

"Maybe we should slow down," I said.

I wanted to laugh out loud at that, but I was too afraid of ruining the moment. It was such a chick thing to say, but I didn't want to push her too far. We'd already established the fact that she was nothing like the girls I was usually with. The last thing I wanted to do was freak her out again.

"Do you want to slow down?" she asked. Her brows bent down in confusion.

"Hell no, but you freaked out last time and I don't want that to happen again," I said honestly.

I felt her body tense up a little and she looked down at me like she was about to lay a massive confession on me.

The expression was there for a brief moment before it cleared.

"I'm sorry I get scared. I wish I didn't, but it's not something I can help."

I hated the thought of her being afraid of anything. When she was with me, fear should be the last thing on her mind. Patience brought out a protective streak in me that would strike down anyone if it meant keeping her safe. So the idea that I put fear in her heart disgusted me.

She looked away from me like she'd said too much, but I laid my hands on her cheeks and forced her to look at me. Her fingers dug into my shirt and wounded eyes met mine.

"Don't ever be scared with me. I'd never do anything to hurt you and I'd destroy anyone who tried."

Two things happened after that.

One: I was smacked in the face with the realization that I had feelings for Patience. It sucked and Lord knows I tried to keep it from happening, but they were there seated deep inside of me where I couldn't get to them to clean them away, and after that point, I wasn't sure I wanted them gone anymore.

Two: She closed her eyes and a single tear slipped down her face as a tiny smile spread across her mouth. She laid her cool hands on my cheeks and looked down at me like I was everything I'd never be and then she leaned down and kissed me like her life depended on it.

A wave of relaxation went through her body and she collided with me emotionally. Her body melded into mine and I wasn't sure where I ended and she began. Her hands were everywhere, in my hair, wrapped in my shirt as she tried to pull me closer, and then up my shirt against my skin.

Breaking the kiss, I leaned down and pressed my lips against the side of her neck. I sucked softly at the smooth skin just under her jaw. She gasped and her fingers dug into my sides. Her pulse was quick against my lips as I ran them down the side of her neck.

She was trembling, but not from fear or anxiety. She was shaking like a girl on the verge of a new experience. She responded much the same way that night at my house in my bed. I loved her responses. I'd never had a girl respond to me that way. She was shy, but still bursting at the seams, and I wanted her to let loose on me.

I ran my hands up her legs and grabbed on to her hips. I pulled her closer and she did the rest of the work as she began to press herself against me and move her hips back and forth.

A husky moan spilled from her lips and she let her head fall back with her eyes closed. It was the most erotic thing I'd ever seen. I'd watched naked women pleasure themselves for me, but Patience was still fully clothed and she wasn't doing this for me; she was doing this for herself. It was a massive turn-on.

I pushed up the bottom of her shirt and ran my fingers across her belly button. Her stomach moved in and out with her heavy breathing. My eyes crashed with hers when I looked back up. There was a tiny strain on her face, and I knew all too well what the strain was about. Her body was strung tight and if I knew anything, it was how to play a taut string. I wanted to release that tension in her and see relief on her beautiful face.

"Is this okay?" I asked when I let my hand move lower.

My voice cracked and it freaked me out how into this moment I was. Being with a girl wasn't anything new for me, but Patience made me feel like some virginal fifteen-year-old punk. I can't say I hated it, but it was different.

She bit her bottom lip and nodded her head yes. My hand slipped lower and I let my finger run just inside her jeans. The lacy top of her panties tickled the tips of my fingers and she made a tiny moaning noise that was probably the sexiest noise I'd ever heard a girl make. I was going slow with her, but going slow was kind of fun. I was teasing myself and teasing her at the same time. As much as I loved a quick, hard fuck up against a wall, going slow with Patience was going to be amazing and I had the distinct feeling I'd remember being with her this way for the rest of my life.

I lifted my finger from her skin and smiled when she lifted her hips and brought her body back to my finger. She wasn't speaking, but her body was talking for her. She wanted whatever I had to offer and at this very moment, I was offering everything I had.

With hesitant hands, she lifted my shirt and pulled it over my head. Her fingers ran across my shoulders and down my chest. Her hands felt amazing on my skin as she softly ran her fingertips over my abs. I reached down and unbuttoned her jeans. I wanted to feel her again.

"Can I touch you?" I asked breathlessly.

I'd asked the last time this happened with her. I wasn't sure why I asked. I'd never asked a female permission for anything in my life, but the tiny voice in the back of my head, the one that was telling me to go slow, was also telling me that I needed permission to touch her. Initially, I just wanted her, but now, after just a tiny bit of touching, my body needed her. No other girl could soothe this ache. It was seated firmly in the pit of my pelvic area and the combination for its release was her touch.

"Yes, please." Her voice was strained and hushed.

And it was like the answer to all my prayers. She let her head fall against my shoulder and I breathed in the scent of her hair. I slid my finger lower and let it dip into her moisture. She was so wet. I'd never felt so much moisture in a woman's body and it was magnificent.

And then her mouth was on mine again and she kissed me hard. Little noises were pressed against my lips as I touched her with experienced fingers. She began softly panting my name and thrusting her hips. Her responsiveness was so sexy, innocent, but definitely sexy.

That was usually the point that I'd strip her the rest of the way naked and get mine, but something about the way she moved her body, her inexperienced movements... I liked making her feel good. As much I wanted my own personal release, I wanted hers more.

Looking up into her pleasure-filled face, her eyes opened and dug into mine. She leaned her head back and opened her mouth for extra air. She was so close; I could see the sweet ache on her face. Her breathing became erratic and she pulled me closer.

A raw sense of pleasure rippled over me when she started to whisper my name over and over again. Her fingers dug deeper into my shoulders and I felt her movements getting stiff. Then the most beautiful thing I'd ever seen happened. She bit down on her lip, threw her head back, and moaned out a long, soul-wrenching release.

Her expression was one of shock when she looked back down at me. Her flushed skin glowed in the moonlight as she came back to herself. I reached up and tucked her hair behind her ears. I went in for another kiss, but her expression changed suddenly and she looked like she was about to be sick.

"Oh my God, what did I do?" she asked.

Panic filled her eyes and she looked down at me like she'd never seen me before.

I didn't know what was happening. I'd never seen a girl react this way before. She struggled to get out of my arms, but something told me if I let her go, I'd never see her again. She began to cry and push against my chest.

"Snowflake? What's wrong? You did nothing wrong." I tried to press my words past her shield of panic.

Still, she continued to look down at me like I was a stranger trying to attack her, and still, she beat against my chest as she tried to get free. I knew I should let her go, but suddenly the idea of not seeing her again made me feel crazy. I needed her to calm down. I wanted to talk this through with her.

"Snowflake! It's me. It's Zeke, and I'd never do anything to hurt you. Please, stop this," I begged.

It was a first for me. I never begged, but she was now hyperventilating and I was scared she'd overdo it and pass out. I released her so she didn't hurt herself and she jumped off of me and slammed her body against the passenger-side door.

She scratched at the door until she finally found the handle. Cold air rushed into my car when she popped the door open and jumped out. I followed behind her, but she didn't get far before she ran straight into the arms of her dad. There were three police officers standing behind him.

The officers stared back at me like I was a wanted rapist. Her dad stared back at me like he wanted to kill me on the spot. And Patience looked back at me like she was begging me to save her.

SIXTEEN
PATIENCE

PROTECTED. PRECIOUS. PERFECT. I WAS all three of those things in Zeke's arms. I'd never known love, other than the love I had for my mom and sister, but when I looked down into Zeke's face after he kissed me, I knew I was in love with him.

I'd fallen for Zeke. He was dark and dangerous, but he was also the safest place on Earth for me. He'd somehow become home base, a place for me to go and gather my thoughts. A place where I could let go of all the bad and take in some good.

I'd never been so close to someone in my life, I'd never revealed the things about myself the way I did with him. I'd even been on the verge of telling him my dirty secrets, things that could change my life, things that could ruin my father and destroy my mother. That's what Zeke did to me; he made me want to exhale everything.

When he kissed me, there was a bonding between us and I was sure he felt it too. He had to. It was so strong. It was as if our souls had collided and began to rebuild the other. It was powerful and it pushed me over the edge and right into him.

I thought for sure I'd never feel anything of the sort, but once he touched me with his fingers and my body experienced a release that it never had before, I knew I was transformed. He intricately placed his fingers in places that only an experienced man could and brought forth a reality that I never knew existed, a place where being touched was wonderful and fulfilling, a place overflowing with relief.

But the minute the feeling dissolved, something tragic happened and turned my beautiful moment into a nightmare. I looked down into Zeke's face and he shyly smiled back at me. Something about the way he looked at me felt wrong. It all felt wrong, and I was waiting for the blow. What I had done was bad and punishment was sure to follow.

The logical side of me knew I was being irrational as I fought to get away from him, but the sick parts of me knew there was no good in what we'd just done. A panic I'd never experienced before swept over me and I went into a full anxiety attack. I wasn't so much trying to get away from Zeke as I was just trying to get out of the car. I needed air. I needed to breathe and the car was too small and he was too close.

Once I was free of the car, I ran straight into the one place I never wanted to be again, the arms of my father. His eyes beat into me and his grip was so tight I was sure he'd snap my arms in half. At that point, all I wanted to do was climb back into Zeke's car and disappear, but there was no running, especially not when I saw the police officers standing behind my dad.

My eyes found Zeke's and something passed between us. I needed help and I wanted to beg him to save me, but that couldn't happen. I could never ask for his help. Asking for his help would require revealing truths, and I could never do that.

"Let her go," Zeke said. His voice held a hint of a threat.

My dad's fingers tightened and I knew it was his way of saying I'd better stay put. I knew my dad was powerful and I also knew he could destroy what little bit Zeke had. Just as Zeke had promised to protect me, I'd do the same for him, so I stood there. As badly as I wanted to run back to him, I didn't.

"Zeke Mitchell, haven't you learned your lesson yet, son? I could have these nice officers arrest you, since I'm sure you have drugs in your car, but I won't do that. All I ask is that you get in your car and go home. Patience is going home, too, and whatever this is between y'all needs to stop. Patience is leaving for college in a few months anyway."

Zeke's eyes met mine like he was searching for the truth. The truth was this was the first I'd heard of any college plans. I hadn't even applied for any since I had no plans of leaving Sydney unattended. If anything, I'd jump on board a local technical college until Syd graduated.

Instead, I shrugged and gave him a tiny, crooked smile that said I was sorry. He didn't buy it. His eyes told me he knew I was playing into my dad's shit. So I plastered on the realest smile I could just for him.

"It's okay, Zeke. Tell Megan I'll text her later. I needed to get home anyway. I had fun. Thanks for the ride."

He looked angry at my words and I knew it was because he felt dismissed by me, but I didn't want him to get arrested again. He'd already been arrested twice thanks to me and there was no way in hell I was going to let that happen again.

"I'm not leaving you," he said with determination.

And in that moment I knew I had to be like Zeke. I had to lie about my feelings and push him away. I cut my eyes at him and then rolled them. Then I said something that made my stomach turn.

"Look, it was fun, but now it's time you go back to your shitty little trailer park. I wanted to see if what they said about you was true, and now that I see it isn't, I'm done messing around with you."

I had indeed hit my mark. The crushed look in his eyes told me it was a direct hit. I didn't wait around for him to respond. I turned away and got in the passenger's seat of my dad's car. Zeke stood there in shock, staring back at my father, until finally he turned, got in his car, and drove away.

The window was cracked and I could hear my dad talking to the police officers. He was thanking them for finding me and thanking them for their service. He was playing the role of good politician so if the stories circulated about his delinquent daughter he could play it up as the good guy who was trying to help his child.

I knew the way these things worked. I wasn't an idiot to that side of life. The cops seemed to fall into the palm of his hand just like everyone else did. It wasn't long until he joined me in the car and another silent ride home commenced.

It was nearly dawn before I was free of my dad. I stood in the hot shower and tried to wash his punishment away. It was the worse one yet, but I made it through thinking about all the wonderful things Zeke said to me in his car.

The next day, I spent most of my time with my mom. She looked good and was actually sitting up in bed watching TV, versus being completely out of it.

"So, are you going to tell me who he is?" she asked as I painted her thin nails with a bright-pink polish.

"What do you mean?" I asked.

She smiled at me and shook her head.

"I wasn't always a sick woman, you know. I remember what it was like to be young and in love. Don't tell your father this, but I was in love before him. His name was Robert and he was wonderful. I fell in love with him almost instantly." She had a happy, dreamy look that made me smile.

"So what happened?" I asked.

"Well, my father told me to stay away from him. He said he wasn't good enough. I guess you could say he was a bad boy." She grinned. "But when it came to me, he was the sweetest guy in the world."

I was shocked by how similar our stories were. Maybe that's what made me comfortable enough to open up to her.

"His name's Zeke," I said with a smile.

"Oh, now we're getting somewhere." She patted my hand. "Tell me more about this Zeke. Is he a bad boy?"

And in that moment I'd never felt more close to my mother. I didn't tell her the entire story of how I met Zeke because I didn't want her to worry, but I did give her a few details.

"I'm so glad I got to see this," she said sadly.

"See what?" I asked confused.

"The look on your face. I didn't think I'd live to see the day when one of my girls would fall in love and I'm grateful that I at least got to see it once."

A tear slipped down her cheek and I couldn't hold mine back no matter how hard I tried. I reached out and hugged my mother's small frame to me and we cried together.

"Do me a favor, Patience," she said to me as she captured my tear-stained face in her hands.

"Anything," I croaked.

"If you love him, don't let him go for anyone and tell him how you feel. I never got that chance with Robert, and I found out ten years ago that he died. I never got a chance to tell him how much I loved him. Don't let that happen to you."

An hour later, my mother slept and I was standing in the middle of the garage next to the dreaded gray Toyota with a set of never-before-touched keys. I took a ton of deep breaths and grasped the door handle five times before I was even able to get in the car.

The inside smelled brand new since technically it was a brand new car. My dad had forced me to drive it once when I first got it and I silently cried the entire time. Even now, climbing inside the car felt wrong. I felt like I was saying what my father did to me was okay. It wasn't, but I needed to get to Zeke and I couldn't keep calling Megan every time I needed to go somewhere.

I knew my way to Zeke's house well. What I didn't know was what the hell I was going to say to him once I got there. He'd probably never talk to me again and I couldn't blame him if he didn't, but I promised my mom I'd be honest about my feelings toward him and that's what I was going to do.

I had the feeling that once I confessed my feelings to him he'd never talk to me again. Guys like Zeke ran from emotions, but deep down I could feel things getting out of hand. Soon, we'd never talk to each anymore anyway. This way I could get my feelings off my chest and have a peace that my mother never got.

When I pulled into Zeke's muddy yard, I parked between his car and his dad's tow truck. I cut my engine and got out. My shoes sank into the dirt as I cut across his small yard. The steps squeaked as I went up. I held my hand up and was about to knock when I heard a loud smashing noise on the inside.

Someone was yelling and then there was another loud noise. Without thinking I grabbed onto the knob and turned it. The door opened easily. Stepping inside the small, shabby space, the first thing I saw was Zeke on the floor with blood on his face. His father was standing over him with fist in the air ready to come down.

Without thinking, I jumped. I latched onto his dad's arm and held on tight as he tried to shake me off. Once I released his arm, I jumped in front of Zeke and stared into his dad's eyes.

He was a big man, much bigger than my own, and he smelled awful, like beer and cigarettes. His grease-covered shirt was too tight and his hair was disheveled like he'd just woken up.

"Who the hell are you?" he asked.

His hot breath struck my cheek and I accidently breathed it in. The smell made my stomach roll and I thought for sure I was going to throw up all over him. The room spun as fear smashed into me, but I'd known fear many times in my life and I wasn't going to let it get the best of me, not when Zeke needed me.

"Don't you dare hit him again!" I growled back at him.

My voice surprised me. How was I able to stand up to this stranger? How was I able to get past the deep-set fear that had taken over me? When faced with my dad I couldn't do this, and I *knew* how far I could go with him. I didn't know this man from a hole in the wall, yet I stood toe to toe with him and dared him to touch Zeke.

He towed over me and his chest bumped into my face. From behind me I could hear Zeke coming to and getting up from the floor.

"No, snowflake," he said through a bloodied lip. "Just let it go and get out of here."

Just like that, so many things made sense now—the bruises I'd seen on him, his anger toward everyone, his quickness to fight another human being. Just as I had my defense mechanisms, Zeke had his. He had shields just the way I did.

Our lives weren't so different. Abuse was abuse no matter its form. One wasn't easier than the other; either way it hurt. Either way it scarred the person on the receiving end. It scarred them and broke them into tiny pieces. Zeke and I were both broken parts of a whole person and no matter what piece you put where, it would fit, because we fit. I'd always known it. We fit.

"Mind your own fucking business, little girl," his dad said.

And then he pushed at my chest with big, meaty fingers and knocked the breath out of me just that easily. Still, I stood my ground.

"You're *not* going to touch him again!" I said with more strength than I felt.

The room spun when the back of his hand connected with my cheek. I landed face first into the foul, shag carpeting. There was a scuffle behind me, so I quickly turned onto my back and tried to get up. My mouth filled with blood and the room continued to spin. Zeke had to be one tough guy if he went through this all the time.

When my vision finally cleared, I looked up to see Zeke beating his father unmercifully. His dad didn't give up and went back in with a punch to his cheek. The thin, paneling wall cracked when Zeke slammed into it, but he shook it off and kept punching his dad in the stomach and face over and over again.

His dad caught him in the stomach and I heard the air squeeze from his lungs as he fell to his knees.

"Come on, you little fucker." His dad baited him. "Is that all you got? I bet your little bitch hits harder than you!"

Zeke crawled from the floor and went on the attack again. He threw punches so fast his hands started to blur. Once his dad fell to one knee, Zeke attacked harder and then out of nowhere, he reached over for the guitar his mother bought him and brought it up over his head. Things started to move in slow motion.

I saw where this was going and I heard myself scream for him to stop, but before the words left my lips, he brought the guitar down and slammed it into his dad's back. There was a loud crack and then tiny pieces of guitar flew everywhere.

He brought it up again and this time he brought it down and cracked the already broken guitar over his dad's face. His dad fell hard and the trailer shook.

Zeke pulled back a broken piece that still had the strings attached. The larger, shattered part of the guitar hung above his unconscious and bloodied father. He looked down at his guitar and then he looked down at the heaping pile of asshole he'd managed to knock out. Sorrow seeped into his big, brown eyes and then he looked over at me. He held the pieces of the guitar up as if to show me what he had done.

It was broken beyond repair, his most prized possession. The guitar his mother bought for him years ago was gone... irreplaceable... gone. I couldn't help but feel like it was my fault. I was the reason he'd lost something that meant more to him than anything else in the world and once he realized that he'd hate me. I hated me.

Dark, unreadable eyes looked back at me before he looked down again and shook his head in what I assumed was aggravation.

"Are you okay?" he asked roughly as he wiped at his bleeding lip.

Me? Who gave a rat's ass about me? I was fine. All I could think about was him and his guitar. He'd told me how special that guitar was and I knew what it meant to him.

"I'm fine. Are you okay?"

"I'll live." He looked like he was about to cry.

"I'm so sorry, Zeke."

The floor shifted as I stood up and went to him. I reached out for his hand and he didn't pull away. Brushing his hair from his sweaty face, his already swelling eye was turning black. He flinched when I ran my finger across the bruise.

"Don't be, you didn't do anything wrong. I should've stood up to him years ago." He sat on the couch and the broken guitar fell to his feet. "What are you doing here?"

I sat beside him and laid my hand on his knee. He looked down at my hand and then looked back at me.

"I came to tell you I was sorry. I didn't mean what I said the other night. I just didn't want you to get arrested."

The side of his mouth tilted up and he blew out a deep breath.

"You could've just texted me that."

I went in for the kill.

"But then I wouldn't have been able to see you."

He turned to me and his eyes took in my face. Reaching up, he laid his palm against my sore cheek. Anger filled his eyes and he breathed hard, making his nostrils flare.

"He hit you. I'm so sorry I let him hit you." His thumb caressed what I was sure was already a forming bruise.

"You didn't let him do anything." I covered his hand with mine. "Do you guys always fight like that?"

He shook his head and closed his eyes.

"No. I usually never fight back. I promised my mom on her death bed that I wouldn't fight him."

"But you did today." I stated the obvious.

Deep brown eyes took me in as he brought his other hand up and laid it on my other cheek.

"When he hit you, I wanted to kill him."

His confession said so much to me. I leaned in to kiss him, but his dad moaned like he was getting up. Zeke jumped from the couch and pulled me up with him.

"You need to get out of here. When he wakes up it's not going to be good."

"I'm not leaving you."

And I wasn't. I refused to leave him in a place where he wasn't safe.

"Fine, let me grab some stuff. Stand by the door and don't move. If he gets up, get out of here and go sit in my car, okay?"

I nodded my agreement and went to stand by the door while Zeke ran to his room and started throwing random things into a bag. A piece of wood on the floor caught my eye. I reached down and picked it up. It was the part of his guitar with his mom's signature.

Quickly, I dug through the pieces of his broken guitar. As if it were fate, I found four quotes that were still whole. The edges were broken and jagged, but still whole. I collected them and put them in my pocket. I was sure there was something I could do with the pieces.

Zeke came back out of his room and grabbed my hand. "Let's get out of here."

Once we were outside, he threw his stuff in the back of his car and turned to me.

“Whose car?” he nodded over to my car.

“It’s mine, kind of.”

“Good. Follow me.”

I nodded and turned to walk away, but he softly grabbed my wrist and pulled me back to him. He ran his fingers through my hair and then leaned and planted a soft kiss on my lips.

“Seriously, snowflake, I need you.”

SEVENTEEN
ZEKE

GO BACK TO YOUR SHITTY little trailer park. I wanted to see if what they said about you was true, and now that I see it isn't, I'm done messing around with you.

Patience's words bounced around my head the entire ride home. The look in her eyes wasn't right, but I couldn't tell if she meant it or not. Either way, I was done. She was right. We were from two different worlds and I needed to stay in my zone.

Once I got home, I went straight to bed, but I couldn't sleep. My thoughts were a scrambled mess. Part of me wanted to go kidnap Patience and keep her safe from her asshole of a father, and the other part of me knew that I should just drop it and hope that she was okay.

When I closed my eyes, all I could see was her face in ecstasy and the way she looked after we kissed. I'd never had a woman look at me with so much emotion in her eyes. I'd also never had someone cut me so deep with their words. I'm not sure when she got that capability, but I was positive it happened during our kiss.

I hated to admit it to myself, but I was falling for her and from the way she looked at me, I thought for sure she felt the same way, but then she freaked out and I couldn't understand why or what was happening.

The one thing I did know was that something wasn't right. Patience was hiding something. Whether it was a severe psychological disorder or the fact that her dad beat her, she was definitely hiding something.

The next day I stayed home all day. I knew it was a bad idea being stuck in the house with my dad, but after the night I had, I had too much on my brain and that last thing I wanted to do was hang around anyone. I'd be shitty company.

I was sitting on the couch, playing my acoustic guitar and thinking about my mom, when my dad came in the door from a tow run. Needing to be out of the same space as him, I got up to go to my room. He never gave me that chance. Instead, he went straight for the fight.

I'm not sure if seeing my guitar with my mom's handwriting all over it set him off or what, but he said nothing. He didn't give me any reason for this fight. I pushed my guitar out of the way and covered myself. Except this time was different, this time he didn't just try to break me; he also broke things around us. He threw a plate against a wall like a Frisbee, and then tossed the coffee table across the room in a heated rage.

"You look just like *her*!" he spat in my face.

My cheek exploded when he brought his fist down on it and I tasted blood, but I ignored it all. I zoned out and I would've stayed zoned out had I not heard Patience's voice.

At first, I thought I was losing my mind. I thought maybe I conjured up the sounds of her soothing voice as a survival mechanism. But then I peeked up and saw her standing in front of me and I knew she was real.

She stood in front of my dad like a petite avenging angel. Her blue glare cut into him as if her vision could cut him in half, and her tiny fists were balled up like she was minutes away from kicking some ass. It was the most heartwarming and frightening thing I'd ever seen.

My dad's large frame towered over here. His shadow crept across her face, and still, she held her ground. Her T-shirt strained against her puffed out chest and her cheeks flushed with anger as she stared him square in the eye.

"Don't you dare hit him again!"

My dad looked down at her like she was a joke at first. Too much beer had obviously riddled his brain. Shaking his head, he adjusted his vision.

I remember telling her to let it go, I remember him pushing her to the side and saying something rude as fuck, but the minute I saw him hit her, a rage that I'd never known struck me. I didn't feel anything anymore. All I knew was he had to die.

I watched as her head snapped to the side before she went down. In that moment something cracked inside me, something other than a rib or a wrist. This time it was something deep set inside my soul. It cracked and crumbled into miniature pieces of fury.

I didn't wait for him to come at me. Instead, I went straight for him. My fist connected to his cheek and for a second he looked at me, shocked. Years of abuse and I'd never so much as lifted my hand to him, but he crossed a line and on the other side of that line was a new me—a me that would kill someone before I let them hurt Patience.

My anger was fueled by years of being his punching bag. I saw images of him hitting my mother, images of his fist coming toward me, and finally, the image of Patience going down after he hit her ran through my mind over and over again. I couldn't have stopped if I wanted to.

He could hit me all he wanted. I'd get my ass kicked every day if that was the way it was, but I drew a thick, black line at Patience. She was the only good thing, a slice of sunlight in my eternal night, snowflakes in my hell, and I'd do whatever it took to protect her from me and my world. I'd kill him for putting his hands on her.

I'd been so blinded by my red-hot rage that I didn't even realize what I picked up. I didn't know that I'd used my most prized possession to take my dad down. Heartbreak unlike any other ripped through me when I pulled back the broken pieces of string and wood, and tears threatened to break through.

Patience knew about my guitar. She was the only other person in the world besides my dad who knew. When I looked over at her and showed her the broken parts of the favorite memory with my mom, her face told me she understood the massiveness of what I'd just done.

My eyes met fair skin that was starting to swell and again I felt my anger rise. Breathing deep, I tried to squash it before I did something *really* stupid. The corner of my mouth burned and the taste of blood was on my tongue, but I was more worried about her.

Every time I looked at her, I felt like my skin was melting from my bones. I didn't find relief until she came to me and touched me. It's so funny. For years my dad abused me and not once had I ever truly felt angry about it, but one hit to Patience and I wanted his blood on my hands.

I thought I'd never see her again, but she was here and she was here to see me. Even after the drama from the night before, she still wanted to see me. So when she said she wouldn't leave without me, I knew I had to go with her. I walked away from my dad's house with barely any money in my pocket and a bag full of anything that would fit.

The strangest thing was, when we got to my car and she tried to pull away, I almost couldn't let her go. The world felt like a jumbled mess. I felt nauseated just being a part of it, but when she was near me or touching me everything stopped spinning and I was filled with a heavy dose of clarity.

Looking through the rearview mirror, I took her in as she followed behind me in the car I didn't know she had. I had no idea where I was going. I just knew as long as she was with me I'd be okay. The idea of needing someone to hold me together scared me shitless, but it was out there. There was no taking it back now. I needed Patience and I couldn't shake the feeling that somehow she needed me too.

My El Camino threw out a puff of smoke when I cut the engine in front of the cheapest motel in town.

Patience stood by the door in the front office as I paid for two nights. I could've stayed with Finn, but I wasn't the kind of person to live up on my friends.

The lady behind the counter handed me my room key then smiled sheepishly at Patience. I grinned over at her when her cheeks filled with fire. She followed me to my room and I held the door open for her as we entered the dark room.

"I should probably go." She picked at her fingernails.

I threw my bag onto the queen-sized bed then turned to her. Covering her hands with mine, I stopped her from picking at her nice fingernails.

"Don't," I said simply.

I wasn't sure if she realized I was asking her to stay, but she looked up at me through those long lashes of hers and I almost forgot I was officially homeless. I almost forgot that I laid my dad out cold and destroyed the last thing I had from my mother. I couldn't seem to remember anything from the last few hours.

Pushing aside a thick piece of blond bangs, I let my thumb skim her swelling cheek.

"I'm so sorry, snowflake." I swallowed hard.

I'd never felt more like a failure in my entire life. I let her down. He should've never been able to get near her.

"You did nothing wrong, Zeke." She covered my hand with hers.

Turning her face into my palm, she closed her eyes and smiled.

"I never thought I'd enjoy this so much," she whispered.

"Enjoy what?"

She rubbed my palm with her cheek again.

"Your touch." She grinned up at me.

"Well, since you like it that much..." I said as I wrapped my other arm around her waist and pulled her close to me.

Her body fit to mine with perfection. It made me question every other woman I'd ever touched in my life. My hand shifted from her cheek and down her neck and my eyes took in her full, pouty mouth. After last night's kiss, kissing Patience didn't seem like a tragedy. If anything, her kisses were tiny miracles. They turned the asshole inside me into a big teddy bear.

The smell of her hair filled me when I leaned in and ran my nose up the side of her neck. She stiffened in my arms, but pulled me closer at the same time. When I got to her ear, I laid a tiny kiss on her earlobe.

"I'm going to kiss you now," I whispered my warning.

I'd been thinking about kissing her since the moment the last kiss ended.

I felt a shiver run through her body and I knew I'd won the opportunity for another kiss. Her skin felt smooth against my lips as I ran them across her cheek to get to her mouth. When I pressed my lips to hers, she leaned into my kiss and exhaled a hard breath through her nose.

It was small, not much more than us pressing our mouths together, but it was enough. Everything was enough when it came to her. Her hand tightened in the back of my shirt and she wrapped her other arm around me. I pulled away first, not because I wasn't enjoying it, but because my mind went into sexual overdrive. I didn't want to get to a point where I pushed her too far.

I nudged her nose with mine and grinned down at her.

"I'm pretty sure I'll never get tired of that," she murmured.

"Only pretty sure?" I teased

"Okay, I'm absolutely positive I'll never get tired of that." She smiled.

"That's more like it." I gave her another quick peck. "But now, I must shower."

Snatching up my bag, I dug through it for a fresh pair of clothes. I handed her the remote to the TV.

"Occupy yourself while I go in the bathroom and get naked and wet." I winked at her.

She laughed and set down the remote.

"Actually, I have to get home." She shrugged. "School tomorrow and everything. You have my number if you need anything."

I didn't want her to leave. My life was getting crazy, and if I were being honest with myself, I didn't really want to be alone. But instead of saying anything and looking like a total punk, I shook my head.

"I guess I'll see you around?"

"Hopefully." She shyly shrugged and looked away.

After Patience left, I took a hot shower and watched sitcoms on the crappiest TV known to man. An hour after that, the sun had gone down and I was dying from boredom.

I picked up my phone and texted Patience.

Me: FYI, you're missing a great party over here.

Patience: I am?

Me: Not really. I'm bored.

Patience: Oh, and here I was thinking you texted me because you were thinking about me.

Me: If I texted you every time I thought about you, I'd never stop texting.

Patience: You're so full of it.

Me: You should be full of it.

Patience: Pervert

Me: You like it.

Patience: Maybe

Me: Come spend the night with me. No sex. Just hanging out.

My phone was silent for almost an hour. I was about to doze off when she responded and I couldn't stop myself from getting excited.

Patience: OK. On the way.

EIGHTEEN

PATIENCE

I WAS NERVOUS THE ENTIRE trip back to Zeke's motel room. What if he expected something I couldn't give? I knew being stuck in a motel room with a guy like him wasn't safe, mostly because I couldn't stop thinking about his hands and mouth, but I wanted to be near him.

When I got home and found out my dad went out of town for the week, I couldn't squelch the excitement that took over me. A week of no dad worries—a week of coming and going as I pleased and not having to play protector... not having to play Patience. I was excited to enjoy my father-free week.

When it came to Zeke, driving the car from my dad didn't seem like such a sin. I hated the car and everything it stood for, but I loved being around Zeke more.

The trip to the motel was quick, and it wasn't long until I pulled in next his car. I couldn't help but feel a little sleazy for pulling up at such a place so late at night. I pulled my book bag out of the back and grabbed my soccer bag that held extra clothes and everything I needed to get ready for school.

"Took you long enough," Zeke said as he leaned a shoulder against the doorframe.

I felt myself blush after realizing he'd been standing there watching me the entire time. Thank God I didn't do anything gross like pick my panties out of a wedgie or something.

He turned and put his back to the doorframe as I started to walk through the door. When I tried to pass, he put his arm out and stopped me.

"What's the password?" He leaned in and whispered.

"Um... I'm a creepy weirdo?" I joked, referring to him.

He laughed. "You are? I had no idea."

I playfully smacked at his chest.

"Just let me in already." I sighed.

He moved his arm, but before I could take a step, he pulled me to him and put his lips against the soft skin beneath my ear.

"For further reference, the passphrase for you will always be 'I like snowflakes on my tongue.'"

His voice against the side of my neck made me shiver. His laughter followed behind me as he stepped in and closed the door.

"You look nervous," he said as he took my heavy book bag away from me.

"I sort of am," I said honestly.

"Don't be nervous. We're just two friends hanging out and watching some TV. It's a first for me, but it seems like I'm doing a lot of firsts when it comes to you."

"It's a first for me, too."

"You've never hung out with friends and watched TV?" His brow creased in with confusion.

"I have, but I've never spent the night with a guy before."

"Well, as long as you don't pull out those damn gym shorts and soccer socks, I think you'll leave unscathed."

I laughed.

"Seriously, my soccer socks?"

"Hell yeah. I've had some dirty fantasies about you and those socks." He winked as he tossed me a pillow, then fell on the bed facing the TV.

"Okay, so what are we watching?" he asked casually, like he wasn't just flirting two seconds before.

We sat up watching sitcoms and talking about our favorite movies until my eyes refused to stay open. At one point, I was almost positive Zeke kissed me on the cheek and told me goodnight, but I was so out of it I couldn't be sure.

I woke up twice throughout the night. Once with Zeke's arms wrapped tightly around me as he spooned me from behind and the second time with my arm and leg thrown across him while he was on his back. It was some of the best sleep I'd gotten in years.

The next morning my ringing cell phone woke me. I reached over to answer it, but I didn't make it in time. It was my eighteenth birthday and I knew it was probably my sister calling to sing me happy birthday. She'd warned me the night before that she would. She wasn't too happy about me "spending the night with Megan" the night before my birthday.

The sun cut through a slit in the curtains and right into my eyes. Outside the window I could hear a couple arguing about money. How I'd managed to sleep through that I had no idea. It didn't seem to bother Zeke since he was snoozing away next to me. I turned toward him and took in his sleeping face.

Happy eighteenth birthday to me!

Dear God, the man looked gorgeous even while he slept. Sleeping on his stomach, his hand was across mine. I pressed my head deeper into my pillow and let my eyes roam over his naked back. When had he taken off his shirt and why the hell did I miss it?

His finger jerked and brought my attention back to our hands. I ran my finger over the nautical star tattoo on side of his wrist. He slept peacefully as I traced the lines of the dark ink. Occasionally, the tip of my finger would bump into a bubbled vein.

He released a sleepy noise and turned his hand over. While the top of his hand was soft, his palms were rough. I laid my palm against his and compared his hand to mine. His was so much larger and tanner. His hands were those of a boy who'd lived a rough life, but when he touched me it was if they were soft as cotton.

Being able to touch him this way was such a big deal for me. I'd always thought that touch was something I'd just have to live without, but with him it was a beautiful thing.

"What's that smile about?" he asked, his voice thick and raspy from sleep.

I hadn't even realized I was smiling.

"It's nothing,"

"It didn't look like nothing." He rolled over "What time is it?"

Shit!

I snatched up my phone and looked at the time. It was after eight a.m., which meant we were both late for school.

I turned to jump out of bed, but he grabbed me from behind and forced me back down.

"No. Sleep," he said into his pillow.

"We're going to miss school."

I very rarely missed school and when I did, it was because of something important like fractured ribs.

"Let's skip. We're seniors. After all the years we've been in school, we deserve a free day."

I settled back into the bed beside him.

"You're a bad influence," I said as I stared up at the ceiling,

"I know and you love it."

His breath evened out after that and I knew he'd gone back to sleep. I slipped out of the bed and got a shower. When I was done, I peeked out of the bathroom to see if he was still sleeping. Once I saw that he was, I opened the bathroom door to let the steam out. I already had on my bra and panties, but the bathroom was so small I couldn't breathe with the door closed.

I pulled on my jeans, then bent down and brushed my teeth. I hummed an Imagine Dragons song as I swished water around my mouth to rinse, then ran my brush through my hair. When I turned to grab my shirt, it was missing. I did a quick scan of the bathroom before my eyes collided with Zeke's. He stood in the bathroom door in pair of loose-fitting jeans. His elbows were braced against the doorframe as his eyes greedily moved over my body.

My eyes went to my shirt, which was dangling from his fingers above his head. He grinned at me and moved it up higher.

"Can I please have my shirt?" I said as I tried to cover myself the best I could with my hands.

It wasn't like I was naked, but still, it was enough nakedness for me. He reached out and pulled my arms away from my body.

"Don't," I said as I tried to cover myself again.

"No. *You* don't. Your body's beautiful."

He threw my shirt onto the bed across from the bathroom door and then he entered the small, steamed-over bathroom. The space shrunk with his large size, but instead of feeling claustrophobic, I felt hotter. Either the steam had gotten thicker or my breathing was getting harder.

Goosebumps covered my arms as he ran his hands from my shoulders to my elbows. Then he tugged me closer and my naked stomach touched his. He looked down at me and bit his lip ring. Pulling my elbows up, he put my arms around his neck, pressing my bra-covered breasts into his chest.

He leaned down and nuzzled my neck with his nose and then I felt his soft lips against my collarbone.

"I love how you tease me," he said as he moved his hands down and pulled my hips closer to him.

"I didn't know I was." My voice sounded weak and nervous.

"That's just it. You do it without realizing it. It's so innocent, but such a fucking turn-on. I'm not used to someone being shy and sexy at the same time."

His lips skimmed my jaw line and then he nipped my chin with his teeth. I couldn't take it. I grabbed the sides of his face and brought his lips to mine. He pulled me harder against him and moaned into my mouth. I felt it in between my legs and my nipples went hard inside my bra.

Pushing against me, he moved me back until the back of my thighs were against the wet bathroom counter. As if I weighed nothing, he lifted me onto it and fit himself between my legs. It felt amazing. Zeke was so good at this stuff. He continued to kiss me. His tongue slipped into my mouth and a tiny sound leapt from my throat.

Kissing was so new to me, but I still managed to keep up. I felt his lip ring press into my bottom lip and he flicked my tongue with his before he began to softly suck on the tip of it. His body was pressing against me harder. I wrapped my legs around him and helped him as he started to rock his hips into me.

The friction of my jeans being rubbing against me over and over again started to feel good. I grabbed onto his hips and dug my fingers into him. I didn't even realize I was making noises until he pointed it out.

"I love it when you whine like that. I can make it better if you'll let me."

He slipped a finger inside the waist of my jeans. I leaned back on the counter to give him easier access. My palm landed on top of my phone and the voicemail from my sister started playing on speaker phone. Sydney's awful rendition of the birthday song filled the heated bathroom and everything stopped.

I swatted at my phone to make it stop, but by then it was too late.

Zeke looked down at me in confusion.

"Today's your birthday?"

"It's really not a big deal."

"Babe, eighteen is a big deal," he said with wide eyes. "Why didn't you say something?"

My dad took away joyful things like birthdays when I was seven, and it was like a nail in the coffin when he took my virginity at thirteen. It was hard to find excitement over something like another year of life when your life was a living hell.

"Because it's *not* a big deal."

Bathroom steaminess forgotten, he pulled me down from the counter and planted a sweet kiss on my mouth.

"We have to celebrate. Let me take you to lunch and a show."

"Both of us are broke. How are we going to make that happen?"

"Listen up, princess, I grew up poor as dirt. I know all about making a dollar stretch. Come on." He grabbed my hand and pulled me out of the bathroom.

I caught my shirt in the air when he threw it at me and then I pulled it over my head. I kind of appreciated the fact that Zeke put my birthday before sex. It said a lot to me about where I was on his list of priorities.

"Okay, first thing's first, I'm taking you to the best restaurant in town."

The best restaurant in town ended up being McDonald's. Zeke schooled me in the ways of the dollar menu and when I pointed out that *Transformers* was one of my favorite movies, he used his skills in persuasion to con the little brunette behind the counter into giving him a happy meal toy of Optimus Prime for my birthday. It was quite possibly the sweetest birthday present I'd ever received.

When we left, he held my hand as we walked to his car. I didn't even think he was aware of it, but I was. I was aware of everything about him.

The show he promised ended up being a trip to the local aquarium. A friend of his ran the front booth so he was able to get us in free. The place was dead, so as we walked around the hallways, we were alone. Still, he held my hand.

"That fish looks like Chet when he plays the drums," he laughed as he pointed out a fish with a squished-up face.

That was how the rest of our day went. When we got back to the motel, it was almost time for Zeke to go to Boy's Club. I hadn't been in a while, but I really needed to get home and check on Mom and Sydney.

We went inside and I gathered up my things. He stood to the side and watched with an awkward expression on his face. I wanted to ask what was wrong, but I didn't want to dig too deep.

Once all my things were packed, I walked to the door. He followed behind me so closely that when I turned around to say good-bye we were face to face. He peered down at me with eyes so dark they looked black, and I sucked in his attention.

"Thank you so much for today. It was by far the best birthday I've ever had." I smiled up at him.

"I'm glad you enjoyed it. I'm sorry I couldn't do more." He reached out and pulled me to him.

"I'm not."

He leaned in and kissed me softly on my lips.

"Goodnight, Zeke."

"Goodnight, snowflake."

NINETEEN
ZEKE

I WAS CONVINCED THERE WAS nothing more gorgeous than Patience with the blue lighting of the aquarium reflected on her face. The radiant smile she wore for most of the day made me forget that my life was in shambles. I felt proud for being able to make her smile so beautifully.

Watching her pack her bag to go home made me sad and it shouldn't have. Actually, I was starting to feel way more for Patience than I was okay with. I hadn't even realized throughout the day that we'd been holding hands most of the time. It was as if I didn't want to be disconnected from her.

That night Boy's Club was a total blow. I enjoyed spending time with the boys, but I'd rather be with Patience or practicing with the band. I really needed to get some playing time in since Finn told me there were going to be some record executives at our show the following weekend.

By time I was done with my hour of community service, I'd texted Tiny, who lived on his own, and arranged to move in with him in a few days, and I'd already talked to Javier about more stuff to sell. Things were coming together and I was starting to feel a load lift from my chest.

That night, while lying in bed watching TV, I could smell Patience on the pillows and sheets. I snuggled into the pillow she'd used the night before and breathed her in. I really loved being around her. I loved her smile and the way her eyes lit up when I did something that made her happy. I loved her laugh and her shy teasing. I loved...

Suddenly, the room came in on me. I couldn't breathe. I sat up quickly and tried to suck in deep breaths, but nothing happened. I jumped out of the bed and ran to the bathroom. Sitting on the counter was one of her hair ties from when she'd taken a shower. The bathroom still smelled like the expensive shampoo she brought with her.

I turned on the cold water in the sink and stuck my hands in to fill them. I bathed my burning face with icy water until my nose felt numb.

How did I let this happen? How was it even possible? I was in love with Patience. I'd never been in love, but I definitely had the symptoms. I sat on the bathroom floor and stared at the purple hair tie on the counter. I couldn't do this to her and I wouldn't do this to me. She deserved so much more than a guy who bought her McDonald's for her birthday and could only afford to do more if he sold enough drugs.

Once I was in bed, she sent me a text I never responded to. She would thank me later, and maybe staying away from her would cure the case of feelings I had.

The week dragged by. I moved in with Tiny in his little shitty apartment on Thursday with plans to go to my dad's house the following weekend and get the rest of my shit while he was at work.

My days were free since I barely went to school anymore. The school year was wrapping up and I only had to take one class for the rest of my senior year. Being held back a year had its advantages. I didn't need many credits to graduate.

Later that afternoon, after Boy's Club, I went to Finn's place to practice. Patience quit texting after I quit responding, and if I were being honest, I'd admit I missed her like crazy. Everything was different in my life, but I still felt like I was spiraling out of control unless I was with her.

"Finn, tell Zeke what you said to that chick at The Pit the other night," Chet said as he took a hard hit from the joint being passed around.

It had yet to come my way, but it had been so long since I smoked. I hadn't even realized my smoking and drinking had slowed while I was hanging out with Patience.

"I asked her if she'd let me go bare back and balls deep on her," Finn said casually.

"And then she punched the shit out of him." Chet laughed through his exhale.

Everyone in the room laughed hysterically. I laughed, too, but I wasn't feeling it.

The joint finally made it to me and, instead of hitting it, I passed it to Tiny.

"Dude, what the fuck? I've known you forever now and I've never seen you pass a joint without hitting it. Are you sick?" Tiny asked.

"Love sick." Chet laughed.

"What's this you're talking about, Chet? You saying our boy Zeke's pussy whipped?" Finn asked with big eyes.

"Fuck you, man. You know better than that," I said as I reached out for the joint.

I took a big hit and then another before I passed it.

Even my boys were noticing the changes in me. Maybe I *was* sick. I know I felt pretty sick.

Once the beer was pulled out, I drank until I couldn't feel anything. It had been so long since I'd been so high and drunk and I fucking loved it. I hated feeling so many things for Patience, and this way I was too drunk to think straight, much less feel.

So when my boy Frankie stopped by with his tattoo supplies, I blamed the alcohol for being stupid enough to get a new tattoo. Getting a tattoo wasn't a big deal, I had them all over me, but the next morning when I woke up to take a piss and I saw a little blue snowflake on the inside of my left forearm, I knew I was in way over my head.

A week went by in a blur of school, Boy's Club, practice, and intoxication. I still hadn't made it over to my dad's so I was still living out of a duffle bag. We played at The Pit a few extra times in hopes that the record executive would be there the night we played, but we never heard anything about it.

When the weekend came back around, Finn had one of his usual parties. I was in the middle of drowning myself in a bottle of Everclear when I saw her platinum hair across the room. I knew sooner rather than later I'd run into her again. Especially since Chet was banging her best friend on a regular basis now.

I couldn't take my eyes off of her. First of all, she'd let Megan dress her again and damn, she looked hotter than shit. Secondly, it was Patience, my snowflake, and I missed her like crazy. She laughed at something Megan said and then ran her fingers through her hair to push it out of her face. All I could think about was the smell of that expensive shampoo she used. When I left the motel, I actually contemplated stealing the pillow case like a psycho.

She must have felt my stare because she turned and her gaze crashed with mine. Her face dropped and her eyes became sad. I knew her sadness. I felt the same. She was the only woman in the world that I'd ever spent time with without sex and I had to be stupid enough to fall for her.

Before she could come talk to me, I walked out of the garage. I couldn't stand looking at her and I hated the expression on her face. Finn's mom was out of the town with her new boyfriend, who was Finn's age, so I shut myself in her room.

Being surrounded by an old eighties-style bedroom set and the god-awful mauve bedding and curtains didn't help my mood. The mauve reminded me of my mom. It was her favorite color to decorate with. Maybe when I went to get my shit from Dad's I'd take her chair, too. It was all I had left of her since I was stupid enough to destroy my favorite memory of her.

I guzzled down the burning liquid and prayed I'd get drunk enough to pass out. I lay back on the bed, and the smell of old lady perfume filled my senses and made me want to gag. The music outside the room was so loud I couldn't think, so loud I almost didn't hear the soft knocking on bedroom door.

"Go the fuck away," I slurred loudly.

The music got louder as the door opened and muffled again once it was closed.

"Didn't I say this room was being used?" I kept my eyes closed as I felt the alcohol taking over me.

"Why are you ignoring me?" Patience's voice filled the room.

I sat up on my elbows and glared at her with drunken, red eyes.

"Why are you following me? Are you into stalking now?" I snapped.

She flinched at my words and I hoped she'd just leave. Being this close to her and not touching her was killing me. I sat up and slung my feet over the side of the bed. I put my back to her on purpose, hoping she'd take the hint, but still I heard her behind me.

"Did I do something?" she asked.

"Nope, you sure didn't. Maybe if you had we'd still be talking."

I knew it was fucked up when I said it, but the urge to be near her was getting stronger.

"So you quit talking to me because I didn't put out?" She sounded appalled.

"Ding, ding, ding!" I stood up and faced her.

The room turned with me and then I got a good look at the sadness on her face and it pissed me off. She moved toward me and I felt my spine stiffen.

She stood there staring up at me like she was trying to see my hidden secret. It was there, just beneath the surface, and it made me uncomfortable having her look so closely.

"Came to try again? Maybe you won't freak out when you get off this time?"

It was like a slap to her face. I knew they would be when the words worked their way down my tongue. Her eyes filled with tears and I felt my heart go flat. Swishing her hair in my face, she turned to leave, but hurting her hurt me and I wanted to apologize on the spot.

I reached out and grabbed her arm and she turned to face me. An apology was waiting just behind my lips, but then she looked down at my arm and her eyes went wide. I followed her gaze and saw she was staring at my snowflake tattoo.

"What's that?" She held up my arm.

I pulled it away and crossed my arms.

"Is that a snowflake?" She pointed at my arm. "Why would you tattoo a snowflake on your arm?" Her expression changed and I saw a bit of hope seep into her eyes. "Is it... did you get it for me?"

Damn right I did! That's what I wanted to say. Yeah, I was drunk when I did it. Sure, I was completely out of it, but they say a drunken man never lies and I had a moment of honesty when I'd branded myself with a symbol for

Patience. She was under my skin always. Why not put her *on* my skin as well?

Instead of giving in, I went deeper into asshole mode.

"Oh, God, here we go. Go ahead, snowflake. Turn it into something it's not. Go tell all your little white-collar friends that the white trash boy from across town is so in love with you he went and got a tattoo for you."

I made it sound as if it were a joke, but in actuality, it was the truth... It was the truth and it sucked.

"You're such an asshole. I don't know what made me think I could ever be in love with someone like you." Her words reached into my chest and squeezed my heart with an iron fist. "Why do you do that? Why do you give me something great and then snatch it away? What would it take from you to allow me to walk away just once feeling like I'm something important to you? Just once!" A tear slipped down her cheek. "You're the only person in the world I want to be important to, but you refuse to just give me a minute of that feeling."

I stood there and listened without saying a word. She had all but admitted she was in love with me. Anything I'd been ready to say was lodged in the back of my throat.

She threw up her arms in frustration. "I'm not going to lie. Yes, I thought the snowflake was for me, but only because you call me snowflake. Parts of me hope you got that tattoo as a memento of a girl you're crazy about, but I know better. You're incapable of having feelings at all apparently. So don't you worry about me having any misconceived notions about where you stand. I know where I place in your life and it's right below your guitar, your shitty car, some skank you banged last week, and drugs!"

I stood there in shock by the vehemence in her voice. The words she said couldn't have been more untrue, but it would be wrong of me to admit such feelings for her. Hell yes, I marked my body with her essence, but I'd been marked by her long before the tattoo. She earned the spot on my body as well as my heart and soul, but I'd never be cruel enough to admit that.

I'd die before I trapped her and made her a prisoner of my world. Patience would give me one hundred percent of herself and I knew she'd run full force into my hell without a thought for consequences. I knew this because I wanted to do the same when it came to her, but one of us had to be smart.

She had a future—filled with college and high-paying jobs. She had a future with rich husbands and beautiful blond babies with sparkling blue eyes and flawless skin. I couldn't offer her more than a minimum-wage life with occasional birthday trips to McDonald's. I'd never forgive myself if I took her future away.

She turned to walk away and without a single thought I rushed her. My body pressed her slender figure to the crappy, rose-covered wallpaper of Finn's mom's room. Her eyes filled with anger and panic. She attempted to push me away and get free, but I grabbed her wrists and pinned her to the wall even harder. I knew what I was doing was wrong. I knew of her irrational fear of being held down, but she felt so fucking amazing and I'd been dreaming of feeling her this way for the last week.

It's sad when you realize just being close to someone you love is enough. Not sex, not a dirty romp in my little single bed, just a moment of closeness—the feel of the rise and fall of her breathing against my chest, the puffs of heated breath as they struck my cheek and lips. It was enough when it came to Patience.

"You don't know anything about what I want or feel. So until you do, I suggest you keep your mouth shut." She struggled again to get free, and her struggle pushed her body closer.

"Why do you hate me so much?" Tears clogged her throat.

Her words cut at my insides.

"You don't know what the hell you're talking about."

"Then tell me. Explain it to me since I'm so clueless. All I know is right now you're looking at me like I'm nothing and it's validating the fact that that's exactly what I am... nothing."

She held back tears. Her face distorted with her effort, but I could see them waiting to rush down her cheeks. She tried again to get free, but I couldn't let her leave me this way. I slammed my palms against the wall in anger and pressed against her again with my body. My arms were like bars holding her in as I tried to press my palms through the wall beside her head.

She turned her head to the side like she couldn't look at me. I wanted to see her eyes. I wanted to see inside her just one last time. I ran my fingers against her cheek and tipped her face toward me with the tip of my finger. She closed her eyes to shut me out.

"Look at me." My voice was a dangerous whisper.

I felt dangerous. I felt like I was about to explode into a million pieces. She had no idea how much she meant to me in such a short time and it pissed me off that she was making assumptions.

Her eyes popped open and looked into mine. I was so close to her. Close enough that I could see the black spots in her blue irises. Her hot breath rushed my lips and I tightened my fingers against her chin.

"You will *never* know the depths of me, so don't even try to explore that far. You'll get lost and you won't survive me. Don't pretend to understand my feelings and emotions. Half the time I don't have any anyway, but when it comes to you, they're limitless, which is more dangerous. I don't look at you like you're nothing. I look at you like you're everything, because you are, and I fucking hate it."

I looked down into her face and my intimate gaze made her pause in her getaway. And then she shocked me by leaning up on her tip toes and pressing her soft lips against mine in the most innocent yet provocative way. It gave me a high like I'd never had before. No amount of drugs could match the burn that pulsated through my blood at the touch of her lips. I closed my eyes, pulled her closer to me, and kissed her back.

TWENTY
PATIENCE

AFTER THE BEST BIRTHDAY I'D had since I was a small girl, I left Zeke's motel room and went home to drama. Mom was sick out of her mind and I felt awful for not having been there with her.

"Why didn't you call me?" I asked Sydney.

"She made me promise I wouldn't. It's your birthday and she said you were probably with your boyfriend and she didn't want to interrupt." A tiny tear rushed down her cheek.

She was too young to be dealing with this. If I could take the pain of our dying mother away from her I would in a heartbeat.

I pulled her to me and wrapped her in my arms. "I don't have a boyfriend. He's just my friend and still, you and Mom are more important. No matter what she says from now on, you always call me."

I walked into my mom's room and was assaulted by the smell of vomit and sickness. She was lying in bed with her head rolled to the side. Had I not seen her chest moving, I would have thought she was dead. I shut the door behind me and the click caught her attention.

A forced smile spread across her face.

"Happy Birthday, baby girl. Again, another thing I'm happy I was able to see. Eighteen years old." She gasped with each word.

Her fevered eyes took me in and her body shook constantly. Damn, it was hard to see this, but I'd be there no matter what.

I plastered on a big, fake smile. "Yep, the big eighteen."

I spent hours in Mom's room with her. I told her about my day with Zeke and she agreed that the McDonald's thing was sweet. She'd have a fit of coughs every now and again and soon she was too exhausted to talk. Once she was asleep, I left her room and went to mine.

There was nothing worse than watching my mother die, but being ignored by Zeke sucked. A week later I still hadn't heard from him. After the first two days of texting and him not responding, I gave up.

My dad came home that weekend and I tried to stay out as much as possible, but there was nowhere to go now that Megan was with Chet all the time. Most of the time I'd stay with Mom and when she wasn't up for company and Sydney was busy, I'd walk to the neighborhood lake and sit until it was late enough to go home and get ready for bed.

Dad must have been busy because he didn't bother me and I was glad for that.

The following week, I went to school like normal, practiced like normal, and had two games. By the time

Friday rolled around, I was ready for the weekend. Megan begged me to go to Finn's party, and after not seeing Zeke for that long, I couldn't take it anymore. I wanted to know why he was ignoring me. I wanted to know what I did wrong.

After cornering him in the room and him sort of confessing he had feelings for me, I kissed him. At first he kissed me back and it was wonderful, but then suddenly asshole Zeke slipped into place and he pulled away.

"Don't kiss me unless you plan on finishing the job this time," he said as he wiped at his mouth with the back of his hand.

When I saw that damn snowflake tattoo on his arm, I was done. I knew the minute I saw it that it was for me, and it was the highlight of my week.

After he broke the kiss, he stormed from the room. I didn't see him at the party again. I ended up being the third wheel to Megan and Chet and holding back tears all night. My life was a complete mess, but at least when I was with Zeke I could forget all that. With him removing himself out of my life, things felt ten times worse.

That night when Megan dropped me off, I crept through my house and tried to make it to my room without being seen by my dad. Tonight was not my lucky night and I passed him in the hallway. He followed me with angry eyes as I walked past him into my room. The door barely had time to click before he was opening it and coming in.

"Where's your sister?" he asked.

I hated that he was asking about her. I hated the idea of him even thinking about her.

"She's at a friend house," I responded with my head down.

I wanted to be strong. I wanted to match his stare like a bad bitch until he left my room, but after everything he'd put me through and after being dismissed like nothing by Zeke, I was weak. I'd always been weak.

He grabbed my chin and slammed my head back.

"If you're going to dress like a whore, the least you could do is look a man in the eye like a whore," he hissed.

I said nothing. I just stared back at him and waited for whatever was to come. The closer he got, the more I could smell the alcohol on his breath. For a brief moment I felt relief since usually when he drank he would leave me alone and pass out, but this time was different. There was wildness in his eyes that felt off.

"I'm so disgusted by you. Just look at you." He motioned to my clothes. "Just look at how you turned out. I'm so glad it's not my blood that runs through your veins."

The minute the words left his mouth, his expression followed his accident. His mouth gapped open like he was going to fix his mistake, but instead, he stared back at me with wide eyes.

"What did you just say?"

The entire house shifted and I felt the blood rush from my head. Surely I was hearing things. Maybe I drank too much at Finn's party. I did take a couple drinks from people I didn't know. Maybe something was slipped in my drink and I was really passed out somewhere in Finn's garage, having a nightmare. All of that sounded better than what I'd heard.

Without fear, I pushed into his space.

"You're not my father," I said simply.

Somehow it made sense, and somehow it made the years of sex with this man a tiny bit better, but still, I felt sick to my stomach.

I looked up at him. I *really looked* at him like I hadn't in many years since I didn't have the nerve. I took in his facial features and his dark-brown eyes. Then my thoughts rushed to Sydney and her green eyes and then my mom… Her eyes were green as well. And just like that, everything was clear.

"You're not. Oh my God, you're not my father."

He didn't deny it. "It doesn't matter. I raised you."

"You abused me my entire life!" I yelled.

As soon as the words flew out of my mouth, he hushed me with the back of his hand. My face stung and my ears rang.

"You've always been a selfish girl, Patience. Do you know that?" He dug his fingers into my cheeks and forced me to look at him. "Are you so selfish that you'd tell your mother something like that so close to her death? Do you really want her to die with that on her chest? Let it go. You liked it as much as I did."

And then he turned and walked away. I stood there and let everything sink in and then I crumpled to the floor with melted bones and cried until I fell asleep.

The next day I stayed in my room for most of the morning. I debated on whether or not to go to my mother and demand to know why no one told me the governor wasn't my real father, but just like I'd never tell about the sexual abuse, I'd never tell her that I knew. It wouldn't change anything, and with my mother on her death bed, I didn't want to give her any reason to not die peacefully.

Then the memory of my mother telling me about her first love sank in. Maybe that was her way of telling me. Maybe that was her way of getting it off of her chest. My real father was a bad boy named Robert that she'd been forbidden to see. How fitting that I'd be in love with a bad boy myself. It was in my blood.

The man I'd been calling Dad my entire life wasn't my dad, but he was definitely Sydney's. She looked just like him, with the exception of her eyes. All these years, I'd been worried about him going to Sydney, and all these years she was really his while I wasn't. Maybe that's why it was so easy for him to do things to me. Maybe the thought that my blood wasn't his own made it okay in his mind to have sex with me. Either way, I'd still keep a close eye on Sydney. The man was obviously sick and sick people aren't picky.

Later that afternoon, the man who was working on Zeke's guitar called and said it was all finished. He didn't want to see me, but I knew what I had for him would make him happy.

I drove to the man's shop. The little bell above the door sounded like my name when it rang. I pressed my forearms against the front counter and fidgeted as I waited for someone to help me.

A little gray-headed man came around from the back with a smile.

"What can I do for you, sweetie?"

"I dropped off a guitar and you called and said it was ready."

I gave him my name. When he came out from the back again, he had a black guitar case in his hands.

"Here you go, little lady," he said as he set the guitar case onto the counter.

He popped open the little latches on the side and opened the case. Inside was the black Fender I picked out. The bits of Zeke's old guitar were intricately added to the front of the new guitar beautifully, especially the part where his mom had signed her name. It was personalized just for him.

He had no idea I'd picked up the broken bits of his guitar. I still felt like it was my fault that his most prized possession was destroyed. The least I could do was replace it, and I thought using pieces of the precious guitar his mother bought for him was a perfect idea.

I paid the man behind the counter an obscene amount of money and then walked to my car with the guitar in hand. Megan told me Zeke was staying with Tiny, so I called her and got directions to their apartment.

The drive across town wasn't so shocking anymore. I remembered going to Zeke's side of the world the first time and thinking how disgusting the place was. I remember thinking I could never live in a place like that, but now, when I drove to anywhere he was, I felt like I was going home, like I didn't grow up in a million-dollar house, like I belonged somewhere for the first time in my life.

The ghetto apartment complex was worse than Zeke's trailer park. I tapped on the door and was shocked when Tiny answered in his boxers.

"Is Zeke here?" I asked.

His eyes roamed up and down my body and I felt dirty.

"No, he went over to his dad's place to get the rest of his shit."

That wasn't good.

"He went alone?" I asked with wide eyes.

He looked at me like I was an idiot.

"Ah, yeah. He left about..."

I didn't even listen to the rest. I rushed to my car and jumped in. Thankfully, the apartment complex wasn't far from the trailer park.

His dad's tow truck was nowhere in sight, but his car was parked in the yard when I got there. I could hear his loud stereo outside the trailer, and I thought it was strange that he'd come to his dad's and play loud music. I knocked extra hard on his door and after five knocks he never came. I was starting to get worried, so I tried the doorknob.

The door opened and I slipped into the small, smoky space. I shut the door behind me and called out his name. Still, I got no answer, which meant either he couldn't hear me or I couldn't hear him. The music was so loud it seemed to be shaking the tiny trailer. The guitar was pulling my arm down, so I sat it up on the grimy, plaid couch and worked my arm to ease the tension that had worked into my elbow.

I heard a noise coming from his room and figured he was back there packing. Maybe he had his shirt off and I'd catch him with only a pair of those deliciously ripped jeans he was fond of. Hopefully they were the ones that barely held onto his hips and showed his sexy tattoos. I'd seen him without a shirt on before and I'd seen every tattoo he had down into his pants line. I wasn't disappointed; nothing physical about Zeke was disappointing.

I found it funny that such a dangerous guy like Zeke would be the one that finally caught my attention. I wasn't the kind of girl that looked for trouble. Especially since trouble seemed to find me at least once a week, but something about him caught me and reeled me in. Getting to know him and seeing the secret parts of him made my attachment to him all the better. He was perfect for me.

The soft floor of the hallway buckled under my feet. The door to his bedroom was cracked so I pushed it the rest of the way open and stepped inside. I'd secretly wished I'd catch Zeke half naked, but when I'd wished that, I'd wished he was alone when I caught him. What I saw before me was like a punch to the ribs.

Zeke was lying on his bed, his hands behind his head as he relaxed against the headboard. The redhead straddling him was pressing herself against him in every way possible. The rhythm of the headboard hitting the brown paneled wall made my stomach turn. The sounds of the creaking mattress made me want to drop to my knees and cover my ears. I knew those sounds well and they brought nothing but nightmares.

I wanted to cry. I wanted to slowly dissolve into nothing and float away in the air, blown around by the clicking, circulating fan at the foot of his bed. The messed-up part was I couldn't be mad. He wasn't mine and as badly as I wanted to be the one having carefree sex with him, I couldn't. No matter how hard I tried, I just couldn't do it.

Seriously? What else could the universe drop on me at this point? I'd all but died inside on several occasions in my life. You'd think finally I'd just drop, but I kept going and I kept running into things that broke down my spirit. Seeing Zeke have sex with another girl was breaking me big time.

In that moment the remaining open doors to my soul slammed shut. Zeke was it for me, and if I couldn't bring myself to give him the part of me that was taken away so many years ago, then there would be no one else. All the thoughts of a physical relationship in my life drifted away. The thoughts of marriage, children, or real life in general were gone in the blink of an eye.

He was only receiving what I could never give him. Proof was purring and bouncing in front of me. I could never be what Zeke needed or wanted. The crescent moon tattoo on her lower back matched the star tattoo on his hand that was now gripping her ass. I couldn't take my eyes off the two tattoos. They were symbolic to me. They were a sign that they belonged together and I was the starless wonder who belonged in the sanitized, padded walls of my supposed safe world. The truth was I was safer in this broken-down trailer park surrounded by drug deals and gang members than I was in my own home.

And then I saw his snowflake tattoo and I died a little more. How could he brand me on his skin that way and then have carefree, meaningless sex with someone else? What kind of person does that?

I stared at the single snowflake. I couldn't take my eyes off of it.

The redhead made a loud whining noise, causing me to avert my attention. I knew in the back of my mind I should slowly exit the room, but I couldn't peel my eyes away from her. The way her long, crimson curls swayed across her hips, the arch in her back, her perfect rhythm as she pleasured him with her body—it was all so hypnotic. She gave herself so freely and I envied that freedom.

I listened to the noises that spilled from her lips as she achieved a passion I'd never know, and it was almost musical. I should hate her, but she was magnificent and seductive, all things I longed to be. I wanted to look away, but something about the scene was strangely beautiful. Take away the fact that my Zeke was having sex with another woman. Take away the fact that my heart was shriveling into a pile of nothing in my chest. She was a girl I'd never be and watching her freedom was breathtaking.

This was how it was supposed to be for a girl. The creaking mattress and the sounds of the headboard hitting the wall were supposed to be a good thing. The redhead was lucky. She didn't cower in fear at the erotic noises. She didn't feel like crying and dropping to the floor in the fetal position if someone touched her. She was exactly what Zeke needed. She was what he deserved and I was not.

Slowly, I backed away toward the door, but before I could look away, I saw Zeke's eyes land on me. The noises stopped and he used his hands to stop her bouncing hips. The embarrassment of being caught watching set in and I felt heat fill my cheeks. I bet the redhead didn't blush like a little girl. I bet the redhead was a real woman, a woman who could say the word penis without giggling.

I felt the doorframe connect with my back. It stopped me from making a quick escape. The redhead slung her head around and with big eyes she looked at me in annoyance.

"Snowflake," Zeke said. His voice was strained and he was out of breath.

A fine sheen of sweat covered his body and all the enjoyment left his eyes as he stared back at me. A strange emotion that bordered heartbreak crossed his expression, but him being hurt made no sense to me. Why would being caught in the middle of hot sex hurt his feelings? Actually, since when did Zeke Mitchell have any feelings? I'd been mistaken for a little while, but it was obvious he'd been right. I was way out of my league.

I felt like I should say something. I felt like I needed to let them know I knew I wasn't supposed to be there, but my tongue seemed to be swollen to the size of a balloon and it felt like it was full of lead. No matter how badly I wanted to smile like it was no big deal and say something witty, I couldn't force my lips to move and my voice seemed to be stuck somewhere in the bottom of my lungs, which I couldn't fill.

"I'm sorry." The words squeaked out of my mouth. They were small and insignificant, like me.

And then my legs didn't feel numb anymore and somehow I managed to turn and step out of the room. The hallway of Zeke's trailer never seemed so long. It suddenly loomed in front of me and I didn't think I'd ever make it to his front door. The sinking floor felt like it was consuming my feet with each step until finally I made it.

The aluminum door caught the wind when I opened it and had it not been for the rusted chain that kept the door in reach, it would have smacked into the trailer. I used the doorframe to hold myself up when a wave of dizziness swept through me. I silently wondered to myself if anyone had ever died from heartbreak. I felt like I couldn't breathe and my brain was misfiring. I couldn't think straight. Little things like moving my legs and walking out of his trailer were too difficult for me to comprehend.

Finally, my motor skills kicked in and I could move again. The cool breeze kissed my cheeks as I stepped out onto the rocky porch. I pushed the door shut and slipped down the wooded stairs. Halfway to my car I felt the sprinkle of rain against my hair. It wasn't until I was safe in my car that I realized there were actual tears on my cheeks.

I silently prayed to myself that they didn't come until I was out of Zeke's house. The last thing I wanted was for him to see me cry. He never needed to know how much I cared about him. He never needed to know the final piece of me that had been holding on flittered away to nothing when I saw him with her.

TWENTY-ONE
ZEKE

WALKING AWAY FROM PATIENCE WAS hard, but it was necessary. The look on her face when I walked away from her would live in my nightmares for a while.

I didn't even tell Finn I was leaving. Instead, I walked out and drove drunk as fuck to the park by the Boy's Club. It reminded me of Patience and I felt close to her there. I could still remember that first kiss with her. It was beyond amazing.

I lifted my trusty bottle of Everclear and finished it. I was so drunk my lips were going numb. I got out and jumped into the bed of my car. I pushed some trash over and lay flat on my back. Staring up at the stars, I passed out.

The next morning, I woke up stiff and hung over. I drove back to the apartment and then stood in the hot shower until I started to feel alive again. When I got out, Tiny was sitting on the couch in his boxers, playing Xbox.

"Dude, what happened to you last night?" he asked without taking his eyes away from his game.

"I got drunk and passed out at the park."

I opened the fridge and downed some tomato juice. Dad swore by it for a hangover. Turns out he was right. I stocked up the minute I knew I'd be doing some heavy drinking. I crashed onto the couch next to Tiny.

"Why do you play this shit, man? It hurts my brain just watching."

"You don't know nuttin' about some Skyrim," he said as he fought some crazy-looking giant on the screen.

"Yeah, you have fun with that. I'm going over to my old man's house to get my shit. I'll be back."

I got off the couch and started toward the door.

"Yeah, see you later."

Not once did he take his eyes off the screen.

A few minutes later, I pulled into my dad's empty yard. I'd never been so happy to see his truck gone. The shitty front porch buckled as I ran up the steps to the front door. The door popped open with little effort and the smell of beer was stronger than ever when I walked in.

I didn't waste any time. I went straight to my old bedroom and started packing my shit into black trash bags I'd grabbed in the kitchen. I was almost done when I heard the door open. I froze. The thought of my dad coming home sucked. It was the last thing I wanted to deal with right now. I'm sure he was sour as shit about getting his ass kicked.

I peeked down the hallway, expecting to see his large frame approaching. Instead, Stephanie, the redhead, stood there. She smiled seductively as she slowly walked down the hallway toward my room.

"What are you doing here?" I asked as I turned away and started packing. "How did you know where I was?"

"I didn't. I was across the street, hanging out with my girl, when I saw you pull up. I thought I'd come over and see if there was anything I could help you with. Finn told me you were moving in with Tiny. I figured you were packing."

She ran a painted fingernail across the top of my old, broken dresser.

"Finn has a big fucking mouth," I said dryly.

"So do I." She grinned over at me.

I didn't miss her meaning. She made it even more obvious when she looked down at the crotch of my pants. I felt my cock get hard under her gaze. It's not like I could help it. It had been weeks since I had a woman and being teased by Patience every time I got around her didn't help. Maybe if I got it out of my system I wouldn't be so caught up on Patience. Maybe all I needed was a good, hard, meaningless fuck.

"Pretty much, you came over here to get laid?" I asked bluntly as I sat down on my old bed.

She laughed. "Well, we can talk, too. I have a lot on my chest that you could maybe help soothe." She smirked.

Fuck it. I was done over thinking shit. It was time old Zeke came back and squashed all this emotional bullshit.

"I think you should come sit right here and tell me all about it." I patted the crotch of my jeans.

She moved like a cat across my room, unbuttoning her top on the way to my bed. When she reached the side of my bed, she was in only her sexy little skirt and a lacey black bra that left nothing to the imagination. It was fucking hot and I should've been all about dipping my cock in that red-hot piece, but my thoughts kept going back to Patience.

She seemed to think I was so much better than this. Well, she was wrong. I wasn't better than this. This was who I was; this was who I'd always be.

Stephanie climbed onto my lap. I worked my hands up her thighs and under her skirt. I was met with stringy panties and a soft, wet spot.

"Take this off," I demanded as I tugged roughly on her skirt.

Her eyes lit up. Women loved that shit. They loved a man who took charge during sex and so, in turn, women loved me. She stood above me, her crotch lingering in front of my face, and peeled her matching black throngs down her legs. Unashamed of her body, she stood above me and let me take her in with my eyes. It was a huge turn-on, but still, all I could think about was how cute Patience was when she was trying to make sure her body was covered. She was so bashful about her beautiful body. Modesty was something I wasn't used to. Honestly, I kind of liked it and strangely, it was more of a turn-on.

Why did I have to keep thinking about her? Why couldn't I just forget about her, deem her a nice girl, and move the fuck on? It was annoying beyond belief and I was already sick of the way she made me feel. Emotions weren't a good thing for a guy like me. Actually, they were fucking dangerous as all get out and I couldn't allow them in my life. If I had to have sex with every girl that passed by, then so be it. I had to get Patience out of my system. I needed her off my skin and the only way to do that was to move on.

I fucked hated this! All of it! My life wasn't supposed to be this complicated, and having pointless sex with Stephanie was going to make things less complicated, I hoped.

I reached up and ran my hands up her legs, then ran my thumb across her wet nub. She sucked in a breath, then leaned down to kiss me. I turned my head and pulled her down on top of me. No way could I kiss her. Patience was the only girl I could stand to be that close to.

I pushed her back and unbuttoned my jeans. She helped as I pulled them down around my thighs. She didn't waste any time straddling me and pushing herself down onto my cock.

I thought the minute our bodies connected I would be lost. I usually lost myself with a good joint and a soaking wet woman, but that didn't happen. Instead, all I saw were shining blue eyes staring back and me and sandy-blond hair instead of red.

I closed my eyes and leaned my body back against my headboard as she moved her body against mine. I didn't really want to, but I think having sex with Stephanie was my way of pissing myself off. My way of proving to myself that I was exactly what everyone around me thought I was—a dog, a loser, not good enough to kiss Snowflake's toes. And I would, kiss her toes, if that was her thing.

For the first time in my life, I was going through the motions of sex. I heard the bed hitting the wall and I knew Stephanie was doing a good job. I heard her moaning on top of me and I knew even though I wasn't really into it, my body was doing a good job. Still, I felt nothing. The achy pressure in my abs and balls that usually came with sex wasn't there.

I felt her warmth and I recognized it was supposed to feel good, but all I could think about was how badly I wished it was Patience on top of me. I wished it was strands of platinum locks resting against my chest as she leaned over me. I wished it was Patience telling me how good I felt, but it wasn't. It was a saucy redhead who knew what she was doing and yet, I wanted it to be over already.

Like a robot I reached up and pulled at the back of her hair. She seemed like the kind that would like that and I got the response I expected. She sped up, the mattress moaning against my hips as she pressed me deeper into its springs. I worked my hands down her back and gripped her ass. Maybe if I pressed her down harder and she moved faster something would happen and I wouldn't have to fake an orgasm. I'd never had to do that before and somehow it made me feel like less of a man.

Movement out of the corner of my eye caught my attention and the world around me paused as my eyes connected with Patience. For a brief second I thought maybe my mind had conjured her up as a sort of reward for a possible orgasm, but the single tear that cut a path down her cheek let me know she was all real.

The look in her eyes burnt me all over. It effectively made me feel like the biggest piece of shit in the world. The hurt she felt was evident and immediately it broke my heart and pissed me off at the same time. Who knew hurting someone I cared about would kill the tiny, living pieces inside? Who knew caring about someone would make me so angry?

I wanted to push Stephanie away and go to her. I wanted to hold her and tell her how sorry I was that she had to see this. I wanted to tell her I was sorry for being me, for not being enough for her, because deep down it's all I ever wanted. I wanted to be good enough and since I had no way of ever becoming even close to good enough, here I was sabotaging any decent part of me.

Her name fell from my lips and then *she* apologized. Why the hell was she apologizing? She didn't do anything wrong. I was the one in the wrong; I was the one that needed a good swift kick in the balls. I was nothing and there she was hurting over me, and then she was gone.

I knew in the back of my head that those tear-filled eyes were going to be the last thing I ever saw of Patience. For years to come, I'd have nightmares about those eyes. I'd lie awake in my bed at night and replay that moment over and over again in my head. It was the moment I broke her, the moment I destroyed myself.

I removed Stephanie from my lap and pulled my jeans up.

"Get out," I said calmly.

"What the fuck, Zeke?" She stood there, naked and furious. "Is this because of that little blond bitch?"

I glared over at her.

"You heard me... Get out."

She dressed quickly with a pissed-off look on her face. Snatching up her shoes and keys, she flew down the hallway of my trailer and slammed the front door.

I buttoned my jeans and grabbed my wallet and keys, then made my way into the kitchen for a beer. I pulled open the fridge and popped the top on a cold one. Turning toward the living room, I threw back my head and took a large swig. That's when my eyes landed on the guitar case sitting on my couch.

I set the beer on the counter and cautiously walked to the couch. I stood above the guitar, finding it hard to open the case and look inside. I think part of me knew that inside was something that would be the equivalent of a kick in the balls. Leaning over, I ran my hand over the letter Z embroidered into the top of the case in bright red. I popped the locks on the side and flipped the lid open.

Inside was a black, 1967 Fender, and while that was enough to make me drop to my knees in front of my couch, it was the bits and pieces of my old guitar that did the trick. The minute I saw the piece with my mother's signature, tears filled my eyes and for the first time in a very long time, I let them fall.

I swiped angrily at my eyes and shut the case. Snatching it up, I took it and the rest of my stuff to my car, setting the case up front with me. Bits of rock and dust flew from my back tires as I peeled out of my dad's yard. I texted her two times on the way to her house, but she never responded.

I didn't remember the ride across town. It was as if I'd driven to the ritzy side on auto pilot. I was stuck inside my head and in a rush to get to Patience—to tell her I was sorry and beg for her forgiveness. I wasn't good enough for her and I still wouldn't drag her down to my level, but knowing she was walking around with a broken heart because of me didn't sit well. Especially considering what she'd given me.

Other than my guitar, she'd given me hope in a hopeless place. She'd given me light when I'd been stuck in the dark so long. She'd done so much for me, and how did I repay her? By hurting her, ripping her heart out and taking a bite out of it. I was the lowest of low.

When I got to her driveway, I cut my loud engine. I climbed out of my car and made my way across the freshly manicured lawn to the front door. Standing at the front door of the governor's mansion felt wrong, but at that point I hadn't even thought about the possibility of running into him. Not until he opened the door and peered at me with those familiar hateful stare did I even think about him at all. He leaned his body against the doorframe and crossed his arms.

"Ah, my friend, Zeke. What can I do for you, young man?" His smile didn't reach his eyes.

"I need to talk to Patience," I said with some force.

He needed to know I was serious.

"I don't think that's a good idea. I asked Patience to stay away from you and I'd appreciate it if you stayed away from her. Plus, she's not here."

His eyes remained on mine while he shut the door in my face.

Two weeks later, I still hadn't heard from Patience. She wouldn't return any of my phone calls and she never texted me back. Megan wouldn't even tell me anything about her. It was the worse two weeks of my life, and no amount of beer or drugs would make it better.

TWENTY-TWO
PATIENCE

IT HAD BEEN TWO WEEKS since I last saw Zeke and I was miserable. The sick part was I honestly had nothing to be upset with him about. Technically, he hadn't done anything wrong, but I couldn't bring myself to talk to him. I was hurt and my world was slowly crumbling in on me.

My mom was dying, my father wasn't my father, and the one person in the world that made everything feel better had hurt me worse than I'd ever been hurt. Life was looking pretty bleak, but instead of falling apart, I kept myself together, smiled on the outside, and went through my days like I had before. School, practice, and games—they're what got me through. I played harder than I ever had before and kicked so much ass on the field that my teammates were starting to call me the beast.

I quit reading his text messages and even started ignoring Megan. I was in a bad place and had no one to help me out.

When I wasn't at school or doing soccer stuff, I was with Mom. She was still occasionally having a good day here or there, but it wasn't looking good.

Finally, after weeks of lying low, Megan showed up at my house.

"What the hell is up with you? I haven't heard from you much in weeks and Zeke won't leave me the hell alone," she said as she flopped on my bed.

"Nothing. I've just been busy with school and stuff. Plus, my mom's not doing very well."

She changed her attitude quickly and just like that she got over me being absent from her life. I loved that about Megan. She was so forgiving and understanding.

"So what's the deal with you and Zeke?" She grabbed a bottle of my fingernail polish from my dresser and started painting her nails.

"Nothing. We were friends and now we're not."

I didn't want to talk about it and I was hoping she'd drop it. Yeah right.

"He's a mess, Pay. You should talk to him. He says you won't answer his texts or phone calls. What did he do?"

"He didn't do anything. I just have too much going on in my life right now to worry about guys, especially one like Zeke."

She left an hour later with a promise that I'd go to The Pit with her the following Saturday night. When Saturday finally came, I went to her house and got dressed. My dad had still been lying low, but I didn't want to walk out of the house with tight clothes and makeup on, just in case he changed his mind about not messing with me.

"Make me as sexy as you possibly can," I said as Megan did my hair.

"Are you sure?" she asked.

"Absolutely."

I left Megan's house in a tight denim miniskirt, six-inch heels, and a halter-top that left nothing to the imagination. I felt like a naughty sex kitten and I meant to play the part right in Zeke's face for the entire night. I wasn't usually a revengeful person, but I wanted him to feel what I felt when I walked in his room and found him with her.

When we finally made it to The Pit, I didn't feel my usual discomfort, which was weird considering what I was wearing. I'd gotten used to the place and the people. We went straight to the bar and ordered drinks and then we made our way to the stage.

Finn was belting out a Three Days Grace song and the crowd was eating it up. The minute my eyes landed on Zeke, I felt warm all over. Seeing him so close made me realize how much I missed him. I watched his fingers move across his guitar and I felt joy when I saw he was playing the guitar I'd given him.

He looked up from playing and scanned the crowd with the angry glare I'd come to love. At first, his eyes scanned right over me, but I knew the moment he realized I was in the crowd. Zeke never gave anything away, but I knew he'd seen me.

I drank, danced, and had a blast with Megan. The entire time, I could feel his eyes on me and I loved it. I could feel his gaze crawl across my flesh and it was turning me on. It was the weirdest thing, but I was definitely getting turned on.

I wasn't sure if it was the alcohol or if I was really losing myself after being torn apart the last few weeks, but something gave me a brave streak. A guy I didn't know came up to me and started dancing behind me and I let him. I was a little disgusted by him, but I knew Zeke was watching so I got into it like I was really enjoying myself.

After that, I flirted openly with three different guys. I was totally bored with it, but there was a lot of smiling and looking up through my lashes. I pretty much just mimicked every girl in the room. I knew my cleavage was out too much and I was aware that every time I lifted my arms most of my stomach was exposed, but I didn't care. I made sure all those parts were available for his eyes. I brought my arms over my head and then ran them down over my breasts and abs.

I looked up at him and he glared down at me. I couldn't tell if I was pissing him off or turning him on. I was fine with either. I picked up my bottle, looked up at him, and licked my lips before placing the bottle against my mouth. Still, his expression didn't change.

"Girl! You are so bad!" Megan shouted next to me.

"I don't know what you're talking about." I grinned.

"Oh, you know what you're doing. I just hope you can handle the wrath of Zeke when he lets loose on your ass." She laughed.

"Please, he better hope he can handle me."

I was definitely drunk. There was no doubt about that.

The after party was at Finn's house and I went along with Megan. Once I was there, someone handed me a red cup of beer. Instead of going to the corner and sipping my drink like I usually would, I was in the middle of everything. I talked to people and flirted with guys. I could feel someone watching me the entire time and I knew it was him.

A guy I'd never seen before started talking to me and I was sure to smile back at him and flirt with my eyes. He was shorter than Zeke and much smaller. With light hair and light eyes, he openly checked me out and licked his lips, and I played right along.

"What's your name?" he asked as he looked down my shirt.

"Patience."

"Pretty name for a pretty girl." He grinned.

"Thank you."

It wasn't long until I'd moved on and was talking to someone else. Originally, it started out as a way to get under Zeke's skin the way he'd gotten under mine, but after getting a lot of attention, I was starting to enjoy it.

I looked around the room for Megan, and she was nowhere to be found. I walked through the garage, checking every corner and still she was nowhere. I walked inside and headed toward the bathroom. When a girl goes missing, that's usually the best place to look. I was halfway down the hallway when I felt someone against my back. I turned around and Zeke was there looking down at me with an angry red face and pinched lips.

"Come with me," he said as he opened a door and pulled me inside.

It was a simple guy's room, but the décor let me know I was standing in Finn's bedroom. A queen-sized bed covered in red bedding was in the middle of the room. A single dresser with a mirror was pushed up against the wall and covered in junk. There were clothes everywhere; the floor was barely visible.

"Are you enjoying yourself?" he asked as he stalked closer to me.

I could hear the anger in his voice.

I liked that he was pissed off. That's no less than what he deserved. Maybe it was because I was drunk or maybe it was because I was beyond repair and as sick and twisted as the man who raised me, but I relished in his anger. If he hated me flirting with other men, then he was getting just a taste of what I'd felt when I walked in on him and his redhead. We weren't together, so technically he hadn't done anything wrong, but damn, it hurt like a bitch. I wasn't usually a revengeful person, but I wanted him to understand my pain.

"Very much," I slurred.

"Are you getting off on making me jealous, snowflake?"

"What if I am?" I matched his stare.

"You're playing with fire. You do realize that, right?" He moved closer.

He towered over me and I had to arch my neck to continue to look him in the eye.

"Oh, boy, I better be careful or I might get burned," I said sarcastically.

He was backing me up and I hadn't even realized it. When I felt the edge of Finn's dresser against my lower back, I put my palms out and pressed against his chest. He pressed harder. Cologne bottles shook and made clinking noises as the dresser shifted.

"If I see one more fucker touch you, I'm going to lose it. You want me to go to jail again?"

He leaned over me and put his hands on the dresser on either side of me, caging me in.

"I have no control over what you do. Just like you have no control over what I do," I said as I pressed against him and tried to move him out of my way.

He didn't budge.

"I can't stand seeing you with them." The muscles in his jaw popped as he gritted his teeth. "It makes me feel like my skin is on fire."

"I know the feeling."

I pulled my eyes away from his and disregarded him. I acted as if I were annoyed and bored, but really, every time he pressed his body into mine I wanted to throw him on Finn's bed and attack him.

"You're mine," he said with so much force that my eyes darted back to his and I looked him up and down like I was about to fight him.

"Excuse me? I belong to no one. Let me go." I pushed again at his chest, but he was like a brick wall.

I really did want to be away from him after that. How dare he throw a claim on me while he was busy screwing anything with a wet hole? Oh hell no! That wasn't happening.

"No," he snapped. His eyes dug into me. "Quit flirting with those guys. You're making promises with your eyes that you can't keep."

I rolled my eyes and laughed sarcastically to myself.

"They'll live." I turned my face away and looked to the side of me when I felt his hot breath warm my cheek. He was so close his breath shifted my hair.

"You look so fucking hot tonight," he said.

He reached up to tuck my hair behind my ear and I pulled my head away from his hand.

"Do I?"

"Hell yeah, you do."

The side of his mouth lifted and his eyes moved down my body and back up.

"I'm getting hard just looking at you." He pressed his hips into me and my insides tightened.

"Then I guess you better find your redhead."

Being a smartass felt good. No wonder he was an asshole all the time.

"Maybe I should." He lifted a sarcastic brow.

And just like that, I went from being a smartass to being pissed off. I pushed at his chest hard with my palms. When he didn't budge, I kept pushing.

"You're such an asshole." I was heated and my breath was coming out in hard, pissed-off puffs.

"Well, you're being a bitch right now so I guess that makes us even," he snapped.

Out of nowhere I reared my hand back and slapped him across the face. It felt good to let my anger out. Had I known it would feel that good to hit someone, I would've gone around beating the crap out of everyone.

His nostrils flared as he glared down at me. A tiny red handprint began to form on his cheek. Maybe I'd gone too far this time. Maybe Zeke wasn't against hitting a girl and he'd hit me back. Instead, he grabbed my cheeks and pulled me into a rough kiss.

At first, I was shocked, but in seconds I forgot what we were doing and I started kissing him back. The dresser shifted and bottles clinked as he pushed me harder up against it. I pushed back against him.

A tiny growl escaped his throat and he grabbed under my ass and lifted me onto Finn's dresser. The back of the mirror slammed into the wall behind it. He pushed my skirt up, gapped my legs more, and pushed himself against me.

I broke the kiss and a growl escaped my lips. I pulled him against me as he went to work on the side of my neck. He bit softly at my collarbone and then dropped a kiss in the same spot. It drove me crazy.

I pushed my hands up the back of his shirt and dug my nails into his back. He made a loud hissing noise.

"Yes, that's so fucking hot."

Things were spiraling out of control. He shoved his hands up my skirt and pushed it up until it was around my waist. I leaned back onto the dresser and thrust my hips at him.

"I know what you want, baby," he said roughly as he pulled my top over my head.

He leaned over me and started to suck on the top of my cleavage. It was rough and raw and I should've been appalled, but I liked it.

I grabbed the back of his head and pulled him to me. Digging my fingers in his hair, I tugged a little when I felt him rip my bra down. He covered my nipple with his mouth and my body went into overdrive. I was overly sensitive and any time he pressed his hips against mine or bit down softly on my nipple, a noise I'd never made before came from my lips and I dug my nails into his skin.

The spot between my legs ached and the only time I could make the ache feel better was when I thrust my hips toward him. I didn't even realize I was doing it over and over again until he stuck a finger in the side of my panties and ran it up and down the inside of me.

"You want me here, don't you?"

"Uh-huh," I responded.

I was so wet. I could tell by the slide of his finger. He shifted his hand and his finger pressed against the most sensitive spot on my body. He started that circular motion that I understood now and I began to breathe in little puffs of air.

"Tell me what you want, baby. I'll give you anything you want," he said as he leaned in and sucked my earlobe.

My hips continued to jerk as the buildup I remembered from before started to climb. I knew it was coming and I couldn't think straight, much less talk straight.

He replaced his finger with his thumb and I cried out when he slid a finger inside of me. It was new. It had never felt like that before. It wasn't forced and my body accepted it with moisture. He knew what he was doing. He knew how to make my body work the right away.

"I want you, Patience. God, I've wanted you for so long now."

I was so absorbed in the rhythm of his fingers, the circular motion of this thumb, the in and out of his finger, and when he added a second finger, I laid my head back against the mirror and began to pant harder.

I wanted more. That was all I could think. I needed more and I wanted all of him. I leaned up and began to claw at his belt. He pulled his shirt up and over his head. I was met with tattooed, tan flesh and I took advantage as I leaned up and bit into his chest.

"Fuck yes," he hissed.

And then he tugged on the hair on the back of my head until I was looking up at him and covered my mouth with his. The room started to spin around us and I was so out of it I couldn't get his belt unbuckled.

He took his hands out of my panties and I whined in aggravation. He swatted my hands out of the way and started to unbuckle his belt. I helped him push his jeans and boxers down and then I felt his hard heat against the inside of my leg.

I reached down and palmed him and he jerked in my hand. There was a popping sound as he pulled at my stringy panties and then they gave as he ripped them off. He pulled me closer to the edge of the dresser and then lifted my right knee up and around his hip.

"Oh my God, baby, if you're not sure about this then please stop me now." His eyes were wild.

"I'm sure. I'm so sure. I want you, Zeke."

Pressing my legs open wider, he leaned down and took my mouth again. His tongue invaded my mouth and he pushed himself inside me at the same time. It was one swift, hard movement and then he was buried deep inside me. The dresser banged against the wall as he began to thrust his hips hard and fast. It was the most amazing noise I'd ever heard in my life.

I wrapped my legs around him and leaned back on my palms. I bit into my lip to try and keep the noises at bay, but I couldn't help myself. He felt too good and I couldn't stay quiet.

He delved his hands into my hair and pulled my lips to his. I leaned up and grabbed onto his hips. I held on as he continued to push inside me over and over again. When he broke the kiss, his eyes connected with mine.

"You feel so good, baby. I love being inside you."

With his words, the ache inside my pelvic region began to climb up into my hips and stomach. It was so close. My lips fell open and I started to breathe hard from my mouth.

"That's it. Come for me, baby. I want to see your beautiful face when you come."

And then I did. My body lit up like the Fourth of July and all my pieces shattered and exploded all around me. Where our bodies were connected throbbed all around him as his movements got faster and he started to pound into me harder.

I could hear myself screaming out the release. I called his name several times and then I heard him say my name. I popped open my eyes and met his. His breathing was accelerated and he was moving so fast and hard. It felt amazing.

Then out of nowhere my body exploded again and I screamed out louder than the first time. My toes curled inside my heels and I was sure his lower back was bleeding from my nails digging so deeply into his skin.

The dresser banged loud and fast and then he leaned his head back and called out my name as he exploded inside me. He kept going for a bit until finally he slammed in me one last time and collapsed onto me. His head was in my neck and his loud breathing was right in my ear.

My body hummed with satisfaction as he wrapped his arms around me and kissed the side of my neck.

"That was amazing," I said through my loud breathing.

He leaned back and looked down at me. Reaching up, he cupped my face and ran his thumb across my cheek.

"You're amazing." His eyes burned into mine and his throat worked up and down as he swallowed hard. "I love you, snowflake," he whispered.

His eyes took me in for my response, but I just stared back at him. His words were so meaningful and soft and I felt them heavy in my chest. He said he loved me and I knew Zeke. He was incapable of lying. If he said it, he meant it.

TWENTY-THREE
ZEKE

I KEPT PICTURING MYSELF BEATING the shit out of every guy she talked to with my guitar. I had to be careful with thoughts like that seeing as how I'd actually done it, but seeing her openly flirt with all those assholes at The Pit was driving me nuts. It was no less than I deserved, but it fucking sucked.

No matter how pissed off I was, I couldn't let it take me over. We were sure there was a record executive in the crowd watching us and I wouldn't be the reason our chance was ruined.

I couldn't stop looking at her. For one, I kept an eye on her just in case some asshole took it a little too far and two, I missed her so much and the fact she'd been ignoring me drove me bat-shit crazy. I'd never had a woman refuse me. Go figured the one I gave a shit about would do it.

I stayed on stage playing even though every nerve in my body screamed to go down there and get her. She was dressed like never before. The denim miniskirt she wore was just long enough to cover her ass and the black top barely covered her tits. She looked fucking delicious and all I could think about was getting her alone and tasting every piece of exposed flesh.

By the time our set was over, I had a massive hard-on pressing against my jeans and my blood pressure felt like it was about to burst my eyes. The fact that she occasionally looked up and cut her eyes at me or sucked on her beer bottle like it was a cock let me know she knew what she was doing. Her show was for me, and I'd be sure to let her know what I thought of her show as soon as I could.

At Finn's house, I waited for the opportunity to get her alone and once I did, I learned some very important things. One, angry makeup sex was the best kind. Two, Patience was a freak. She ripped at my skin and growled and I fucking loved it. The sweet, shy girl was replaced by a seductive goddess and that goddess liked it rough.

The most important thing I learned was that she loved me. I had an idea that she cared about me, but I wasn't sure it was love she felt.

Her face when I confessed I was in love with her was priceless. Her eyes lit up in shock and a tiny smiled played at her lips. She was flushed from our wild sex. A tiny sheen of sweet shined on her forehead and above her top lip. She looked amazing and satisfied, but more than anything, she looked happy.

"I love you, too," she whispered.

And just like that I was a taken man. My heart would always belong to Patience and as long as she would have me, I was hers for the taking.

"Come home with me tonight," I said as I caressed her waist with my thumb.

She closed her eyes and took a deep breath.

"If you don't stop doing that, I'm going to want more." She grinned up me.

I chuckled.

"Baby, I'll give you anything you want."

"Anything?" she asked with a raised brow.

"Anything." I leaned in and softly kissed her.

And I would, too. I'd make sure from this point on not to screw up when it came to my snowflake and no matter what, I wanted to make her happy.

We held hands on the way to my apartment and we barely made it to my room before we were at it again. This time it was up against my bedroom door with my pants around my ankles and her skirt around her waist. She was insatiable and wild, and I loved seeing her with so much happy freedom.

The next morning, I woke before her and watched as she slept peacefully in my bed. Her platinum locks were spread across my pillow and occasionally she let out a soft snore. As I looked down at her, I knew I was the happiest I'd ever been in my life. It would never get any better than this.

I ran my fingers through her hair and she moved closer to me with a soft moan. I lay there with my fingers in her curls and contemplated my next move. Once I graduated, I would go to work. Selling drugs had to stop. A drug dealer was no good for Patience and I wanted to be good for her.

The drinking had to slow down too. I was headed on a one-way track to being my father, and I'd have myself admitted somewhere before I became a disgusting alcoholic like him. There were many changes I wanted to make, things that were good for me and things that were good for Patience.

I didn't realize she was awake until I felt her softly kiss my chest. I pushed her hair from her face as she nipped at my nipple ring. I loved having her mouth on me and I hissed out loud when she sucked the ring between her lips.

"You're trying to kill me, woman. Will you at least feed me before you take advantage of me again?" I smirked down at her and ran my finger down the side of her face.

"Feed me he says," she joked. "Didn't you get enough to eat last night?"

I threw my head back and laughed. I'd created a monster, a sexy, soft-skinned monster that was slowly starting to straddle me.

"I'll never get enough of you," I said against her lips as she leaned down and started to kiss me.

Thirty minutes later, Tiny was beating on my wall and telling us to shut the fuck up. Two hours later, we were in my car headed to her house. She had on my clothes and wet hair from the shower. I was sure her screams combined with the bathroom acoustics left a fabulous impression on the people in the apartment next to us.

"Are you sure you don't want me to go in with you?" I asked as I drove her to her house.

She needed clothes and girlie stuff, and while she looked fucking hot in my boxers and T-shirt, she couldn't wear that stuff out.

"Yeah, I'm sure. I'm just going to run in, get some clothes and stuff, check on my mom, and then I'll be right out. Fifteen minutes... tops."

She gave me a sweet peck on the lips before she jumped out of my car and ran up the sidewalk to her front door. She disappeared inside the white mansion and I sat in my car listening to Radiohead and tapping the steering wheel.

I looked down at my radio clock and fifteen minutes later, she still hadn't come out. I didn't think anything of it, but once thirty minutes passed, I got out of my car and walked up to the front door. She'd told me to stay put, but something wasn't right. She would have at least texted me and told me it would was going to be longer.

I knocked at the front door, but no one ever came. My nerves were jumping around inside me and my instincts were telling me something was definitely wrong. I reached out and tried the knob and the door popped open. I guess when you lived in a neighborhood like this one, locking your front door wasn't important.

I walked into the massive space and looked around at all the expensive furnishings. As I continued to walk, I passed a living room and an office. I heard voices nearby so I followed them and found myself in the kitchen.

I saw Patience and her father talking. They didn't know I was there and while most people would have announced themselves, I was seriously thinking of backing out and going to the car. Now that I saw she was fine, I was more worried about the governor getting pissed about me walking into his house without being invited in.

Patience was my girl now, and the last thing I wanted to do was piss off her dad or end up in jail again.

I started to back away, but something odd struck me—the way his hands were touching her. He was too personal. Not the kind of personal a father was to his kids, but the kind of personal a man was to his woman. It made me sick to watch.

She reached up and batted his hand away and his eyes got angry. Then I took a good look at her face and I saw fear there. She was afraid of him and his hands, and just like that, I knew. All the pieces of Patience were clear to me and slowly I collected them.

I thought back to her shyness and the way she freaked out about being touched. I thought back to the guilt I saw on her face when I gave her an orgasm in my car that first time. Her constant need to rush home, the bruises, it all made sense to me now. Then something else hit me and I thought for sure I was going to be sick. Patience wasn't a virgin. I'd been with a virgin before and she definitely hadn't been one, yet before, she would barely let me touch her. There was no way in hell she'd had sex with another person unless it was forced her on. Her dad sexually molested her. It was all so clear to me now and I couldn't even believe I hadn't seen it before. Her father touched her inappropriately. That bastard touched my Patience.

He jerked her up and spun her around over the kitchen table. She kicked and fought back, but never made a sound. He started to pull down her shorts, and just like that I wanted to kill him. He had to die. He deserved to die.

"You got about two seconds to get your fucking hands off of her before I come over there and kill you." My voice echoed in the kitchen.

Both of their heads snapped in my direction and he let her go instantly. There should've been relief in her eyes, but all I saw was her starting to panic even more.

"You sick son of a bitch." I started across the kitchen.

Patience jumped in front of me before I could get to him and I stopped and looked down at her. Her eyes were wide and she placed her hands on my cheeks.

"Everything's fine, Zeke. Come on, let's just go." She talked to me like I was about to jump from a cliff.

"No! Everything's not fucking fine. That bastard's been molesting you, hasn't he?"

I knew I was being loud and I didn't give a shit.

She started shushing me and I looked down at her like she was crazy.

"Don't tell me to be quiet." I was getting even angrier that she was still afraid of him.

She never needed to be afraid again. I'd kill the son of a bitch if he even looked at her the wrong way.

"Don't be scared of him, snowflake. If he even thinks about touching you, I'll kill him." I looked him dead in his eyes when I said it.

"I'm not sure I know what you're talking about, young man." He attempted to deny it. I got even louder and Patience shushed me again.

"Why are you telling me to be quiet? Who gives a shit who knows? He needs to go to jail, Patience. He belongs in jail."

"Zeke, please stop. My mom will hear you." Her eyes filled with tears.

And then another thing became clear to me. She was hiding it because of her mother. Her mom was dying and Patience, being the most selfless person I knew, would rather hold on to the dark secret than let her mother die knowing what was happening to her.

"You need to leave," her dad said sternly.

"No, what I need to do is come over there and beat you to death." My chest pressed up against Patience's tiny palms as I felt myself losing control.

"I have a gun in my desk drawer that says you need to leave," he snapped with angry eyes.

Then I felt myself moving toward him. A threat was a threat and he'd just thrown one down on me. I stood toe to toe with him and I enjoyed the fear that crept into his eyes.

I felt Patience tugging at my arm.

"Please, Zeke, please just go," she said over and over again.

I didn't blink as I stared into his eyes. "I'm not going anywhere without you."

I wasn't. There was no way in hell I was leaving her in that house with that fucker. Especially considering I'd probably just made things worse for her.

"Fine." She was panicking. "Please, just let's go."

And then I was backing away from him as she pressed against my chest with her hands. My eyes never left his face. I'd never wanted to rip the flesh from someone so badly in my life.

I didn't breathe again until we were in my car. I turned to her and she stared back at me with wide eyes.

"You should've told me." I wanted to cry.

The sadness I felt for her combined with the raw anger I felt toward her dad was overwhelming.

"I'm sorry," she whispered.

I pulled her to me and held her in my arms as she started to cry.

"Don't ever apologize to me for anything. If anything, I should apologize. Had I known, I would've handled things differently."

The front of my shirt was getting wet from her tears. I pushed her hair from her damp cheeks and kissed her forehead. I vowed in that moment to take care of her. There was no way in hell I was letting her go back to that house, not until that fucker was under the jailhouse or dead.

I pulled away and looked down at her. "Where's your little sister?"

I hadn't even thought about her little sister until then. She spilled her guts. Right there in the front yard of death and the devil. She told me about the years of being abused, about finding out the governor wasn't her father, and about her fears for Sydney. She explained that she didn't think he'd touch Sydney because she was really his. I didn't buy it. He was obviously a sick man and sick men could give a shit less about who their victim was.

Still, she said she kept a close eye on her sister and only stayed away when her sister did. It was strange finding out these things about Patience, things that made who she was even more understandable. We'd both grown up in fucked-up environments and we'd both saved each other. We were meant to be together, and I'd soothe her hurt the same way she'd soothed mine.

"I understand if you never want to touch me again," she said through tears.

I looked down at her like she was crazy.

"That, you will never have to worry about." Her lips felt soft and moist against mine when I gently kissed her. "Let's get you home." I pulled out of the driveway.

"Home?" she asked.

"Yes, home. No way am I letting you come back here. We're going to go home, figure out what our next step should be, and then we're calling the police."

"I can't, Zeke. It would kill my mother."

"You can't guarantee he'll never touch your little sister, snowflake, and you can't follow her around until she's old enough to move out. You have a life to live too—one that I hope you'll share with me. Do this for her? Please, do this for us."

She looked down at her hands and nodded. I pulled her closer to my side as I drove back to the apartment.

TWENTY-FOUR
PATIENCE

I FINALLY DID IT. I fought back. Mostly because I knew Zeke was waiting in the car for me, but also because I refused to let him touch me again. I refused to let him turn what I'd done with Zeke into something disgusting and perverted. If he touched me, it would take away all the magic from the night before. I was free. Zeke had released me, and there was no way in hell I was letting this man put his hands on me.

I'd made it to my room and packed a duffle bag without seeing my dad. I visited with my mom and told her Zeke and I were together and in love. I did all that without seeing him. It wasn't until I made my way to the front door that he blocked my path and pulled me into the kitchen.

He'd called me every name in the book. He pulled and tugged on my arms and came close to snapping my wrist, but still I fought back with every ounce of strength Zeke had given me. And when he turned me over the table and started to rip at my shorts, I knew I would continue to fight until I couldn't anymore.

When Zeke's voice stopped everything, I knew it was the end of pretending. There was no more hiding it. There was no more keeping it under wraps to protect my mom and sister. Zeke would never go for that. He'd want my dad either dead or in prison, and by the look in his eyes, I was sure he was seconds away from killing him.

It wasn't until we were back at his apartment that I felt the pressure leave my chest. So much had happened in my life and I was nervous it was all about to be revealed for the world to know. I was going to go to the police and I was going to report my dad. I had to. Zeke was right. There was no way of being sure he'd never touch my sister, and maybe it was selfish of me, but now that I was with Zeke, I wanted to live my life. I couldn't do that if I was chained to that house like a mini guard dog for my sister.

The main thing was I wanted to be the one to tell my mother. It felt wrong for her to hear it from some impersonal police officer. I wanted her to know it wasn't her fault. I wanted her to know that I should've said something. She was sick and I never expected her to save me since I never said anything. If my mother was going to die with my secret heavy on her chest, then I at least wanted to help soothe it as much as possible.

She, better than anyone, understood the importance of some secrets. She'd walked around my entire life knowing my father wasn't my father, but that secret couldn't cause bodily harm to another human being—mine could.

So after having a major heart to heart with Zeke and telling him things I never thought I'd say out loud, I lay in his arms with my eyes open until I knew he was asleep. I wanted to speak to my mother before I went to the police station the following day, and I knew there was no way in hell Zeke would let me go back to that place until my dad was firmly behind bars.

I crept out of bed and dressed as quietly as possible. I palmed his keys so they didn't jingle and then I tiptoed through the apartment and out the door. I was scared his loud-ass car would wake everyone when I cranked it, but it was two in the morning and everyone's windows were black.

The drive to my house was a long one. The entire time, knowing what I was on the way to do, my heart was in my throat. It was the middle of the morning so my dad would be asleep and I'd have to wake my mother, but this needed to be done.

I unlocked the front door and closed it softly behind me. The stairs creaked under my feet as I snuck up the stairs. The long hallway that cut across the house felt longer as I made my way to my mother's bedroom door. I passed Sydney's room and a strange noise brought me to a halt. I knew I needed to get in and get out, but I was positive I'd heard a noise come from Syd's room.

I stepped up to her door and slowly pushed it open. The house shrank as I took in the scene in front of me. Dad was on top of Sydney. She wasn't supposed to be home, but she definitely was, and while I'd thought that maybe because she was his real daughter, he wouldn't touch her, I'd never been more wrong.

His heavy frame covered her tiny body. I was faced with his bare back as he held her down. Her long legs ending with pink toenails peeked out from beneath him. I couldn't see his hands, but I knew he was covering her mouth. Her screams were muffled. I remembered the taste of his salty palm against my lips.

I wanted to scream for her, but my vocal chords felt broken and no sound came from my opened mouth. On their own, my legs moved me. I felt myself leaving the room and walking down the hallway. I took the stairs and somehow managed to keep myself from falling down them. I was in shock and my body felt foreign.

The doorknob to my father's office felt cold against my heated palm. I knew where the key to his lockbox was hidden. I could remember going down there many nights and contemplating ending all the pain. I could remember unlocking the lockbox and holding the cold steel against my palm. It felt just the same in my palm now as it did all those many nights ago.

It was like I watched someone else's movements, like a movie on the big screen, as I worked my way out of the office and back up the stairs. I was so far away from everything that nothing I did felt real. The stairs didn't feel real, the hallway floor didn't feel real, and when I stepped back into my sister's room, that definitely didn't feel real. But it was; everything I did was real. Everything I saw was real.

I stood there for a minute as he started to rip at her nightgown. He released her mouth to use both his hands and her soft cries reached my ears. They didn't last long and I got a glimpse of her face and closed eyes as he shifted on top of her. She had passed out from fear. I could remember doing the same when I was young. I remembered waking up with my clothes all skewed and knowing my body was different somehow.

All of a sudden, I was back in control of myself. I felt the weight of the gun in my hand as I lifted my arm and pointed it at his back. Ten years of my life came crashing into me. The memories of his body on top of mine, his intrusion, his smell, and the way he sounded—all of it invaded my mind at once. It gave me all the determination I needed, and in that moment I knew I was going to pull the trigger if it meant keeping Sidney from going through the same.

The force of the gun kicked my hand up. The sound was so loud it blocked out my hearing for a few seconds until all I could hear was the loud constant beep and buzz of my ears ringing.

His body jerked and he turned with wide eyes. Standing, his full naked body faced me and I felt nauseated by his nudity. He reached back and grabbed his back before bringing his bloodied hand around for inspection. I had indeed hit my mark, but now that I had, I wasn't satisfied that he was still walking. If he was still walking, then that meant he could still perform. If he could still perform, then that meant Sydney still wasn't safe. As long as he was breathing I could never be whole and she'd never be safe.

I matched his stare as I once again lifted the gun and aimed for his chest. It would only be the second time I shot a gun in my life and I'd be sure I didn't miss. I squeezed the trigger once more and again my hand jerked up. His body crumpled to the floor in a mass of blood and naked flesh. I looked over at Sydney, who was thankfully still unconscious. There was blood spatter on her pretty face and covering her pink bedding.

My tunneled senses expanded and once again I could take in everything around me. The popping in my ears remained, but now the beating of my heart was added to the sounds around me. The smell of sweat and blood filled my nostrils and the taste of bile filled the back of my throat as I felt myself getting sick. All those things slammed into me all at once and yet I felt so much lighter, as if a thousand-pound weight had been lifted from my chest.

I stepped up closer to his bloodied body and while I knew I should've felt sadness by the fact that I was probably going to spend the rest of my days in prison, all I could think about was how free I was going to be for the rest of my life.

"Snowflake," Zeke whispered from behind me.

I swung around and he put his hands up like he was afraid I was going to shoot him. His eyes were wide as he stared back at me. Soon, Finn and Tiny were standing behind him, looking into the room. The three of them surround me as Zeke slowly reached in and slid the gun from my hand.

"Oh my God, what did you do, Patience?"

Words were stuck in the back of my throat and I had to push them out. My voice sounded like it was a million miles away. "He was hurting Syd."

His eyes looked past me and took in my sister's unconscious body and my dad's dead one. Then his dark eyes crashed into me and a shadowy, sad expression covered his face.

"Finn," he called over his shoulder. His eyes never left mine.

Finn's white face appeared next to Zeke. "Yeah, man?" His voice shook.

"You're my boy, right? You'd do anything I asked you to do, no questions asked?" Zeke asked.

Finn swallowed hard, then shook his head yes. "Yeah, dude, I got you. Whatever we need to do, let's do it and get the fuck out of here."

Zeke reached out and ran his finger down the side of my cheek. His eyes filled with tears as he leaned in and softly kissed me. "Take Patience and leave," he said sternly.

"Zeke, don't do this man. You're going to ruin your life," Finn said with wild eyes.

Zeke shot him a final look and Finn held up his hands and shook his head.

"If this is what you want," he said with finality.

My head whipped back and forth between the two until finally it sank in. Zeke was going to try and take the blame.

"No!" I screamed out when Finn grabbed my arm.

I tried to pull away, but then Tiny was next to me, pulling me as well.

"I'll tell them the truth. I'll tell them I did this. Please, Zeke, don't do this," I called out as I struggled against their tight hold.

They pulled me away from him and my feet dragged across my sister's pink carpeting.

"Who do you think they'll believe?" Zeke asked. "A guy like me from the wrong side of the tracks who's already been to jail? Or you, the governor's daughter who's stupid enough to try and protect her boyfriend from prison?"

I grabbed the doorframe as Finn and Tiny pulled at my body.

"No!" I screamed out once more.

He was right. It didn't matter what I said. If he confessed and told them I was only confessing to save him, the cops would definitely believe him. Again, our backgrounds were biting me in the ass.

My fingers were turning purple as I gripped onto the doorframe. His eyes burned into mine and a single tear fell down his cheek. He sniffed once and wiped it away with the back of the hand that was still holding the gun.

"I love you, snowflake. Always."

Finn pulled one last hard time and my fingers slipped away from the doorframe. I screamed, not caring who heard me as they pulled me down the hallway, then down the stairs.

TWENTY-FIVE

ZEKE

I WOKE UP FROM MY nightmare about Patience being pulled away and into the darkness with her name on my lips. The thick comforter was stuck to my sweaty chest, so I peeled it back and let the cool air rush over my sticky skin. Reaching over for her, I pulled back a pillow.

With wide eyes, I sat up and turned on the lamp next to my bed to see that she wasn't there. Instantly, I felt like something was wrong. I jumped out of bed, wearing just my boxers, and went through the apartment, switching on lights, looking for her. She was gone.

I ran back to my room and threw on some clothes. I searched for my keys, but I couldn't find them anywhere. Then I realized that if she wasn't there, she was in my car. I ran to the window and ripped back my curtain. The streetlights out front shined into my empty parking space.

"Shit!"

I burst into Tiny's room and flipped on his light. He looked up at me like I was crazy, with sleep-filled eyes and wild hair.

"Get up. Get dressed. Shit's going down, dude, and I need you to have my back.

Five minutes later, we were in his car and on the way to Patience's house. There was no doubt in my mind where she'd gone. I could only hope I made it there before she got hurt.

I texted Finn when we left the apartment and he said he wanted to go, too, so since his house was on the way, we stopped to get him. We stuck together, and if the shit was going to hit the fan, I wanted my boys there to at least get Patience out of the way. We pulled up and he jumped in.

It felt like it took forever to get to her house, but soon we were pulling into the driveway. My car was parked up against the garage and then I knew for sure going there had been the right thing.

Finn and Tiny followed behind me. The front door was unlocked and as soon I as stepped through the doorway, I heard a gunshot.

I didn't know where I was going, but I ran toward the sound. The house was so big and I found myself standing in front of a long hallway at the top of the stairs. I stood there waiting to hear something and then another shot rang out. My feet moved before I thought as I ran to the door where the shots were coming from. I heard Finn and Tiny on my heels. We could've been running into our deaths for all we knew, but it didn't matter. All that mattered to me was getting to Patience and helping her.

When I got to the doorway, I looked in and felt instant relief when I saw her standing there facing away from me. Then my eyes took in the scene, her sister lying in bed with her clothes ripped and her father's bloodied body on the floor.

When I saw the look on her face, I knew what I had to do. Her skin was paler than usual, whiter than her hair, and her eyes were wide with shock. I wanted to hold her to me and tell her everything was going to be okay, but I knew we had to move fast.

Words couldn't describe the way it felt to watch her being pulled away from me knowing I could never be with her again, knowing that once I took the blame for this, my life would never be the same. She came into my life and washed away all the bad, and I loved her with every part of my soul. It was the least I could do.

I could hear her screams down the hallway and I waited for someone to show up so they could call the police on me, but she went silent and no one ever came. I stood there looking over the two bodies, one unconscious and one dead, and thought about what my next move should be. I dug into my pocket and pulled out my cell phone. The text messages were still open and I stared down at all the "Where are you?" messages I'd sent to Patience.

I cleared the screen and pulled up the dialer to call someone. I typed in the number nine, but stopped when I heard someone come up behind me. I spun around and came face to face with who I could only assume was Patience's mom.

She gasped for air as she held on tightly to her IV stand. A purple handkerchief covered her balding head. She struggled to stand and I could only imagine what it took for her to get out of bed and come to this room. She stared back at me with fevered eyes and pale skin.

Her watery eyes took in the room. They grazed across Sydney passed out in her bed and then down at her husband's crumpled body. Her shaking hand came up and covered her mouth as she started to cry.

"I'm so sorry," I said into the silent room. "I couldn't let him hurt her." I pointed over to Sydney's body.

"Is she... is she dead?" Her voice was as frail as she looked.

"No, ma'am, she just passed out, I think."

I saw relief run through her body. She took in the room, her husband's naked body, her daughter's ripped clothes, and I saw it in her eyes the moment she realized what was happening.

"How did you know?" she asked.

There was no point in lying to her.

"Patience told me. He's been molesting her since she was a little girl."

I hated that it sounded so cut and dry, but there was really no other way to say it. Her legs buckled like she was going to fall. I moved quickly and caught her. I pulled her over to a white, padded chair that was in front of a desk in the corner and helped her sit.

"How do you know Patience?" she asked with tears on her face.

"She's my girlfriend," I said firmly. "I'm in love with your daughter, ma'am."

A tiny hint of a smile touched her lips.

"You're Zeke?"

"Yes, ma'am." I nodded.

She reached out and patted my cheek softly. Her paper-thin skin felt cold against my cheek.

"She loves you, too." She sighed. "Zeke, do me a favor, son."

"Anything."

It was the least I could do considering she thought I killed her husband.

"Hand me that gun, call 9-1-1, take Sydney with you, and promise me you'll take care of my girls."

My brows pulled down in confusion.

"I'm sorry, I don't follow. Who's to say you won't shoot me if I give you this gun?"

It was a valid question. I didn't know how much of my story she believed. For all she knew I'd broken in and shot and killed her husband and her daughter.

"I've had my suspicions that my husband was a sick man. I should've said something and saved my girls. This is my fault and it's the least I can do." Her shoulders dropped. "I'm dying, Zeke. I have days at the most, and now my husband is dead. If you go to jail for life simply for doing something I failed to do, then who'll care for my girls?"

She smiled sadly at me as she reached down and used what little strength she had to pull the gun from my hand. I knew I should've stopped her, but she was right. Patience needed me. Especially considering her mother was going to die soon.

She used the thick cotton of her robe to wipe the handle of the gun and laid it in her lap.

"Now, be a good boy and do as I said," she rasped.

I nodded and backed away.

I pulled out my phone and called the police. I told them someone had been shot, gave them the address, and then hung up. She smiled up at me and shook her head as if she agreed that what we were doing was right.

I turned away, picked up Sydney's limp body, and then turned to walk out of the room.

"Zeke." She stopped me. "I'm so glad Patience has someone in her life like you. Tell my daughter I'm sorry I didn't protect her and tell her I love her." Tears flowed down her sallow cheeks.

"Yes, ma'am." I adjusted Sydney's body in my grasp and walked away.

I hated leaving her there so sick and frail, but it was what she wanted, and while I would've been more than willing to take the blame for killing that sick son of a bitch, Patience needed me. I'd always be there for her no matter what.

Thankfully, Sydney was out the entire ride back to my apartment. I'd never been formally introduced to her and I didn't want her waking up and showing her ass, thinking I was kidnapping her. Not to mention, she'd gone through something pretty traumatic already.

I wasn't sure what story Patience wanted to tell her, but either way, when she woke up she'd find out her father was dead. Had it been me, I'd be happy the bastard was gone, but she might not take it so well. The girls' lives were going to change from this point on, and I planned on being there to help them through every step of the way.

When I walked through the door, holding Sydney's body, Patience stood from the couch and pushed Finn and Tiny out of her way. They'd been doing a good job guarding her apparently, and she looked pretty pissed about it. She ran to me and pushed Sydney's hair from her face, and then she looked up at me with a look of confusion.

"What happened?" she asked with wide, accusing eyes.

"Here, give her to me. I'll put her in your bed," Tiny said.

I handed Sydney over to him and he turned to take her to my room. Finn nodded his good-bye as he turned and left the apartment.

I reached out to Patience and attempted to pull her into my arms. All I wanted was to be close to her. We'd almost been pulled apart tonight and I wanted to feel her against my body, but she put her palms against my chest and stopped me.

"What happened, Zeke?" she asked again in aggravation.

The sun was beginning to peek through the living room curtains and bathe her face. There were tear stains on her cheeks and her hair was a ratted-up mess, but she was still the most beautiful thing I'd ever seen.

"Your mom, she heard the commotion and came to the room."

Her eyes got large and she started to panic.

"Is she okay? We have to go to her. What did the cops say? Why didn't they arrest you?"

I looked at her with sadness in my eyes. I knew what I was about to tell her was going to upset her, but I just hoped she could see as her mother did.

"She took the blame, snowflake. She asked me to give her the gun, and then she told me to call the police and bring Sydney to you."

She exploded.

"And you let her! You let a dying woman take the blame for killing her husband!"

She pulled away from me and started digging through my pockets for my keys.

"It's what she wanted, baby. I told her I shot him to protect you and she said since your dad was dead and she'd be dying soon, she wanted me to take care of you and your sister."

She wasn't hearing me. She was too busy trying to get my keys. When she finally got them, she ran toward the door. I caught her around the waist and she struggled against my hold.

"Don't do this, Patience. It's what she wanted."

She growled at me and beat me in the chest. I was afraid I was hurting her so I loosened my hold a bit and she took the opportunity to get away. I ran after her and tried again to stop her, but finally she got away and ran to my car. When she locked the driver's door and started to crank the car, I ran around to the passenger's side and jumped in.

I spent the ride to the police station trying to talk her out of whatever it was she was planning on doing, but she wouldn't even look at me, much less talk to me. It was like I wasn't even in the car.

"Baby, please stop the car. I don't want to lose you. Just think about this. Your mom was right and it's what she wanted. I promise I wouldn't have done it had she not asked me. She wanted me to tell you she was happy you had me and that she loved you."

That got a response from her and more tears slipped down her face.

By the time we made it to the police station, the sun was up completely. There were reporters everywhere outside the station, waiting for the news on the governor. Thankfully, none of them noticed Patience. With her head held high, she went into the police station in a heated rush. I was right behind her, begging the entire way to please think things through. Still, she ignored me.

When we got to the counter, a young officer looked down at her with concerned eyes.

"Is there something we can do for you, ma'am?"

I didn't miss the fact that he looked over at me with suspicious eyes. I was sure it looked like she was running from me because I was a danger to her, when all I was trying to do was save her.

"Yes, my mother was brought in for murdering my father, the governor, last night. I'd like to confess and have her released immediately. She's sick and she doesn't belong behind bars."

She was beginning to raise her voice and cops were turning and looking over at us. An older detective came over and ushered us into a small questioning room.

"Where's my mother? I want to see her right now," Patience demanded.

The detective looked at her with sad eyes and I knew right away he was about to give her awful news.

"Ma'am, your mother never made it to the station. When we saw the state she was in, we called in an ambulance to have her taken to the local hospital instead. But she never made it to the hospital. I'm sad to tell you she died in the ambulance."

I reached out and pulled Patience to me as soon as he said those words, but she pulled away from me and slapped me hard across the face. She looked at me like I was an intruder, like I wasn't the man she was in love with, and my heart broke. I understood she was upset and I needed to let her grieve the death of her parents, but still, it hurt like hell.

She turned back to the detective.

"I killed my father! Do you hear me? I killed him. That bastard sexually molested me all my life and I wasn't about to let him do it to my little sister. Arrest me, damn it! Arrest me!" She was crying hysterically.

The detective calmly sat her down in the chair and handed her a tissue.

"Miss Phillips, this is off the record. I'm going to pretend I didn't hear that. It's in the books that your mother killed your father and the case has been closed. If what you say is true, then the bastard deserved to die. Let's not ruin your life because you were protecting yourself and your sister. I can keep a secret if you can."

With luck that I didn't know we had, Patience and I walked out of the police station and weren't sentenced to life in prison, thanks to the detective who decided to turn his head.

He was right. There was no need for Patience to ruin her life over that asshole, especially when the blame had already been set and her mother had already passed.

When we got back to my apartment, I followed behind Patience and shut the front door. For the first time since I'd told her about her mother's confession, she turned and acknowledged me.

Her pale skin blanched and I thought for a minute she was going to be sick. I stepped toward her, and she held her hand out to stop me.

"I'm going to go be with my sister. Stay away from me, Zeke. I can't do this anymore."

The room around me disappeared and for a brief second, it was only us. All the air in my lungs rushed out and I suddenly felt like I was breathing though a tiny coffee straw. Too much. Too many things were going on around us and I just wanted it all to stop. I wanted to be alone with my snowflake and shut out the rest of the world.

She wrung her hands and shook her head. No tears came to her eyes. She showed no expression whatsoever.

"We're over," she said clearly.

She said it as if she wasn't gutting me, like she had no care for me at all. She was a stranger, not the girl I'd come to love so much. The broken girl was smashed, and I watched as the pieces of her flittered away and out of my reach.

She didn't even look me in the eyes, and just like that, Patience had killed twice in less than twenty-four hours. I was sure my heart had stopped and I was positive I was dying as she walked away from me, went into my bedroom, and shut the door behind her.

TWENTY-SIX
PATIENCE

THREE DAYS LATER, MY MOTHER was buried at a private burial. Sydney stood beside me and held my hand as we watched them lower her pretty pink coffin into the ground. I felt numb inside. I couldn't cry even though the tears were choking me. Her death was expected, but I'd hoped she would die warm in bed at home.

As for my father, I ordered that he be cremated and his ashes spread over the Atlantic. He didn't deserve that much, but since the news stations were making a big deal out of everything, I figured it would draw more attention if I didn't do at least that. Had it not been for the reporters, I would've left his ass on ice in the morgue.

They both had life insurance on them, but I couldn't touch it yet and something told me I was going to have a hell of a time with it. Not that the money mattered, but it would help with Syd and she was all I cared about anymore.

My Aunt Sarah in Florida got custody over Sydney and even though I called her and begged her to let Sydney stay with me, she refused and I had to pack my sister up and send her to Florida. It was the hardest thing for me to do. I'd spent years protecting her and there I was, sending her off to live with a virtual stranger.

It was just as well. Rumors about what happened in the governor's mansion were beginning to circulate. Fingers were being pointed and guards were being questioned by reporters. So I promised Sydney once all was settled with our parents' possessions and properties, I'd move to Florida, too, and I would. I wanted to get the hell out of this town and leave everything behind, everything including Zeke.

I couldn't get past that fact that he'd allowed my mother to take the blame for my father's murder. I couldn't let it go that he was the reason she died in the back of an ambulance and that Sydney and I didn't get to say a proper good-bye. I loved him, but I hated him for doing that to me.

He called continuously and texted constantly until finally I had my number changed. I didn't want to hear his voice. I didn't want to talk to him. I just wanted everything to go away. I didn't want to feel anything for anyone anymore, anyone except Sydney.

I was now able to drive the gray Toyota, so I drove over to Megan's to tell her good-bye before I left for Florida.

"I've missed you so much," she said as she hugged me tightly.

I told her the truth about everything. I wasn't worried about her telling people. She agreed that my father deserved what he got, but what she didn't agree with was my decision to leave Zeke.

"He's a mess, Pay. At least he was the last time I saw him. Me and Chet called it quits," she said sadly.

I pulled her into a hug.

"Oh my God, Megan, I'm so sorry. I've been an awful friend, but I've just had so much going on."

I felt horrible for not being there for her, but with everything that happened, I barely had time to think about myself, much less anyone else.

"Girl, please." She swatted at me and rolled her eyes. "With everything you've had going on; the last thing you needed to worry about was my stupid love affairs."

We cried when it was time for me to leave and we promised to stay in touch through phone calls and texts. She even promised to come down to Florida for a week or two during the summer.

An hour later, I was on the road and on my way to my new life. The interstate stretched in front of me and for the first time in days I was able to lose myself in my thoughts. I'd cry for an hour, and then I'd get angry. I experienced a wide range of emotions in the six hours it took me to get from South Carolina to Florida.

By the time I passed the sign for Orlando, I was emotionally and physically exhausted. I was so lost in my thoughts that I didn't even notice the change in scenery. Not that there were many changes; Florida wasn't much different from South Carolina. It was hotter and the houses were flatter, but not much different.

My sister ran into my arms when I got out of my car. I'd never been happier to see her sweet face. My life was wreck and she was the only person I really had left. Somehow she looked older to me, as if the drama from the prior days had changed her all around. I didn't like the transformation in her. I wanted her to stay young and happy for as long as possible, but now there were lines forming in the baby-soft skin under her eyes that told an in-depth story of a life no girl should ever know.

"It's about time you got here, girl!" Aunt Sarah said.

She was tan and barefoot. Her dark hair was braided over her shoulder and cut across the strap of her yellow tank top. Dream catcher earrings sparkled in the sunlight and there was a sun and moon tattoo on her right shoulder. Needless to say, she was nothing like my mother, yet her eyes were an exact match. Her eyes hurt my heart. It was almost like my mother was looking back at me.

Aunt Sarah welcomed me with open arms and a smile that looked rehearsed. I wasn't the innocent nine-year-old I was the last time she saw me, and she could probably see the tension in my face. I'd come so far, brought myself from the brink of hell, and I had been transformed. I wasn't the soft, scared little girl that I'd always been. My father had scarred me, and those scars were forming a hard outer shell I was afraid no one would ever puncture again.

We ate spaghetti for dinner and Aunt Sarah cooked it just like my mom used to. I slurped noodles and secretly cried inside with the memories of my mother when she was vibrant and able to stand in the kitchen and laugh with Syd and me.

"So do you think you'll like Florida?" Aunt Sarah asked around a mouthful of sauce.

She was so laid-back and marched to her own drum. I found her joyful, hippy attitude refreshing.

"Yeah, I think I will," I said as I poked at a meatball. "I promise to get a job as soon as I get settled."

"What about college?" Her brows pulled in.

I looked down and the only response I gave was a tiny shake of my head. There was no need to go into the college discussion since it was the last thing on my mind. College wasn't important; taking care of Sydney and myself was.

"Well, don't you worry yourself about a job right now. Get settled in and once you feel up to it, I know a few places that are hiring." Aunt Sarah smiled over at me and reached across the table to give my hand a squeeze.

The first night in Florida the nightmares started. I woke up in a cold sweat with the fear of my father standing above me. I ripped the covers from my moist skin and tried to go back to sleep. Instead, I rolled onto my side and watched the sun rise.

These nightmares continued from that night on, and I was starting to think I'd never sleep again.

It was exactly a week later that I started missing Zeke like crazy. The dark fog of my mother's death and the drama were beginning to clear and I realized I needed him more than I thought. I missed his voice, his smile, everything about him, and being so far away from him only made it worse.

After dialing his number and not hitting the send button several times, I got up the nerve to call his cell. His number was disconnected. Thoughts of him doing something stupid and sinking into a drunken state and getting himself killed invaded my mind.

I couldn't shake the feeling that something awful had happened to Zeke and I was starting to freak out. What had I done? Yes, I was in the middle of a distraught moment, but I pushed away the only man I'd ever loved, a man who was willing to serve life in prison for me.

In the sudden moment of clarity, what my mother did made sense. I could see it from her point of view. Why let your daughter or the man your daughter loved serve jail time over something that was well deserved? She knew her time was coming to an end and she knew we had long lives ahead of us.

I called Megan in a panic.

"Hey, Pay!" she sang into the phone.

"I'm trying to contact Zeke, but his phone's been disconnected. Do you know how I can reach him? Maybe you could call Chet and get his new number?"

She was silent on the other end and I heard her take a deep breath. Every bad thought I could conjure ran through my mind. What if something happened to him? I couldn't handle losing another person that I loved. I wanted Zeke and I wanted him here in Florida with me.

"Pay, I don't know how to tell you this, but literally the day after you left, the big news was that Blow Hole got picked up by a label out of California."

All the bad thoughts disappeared and happiness filled me for the first time in what felt like ages. Zeke was probably ecstatic and I hated that I wasn't there to celebrate the milestone with him.

I closed my eyes and envisioned the smile I'm sure he had when he heard the news. I loved the way his lip ring would tug on his bottom lip and I adored the tiny dimple on his cheek that peeked out when his smile was big enough. I could almost hear his deep, amused laughter, and if I pushed my mind far enough away, I could almost feel his fingers in my hair.

I popped my eyes open and smiled into the phone.

"That's great, Megan. I bet they're happy. Why would you be afraid to tell me that?"

Again, she was silent on the other end.

"Well, because he's gone, Pay... All of them are. They hauled ass to California."

And just like that, my smile disappeared. The floor shifted beneath my feet. Zeke was thousands of miles away instead of hundreds, and his loss was sinking in and leaving me in a state of distress.

I didn't even remember hanging up with Megan. Zeke was gone, off living his dream, and I'd probably never hear from him again. The only real connection he had in South Carolina was his father and they didn't even talk anymore. I had no way of getting a message to him. He ran away to California, thinking I hated him. He was there surrounded by bleach-blond California bimbos and knowing him, he was probably taking out his heartache and anger on one of them in the form of rough sex at that very moment.

The weeks flew by from that point on. I lived my life in a never-ending state of depression. My sister and aunt commented on my behavior, but I couldn't help it. He was gone and I couldn't find a way to reach him.

I got a shitty job at a restaurant close to my aunt's house and since school was out, Sydney spent most of her time with Aunt Sarah at the beach. Every day was the same—wake up, go to work, come home, sleep. But no matter what I was doing, I thought about Zeke.

Between the depression and not playing sports anymore, I gained five pounds and my jeans started to get snug. I'm sure it had more to do with the ice cream I used to soothe my pain, but at least it was better than drugs and alcohol.

My high school diploma was forwarded to me and again, Aunt Sarah went into her college speech. College was the last thing on my mind and even though I'm sure my mother was rolling over in her grave every time I thought it, I knew in the back of my mind I was never going to attend. I didn't want to think about school or sports. I just wanted to wallow in my crappy life.

The recurring nightmares had started to take their toll on my sleep habits and I was finding that I was sleeping less and less. When it wasn't a nightmare about my mother's death, or the dreaded one that included my father and his disgusting hands, I'd have nightmares that I was surrounded by fire and melting away to nothing.

The sleep deprivation was becoming noticeable every time I looked in the mirror. The dark circles around my eyes were a direct contrast to my light skin and even lighter hair, and the bloodshot look in my eyes reminded me of the girls who used to throw themselves at the boys at The Pit.

"More nightmares?" Aunt Sarah asked when I finally made an appearance in the kitchen.

I pulled open the refrigerator and grabbed a strawberry -banana yogurt. Rifling through the silverware, I found my favorite spoon before collapsing in a kitchen chair.

"How'd you know?" I asked around a mouthful of pink yogurt.

She wiped at the kitchen sink and shook her head. "I heard you scream this morning. I think maybe you should talk to someone. I think it could be good for you, Pay."

She followed up with an apologetic smile that told me she felt sorry for me.

"I don't need a shrink. The last thing I want to do is sit in front of some quack who's probably worse off than me and spill all my deepest, darkest secrets. No thanks. Besides, I think I'm doing great. There's nothing wrong with me. I had a problem, I dealt with it, people died in the process, and here I am in the great Sunshine State with the best aunt alive," I said as I jumped up, threw my yogurt container in the trash, and gave her a tiny peck on the cheek.

It was my way of saying the conversation was over. Did I have nightmares? Yes. But so did the rest of the population. It was normal to dream. I'd been through some crazy stuff, but I'd always dealt with it my way and that's what I'd continue to do.

I grabbed my bag on the way to the door and threw it on my shoulder as I snatched up my keys.

"Patience, I think you need help," Aunt Sarah said in a tiny voice.

She spoke to me as if she were poking a dangerous animal, and it made me wonder if I'd become so aggressive since my world tumbled into chaos that the only family I had left was afraid to talk to me.

I didn't respond as I slipped out the front door and went to my car. Work. Work would make me forget and so work is what I'd do for the rest of the day, even if I had to cover other shifts.

Technically, I didn't have to work. My parents' life insurance was enough to cover everything Syd and I could ever want, but working centered me out, and at this point in my life I needed to feel secure and centered more than anything.

Getting the life insurance had been hell since it was on record that my mom murdered my father. Aunt Sarah hired some of the best lawyers Florida offered and before we knew it, the money was deposited into an account and ready for us to live off of.

The rumors continued to swarm around South Carolina and a few even reached Florida, which made me sick to my stomach. It was a big government cover-up and anybody who was anybody was pointing fingers and making suggestions about how the governor really died.

I wanted more than anything to push that part of my life away and start feeling alive again, but the memories of Zeke wouldn't let me go. His smile, his eyes, everything about him seemed to brand my mind and burn my heart.

Megan kept her promise and called often. Part of me had an inkling that Sydney was putting her up to it. Syd was more worried about me than Aunt Sarah and something told me she was calling Megan and filling her in on the fact that I wasn't doing as great as I'd let on.

To add to the pressure of going to a shrink, I was also being bombarded with soccer scholarships that I tried to hide from Aunt Sarah. I missed playing soccer. Feeling the joy of getting a goal had always been one of my favorite feelings. That is, before Zeke came into my life and showed me that he could make me feel a ton better than that.

"HEY, PATIENCE, DO YOU THINK you could cover my shift this Saturday?" Tarah asked as she wiped up a table that had left a big mess.

She was only a year older than me, but had a two-year-old son at home and he seemed to always get sick.

I didn't even hesitate. "Sure," I said with my signature fake smile.

My little shitty job at the restaurant by my aunt's house was a lifesaver. It was a mind-numbing job that took little to no effort, but it was enough for me.

Months went by and while I was starting to feel more alive, I was still followed around by the black cloud of sadness. It was made worse the day I heard Blow Hole's first song on the radio. The guitar stuck out to me more than Finn's loud voice. Damn, I missed Zeke.

SIX MONTHS LATER, SYDNEY WAS comfortable in seventh grade at her new school and I was working double shifts at the restaurant. I stuck all the extra money into a savings account and pushed through.

I was at work when I overheard some girls at a table talking about a rock festival that was coming to Orlando. One of the girls threw out the names of the different bands that were coming.

I was wiping down a table that had just left without a tip and my hand paused when I heard her say the name Blow Hole. My feet moved before the rest of me as I left the table and rudely interrupted their conversation.

"Excuse me, did you just say Blow Hole was going to be at some rock festival around here?"

The girls looked at me like I was crazy. Maybe I was, but love made you do crazy things and regardless of everything that had happened in the previous months, one thing remained the same. I was in love with Zeke Mitchell.

"Uh, yeah, it's this weekend. The tickets are still for sale I think."

I didn't even listen to the rest. I turned and went for my purse. I told Gladys, the lady who owned the place, that I had a family emergency and then I drove home as quickly as possible so I could get on my aunt's computer.

I Googled rock festivals in Orlando and, sure enough, it was there. I pulled out my wallet and bought a ticket to Orlando Rockfest with plans of hopefully seeing Zeke. For the first time in months, I felt like I had something to look forward to. I felt happy. I just hoped it wasn't too late and I really hoped he wasn't seeing someone new and had forgotten about me.

The rest of the week dragged. The weekend had never seemed so far away. I spent the afternoons after work helping Syd with her homework and when I wasn't helping with homework or working, I'd do housework for Aunt Sarah.

When the weekend finally came, I dug through my closet for anything Rockfest friendly and took extra time getting ready. I hadn't cared about my appearance in months and it was nice to see myself looking somewhat normal again.

Since I was going to Rockfest alone, I waited until later in the afternoon when Blow Hole was planning to take the stage. My fair skin and the Florida sun didn't like each other very much. I'd already suffered several bad burns since I moved there and I had freckles on my shoulders that never existed before. The fear of skin cancer was a very real fear in a heated place like Florida.

When I got to the festival, the band before Blow Hole was still playing. I stopped by a drink stand and grabbed a bottle of water and then pushed my way through the crowd with hopes of getting as close as possible to the stage. I could only hope he'd be able to spot me in the large crowd and I prayed if he did spot me, he wasn't so upset with me that he'd ignore me.

My heart rate sped up when the band said their good-byes and I knew I'd be seeing him at any moment. A DJ from a local radio station loudly introduced Blow Hole, and when Zeke and boys came out on stage, the night sky lit up with lights and the girls went crazy. It was then that noticed all the "I'm a freak for Zeke!" T-shirts the girls wore. I wasn't afraid to admit that I was totally jealous.

He picked up his guitar and hooked the strap around him. He looked different, yet somehow he was the same. There was a tension around his eyes that was never there before. While he'd always had the look of an angry asshole, what I saw on his face was different. It wasn't anger; it was pain. He wore the heated expression of a man who'd had his heart ripped out, and I swallowed hard knowing I'd been the one who did the ripping.

Once they started playing, it was near impossible to get to the stage. Girls swarmed and a mosh pit formed right in the front center. No matter how hard I tried, I couldn't squeeze myself through. My toes were stepped on and some people pushed me back as if I were trying to become a part of the wild crowd. Guys grabbed at me and girls rubbed themselves on me. It was the most annoying thing ever.

Finally, after spending three songs trying to get close to the stage, I gave up. If this was going to be the last time I ever got to see him, then I wanted to actually *see* him. I wanted to see his expressions and I wanted to watch him play. I always loved watching him play and I wanted to take advantage.

The entire time so far I'd spent trying to move closer and I had yet to just stop and look at him. I missed him so much and I had no pictures of him. I was starting to forget what he looked like. There had been times when I would close my eyes and try to see his face, but all I saw was the blurry image of a guy with dark hair, yet no distinguishing features.

I took in his dark jeans and ripped T-shirt. His midnight bangs hung down into his face as usual and the light kept catching his facial piercings and making him shine. He was gorgeous. He was everything I ever wanted and I'd pushed him away and ran from everything he stood for.

I smiled when I saw he was still using the guitar I got him and I smiled even wider when I was able to see a tiny spot on his forearm from far away that I knew was my snowflake. But the longer I stood there, the more I realized that what I was trying to do was impossible. I should've been smart and came earlier. I should've braved the hot Florida sun for Zeke. At least that way I would've been guaranteed a front spot and could've gotten his attention.

Their last song was playing about the time I felt myself start to tear up. I'd failed and it was so hard to see him so close yet so far away. He was right there, yet I couldn't touch him. I wanted to touch him. I wanted him to hold me. I wanted to feel whole again and Zeke was the only person in the world who could make me feel that way.

When their set was over, they said their goodnights and left the stage. Watching him walk away was so hard. Knowing I'd lost my chance was even harder. When I couldn't see him anymore, I turned to leave in hopes of getting out before the swarms of people headed to the parking lot.

The whole thing was a bad idea. If anything, I was leaving feeling worse than I did before, but I had to at least try. Zeke had been responsible for putting me back together and now I was more broken than I was when I first met him. I didn't need him to live, but he sure as hell made me feel alive.

It was pitch black outside once I was far enough away from the show. People sprinkled the parking lot and the smell of burnt rubber filled the air around me as people walked by with joints hanging from their lips. A girl was throwing up next to her car while her friends laughed hysterically. The sounds of her retching made my stomach turn.

I passed by a bunch of buses and the smell of diesel fuel replaced the familiar smells of Finn's garage. The roaring of the buses drowned out the loud groups of people leaving the festival.

As I passed the buses, I thought maybe I could catch him on the way back to his bus, but I didn't know which one was Blow Hole's and everyone else seemed clueless about who was in what bus, too. There were people already lined up around the buses, trying to get a glimpse of their favorite band, so I didn't even bother. I was emotionally exhausted and the thought of going home and crawling in my bed to cry seemed like the perfect thing to do.

I was lost in thought and kicking at the white rocks of the parking lot as I walked to my car. I didn't see the dark shadow of a man as he stepped out in front of me until I was right up on him. I gasped and pulled back, but it was too late. He wrapped a rough hand around my wrist and pulled me into the darkness between two buses. Another hand covered my lips before I could scream and the salty taste of skin filled my mouth. It was so dark I couldn't see anything, but I could feel the warmth of a hard body as it pushed up against me and pressed me up against the back of a bus.

A single finger softly pushed a lock of hair out of my eyes before a hot hand ran down the side of my face and cupped my cheek. Warm, minty breath struck my nose as he moved his face close to mine and nuzzled my chin.

Great, I was being raped by a romantic. Some crazy druggie had singled me out, saw that I was alone, and now he was going to take advantage of me. Life had been hard. Awful things had always happened to me. What else could possibly be added to the top of the shitty Patience pile?

Then I heard a familiar deep chuckle. It vibrated its way down my spine and left my knees weak. Warmth rushed down my skin as a tiny kiss was planted on the side of my neck. Then a whisper of breath echoed against my ear.

"Damn, snowflake, if you get any hotter you'll melt."

Happiness erupted from every pore in my body. I threw my arms around his neck and pressed my body hard against his. I felt the tension that I'd been carrying around for months slowly leave me. I felt like I could breathe for the first time in forever, and when his hand moved away from my mouth and his lips were on mine, I felt whole again.

TWENTY-SEVEN
ZEKE

MY DREAMS WERE COMING TRUE. The guys and I were getting everything we wanted. A damn good record contract was signed with LA Records. The only downside was that we had to move to California. I'd always been a South Carolina boy and the West Coast had always seemed like a million miles away. Maybe getting far away was exactly what I needed.

We were in the middle of recording our first record, and I was able to buy a new car with the advance we got from the label. It should've been the happiest time in my life, but everything felt wrong. I never felt as comfortable in my new shiny mustang as I did in my busted-up El Camino, and somehow I felt like I was disrespecting my memories of Patience by getting rid of my old car.

The thing about having your dreams come true is that it only felt good to enjoy it if the person you loved was there to enjoy it with you. The person I loved was long gone. She'd dropped me like the nothing I was and moved on as if I'd never existed. I'd been in worse predicaments; I'd had my ass handed to me on more occasions than I could count by my dad, but none of that hurt as bad as missing Patience.

Missing her made me delusional. Every woman I passed was blond. Every girl had her signature blue eyes and sometimes when I was in a crowd of females, I was almost positive I could hear her laughter mixed into the group.

Of course, that could've been all the drugs and liquor I'd been consuming since I moved to California. I'd always turned to drugs to numb my pain and usually the shit worked—not so much this time. No matter how much I smoked or how much I drank, the pain of Snowflake's loss never lessened.

On top of missing Patience, I missed home. I missed South Carolina. Mostly because it was hot as hell in the West, but also because when I was home, I could see things that reminded me of her. Nothing in California held a memory, and once I got rid of my El Camino, it was as if she never existed. I fucking hated waking up and looking around at my unfamiliar world.

Leaving the East Coast without being able to say goodbye to my snowflake was by far the hardest thing I'd ever done. I called and texted until I couldn't call and text anymore. The day I found out her phone was disconnected, I went on the warpath and destroyed anything I could get my hands on. I had to buy Tiny a new Xbox and flat screen, and I had to get ten stitches in my knuckles thanks to the hard-ass tile on the bathroom wall.

It was hell. I thought I knew hell all my life, but I was never more wrong.

I searched for her and even asked Megan what the deal was, but nothing. It was as if she'd disappeared off the face of the earth, and I felt like I'd disappeared with her. I didn't want to exist without her. I wanted to crawl into a dark whole and die quietly. But every time I thought about taking the easy way out, I'd think about the fact that she was out there somewhere and one day, no matter if it was years away, she might need me. If that day ever came, I wanted to be there waiting for her. I'd always wait for her.

When I was packing to leave for California, I found her Happy Meal Optimus Prime toy from her birthday, and I cried a little. I wasn't much for crying. To me, crying was for weak assholes, but sometimes something would send me over the edge. A cheap McDonald's toy did the trick that day. After the toy, it was a song on the radio, and after that, it was just the memory of her smile.

Another thing that killed me was my guitar. I used to love my guitar, but every time I played it, I thought about Patience. I could've bought a new one, but I couldn't bring myself to do it. As much as it hurt to play it, it hurt more when I thought about sticking it in a closet.

I couldn't bring myself to regret the choices I'd made for her. The thought of her living in a prison cell for killing that sick son of a bitch made me sick to my stomach every time. I ran the conversation I'd had with her mother before leaving Sydney's room through my head over and over again. What I did was the right thing. Even if Patience couldn't see that, it was the right thing.

Weeks later, my tears had long dried up, but the deep ache in my chest that I carried around left me feeling hollow, even more so than I'd always been. It was as if I'd been allowed a tiny glimpse of real life before I was given the kill shot. I'd always been sort of dead inside, but it was different. This time I was dead and rotting from the inside out.

The first time I heard one of our songs on the radio should've been a beautiful moment, but all I could think about was whether or not Patience would hear it. I was slowly losing my mind and nothing or no one could make it better, no one but her anyway.

"Dude, you played the wrong chord again." Finn complained. "Snap the hell out of it, man."

The guys were constantly complaining since I kept screwing up. It was so unlike me and I couldn't let it continue any longer, so I pushed back all of my memories of Patience and swallowed down my emotions. I delved deep into the music and forgot about everything else.

Months later, I was still pretending. I pretended to be happy, smoked entirely too much green, and drank like a fish. When the guys brought home girls, I flirted and fooled around often, but I could never bring myself to have sex with any of them. I thought for sure stepping into my old self and fooling around with girls would make me feel normal again, but nothing I did helped, and I'd always end up spending the night afterward hating myself and feeling guilty, like I'd cheated or something.

It was a tragedy what Patience had done to me. I was more broken now than I was before she fixed me. I couldn't seem to dredge up any form of emotion. I used to be angry, but now I didn't care enough about anything to get angry. I used to be ready to fuck at the drop of a hat, but the thought of being with anyone but Patience felt all kinds of wrong, and for a brief time in my life I was able to laugh, but now my face was stiff with no expression and it hurt to even think about a smile.

Time went by in a slow and unbearable haze of nothing, and soon I only thought about her every hour versus every minute of every day. When we were invited to Rockfest in Orlando, Florida, I was excited, but more so because I knew by being on the East Coast again, I was also going to be close to Patience.

It was a never-ending cycle of emotions that I was sick of being on. As far as I was concerned, emotions could suck a fat one in hell and hopefully gag. I'd been strung through the wringer all my life and I was fucking tired.

When it was time to go to Orlando, we stepped onto a commercial airplane headed east and I popped a pill and slept through most of the trip. Sleeping was my favorite thing next to drugs. When I wasn't playing, getting high, or partying, I was sleeping.

We switched planes in Texas and I watched as the skyline changed from day to night. A wall of humidity slammed into us when we stepped out of the airport in Florida. By the time we got to the nice-ass hotel by Disney World, I was so fucking tired I could barely keep my eyes open.

We spent the rest of that week getting drunk off our asses and hanging out at all the kickass clubs in Orlando. Four single guys could get into some serious shit around those parts, and I should've been enthralled by all the beach bodies surrounding me, but still there was nothing. I did, however, feel closer to Snowflake, and that was better than I'd felt in a long while.

Women were everywhere trying to get a piece of me, yet I went to bed alone every night while I listened to the guys in their rooms with whatever girl they brought back to the hotel to bag. It was hell and I hated it.

By the time the weekend came and we were setting up for Rockfest, the weather was starting to cool to a nice ninety degrees. I was still hot, but just not hot as fuck. There was a big difference.

The crowds came in swarms and we were set to play later in the day. I hung out with other bands behind the stage setup and smoked way too much weed. A few times I'd peek out into the crowd in hopes that I'd feel some kind of excitement about playing. Music didn't do it for me the way it used to, and a few times I'd even contemplated leaving the band. If it weren't for the fact that the boys were more like brothers to me, I probably would have.

Once it was time for us to go up, the crowd had doubled. More than half the people were drunk and burnt from being out all day in the Florida sun. Women were on men's shoulders with their tops off and the smell of weed circulated around the crowd.

People jumped up and down with our music while Finn dominated the crowd. Girls with T-shirts that said, "I'm a freak for Zeke!" jumped around without bras on in the front row. I nodded down at them to let them know I hadn't missed them, and they smiled and blew kisses up at me.

I looked at women so differently. They weren't ass waiting to be bagged anymore; they were human beings. I had Snowflake to thank for that, or to hate for that—I hadn't decided yet.

All in all, it was a good show. We played our hearts out and the music sounded better to me than it had in a while. Not once did I play the wrong chord or stop playing altogether to drink my beer, and I could tell the guys were happy that things were going so well.

The sky was turning black as night set in and the area became even cooler. Our music vibrated the star-filled sky and sound waves from the crowd pumped us up. Toward the end of our set, Finn jumped out into the crowd and surfed until they threw him back on the stage. Everything felt normal for just a bit, but when we played our last song, sadness settled over me because I knew we'd be leaving the East Coast in a few days and I'd once again be thousands of miles away from Patience.

I scanned the crowd once more as I played my final solo for the night, and I was caught off guard by a flash of platinum hair. One minute it was there and the next it was gone. I was positive I was seeing things when suddenly the crowd cleared once again and my eyes collided with Patience.

After months of feeling like I was suffocating, I felt like I was able to breathe again when I saw her looking up at me from the crowd below. She looked as lost as I felt, as dead as I was, and I wanted to jump down into the mosh pit and kill anyone who stopped me from getting to her.

My insides were waking up and I felt more clearheaded than I had in months. The liquor and drugs that I'd taken before going on stage were burned off by the adrenaline rush that occurred when I saw her face. The air felt lighter and the breeze that I hadn't felt earlier touched my skin, cooling me from the head down.

She stared back at me with an aggravated look on her face. She looked different, thicker in some places and tanner, but she was just as beautiful as the last time I saw her. The crowd around her seemed to disappear and all I could see was her standing there alone as if she were a mirage for a dying man. That's what I'd been since she left me, a dying man, and until she was mine again, I'd never be alive.

I continued to play as I watched her struggle to get to the front, and then finally she gave up and stared at me. From so far away I couldn't see her eyes, just as I'm sure she couldn't see mine, but my heart felt her presence and it took everything I had in me to stay put on that stage.

I lost her in the crowd and wasn't able to locate her blond hair again. I frantically searched the crowd and once we were off the stage, I attempted to go through and try to find her, but I could barely move it was so packed, and I kept getting stopped by drunk girls who kept trying to rub their tits on me.

We followed the crowd to the buses and I was on the verge of losing it. She was so close. She was there and I couldn't see her or get to her. I pushed at random people and got looks of horror as people thought I'd lost my mind, but there were too many and I couldn't get through. I was almost on the bus when I saw her cutting a path through the parking lot. Darkness covered the lot, yet the stars still seemed to glisten in her platinum locks.

She was alone. What was she thinking walking around a dark parking lot alone? Hadn't she been through enough? Seeing her there, walking as if she were untouchable, pissed me off. I was angry that she'd put herself in danger that way and I wanted to shake her and hug her at the same time.

I put my head down and slipped through the crowd. Hiding in the darkness between our bus and the one in front of it, I waited until she walked by. The sounds of whistles and loud music filled the parking lot. The smells of diesel fuel and beer filled my nostrils and somehow reminded me of The Pit and home.

I didn't have to wait long, and once I saw her walk past, my soul sang with joy. I didn't think twice as I reached out and pulled her to me. Her body stiffened in my grasp and I knew I'd scared her. The last thing I needed was her screaming and calling attention to us, so I covered her mouth with my palm.

I could hardly believe she was here in my arms. Her soft baby-powder scent made me forget all about the other smells that surrounded me. I pressed my body to hers and it was like stepping into heaven, and I was touched by warmth a sinner like myself had no right to feel. She had always been my heaven, a light that the darkness in my soul should never be able to see, but there she was, in my arms, filling me with an unimaginable sense of right.

Years of shadows and darkness were erased in that very moment. I held my source of freedom in my arms and the weight that had settled on my chest months before was gone in an instant.

I vowed that no matter what happened over the last months, she'd never leave my arms again. Nothing in the past mattered. All the bad that had occurred in our lives was struck from the record and prepared to be long forgotten. As long as she would have me, and even if she decided she'd never want me, I'd be hers.

Her breath was heavy as she struggled against me, and part of me didn't want to let her loose. Her body fit to mine as if I were a memory, a habit that she'd forgotten but could pick back up as if I were branded in her brain. I was a bad habit, the worst kind of habit, but I was too far gone. My addictive personality had inhaled Patience and I'd never become immune to her high.

It felt too good to be so close. After I released her, the few seconds that followed were golden as she wrapped her arms around my neck and kissed me back. And when she pulled away and whispered that she loved me, all the tiny scars inside me blended together and dissolved leaving pure happiness that only my snowflake could invoke.

EPILOGUE

THE LOCAL DJ INTERVIEWING BLOW *Hole looked a little like Santa Claus. Except instead of a red suit, he wore black leather, and instead of a jolly hat, a blue bandana covered his gray curls.*

"So, Zeke, we get a lot of questions in about some of your tattoos. I was wondering if you could tell us what the three snowflakes on your forearm represent."

Zeke's lip ring pulled when his smile widened. It was strange to see him smile so openly in front of people. He looked over at me and winked as he lifted his arm onto the counter in front of him to show the DJ his tats.

"The big one here is for my girl. When we first started dating, she reminded me of a snowflake princess, so I started calling her snowflake. I still call her that now. The two smaller ones are for our two daughters. They're just as blond and beautiful as she is."

"Snowflake, huh?" the DJ asked. "It's a wonder she doesn't melt in this California heat." He laughed.

Zeke's eyes met mine from across the room and the love that lived there sparkled. The side of his mouth tilted in the secret smile he reserved just for me.

"Well, we went through the depths of hell to be together. If she hasn't melted yet, I don't think she ever will."

KEEP READING FOR A SNEAK PEEK OF...

PERFECTING PATIENCE

BLOW HOLE BOYS, BOOK 1.5

&

FOR A LOOK AT...

FINDING FAITH

BLOW HOLE BOYS, BOOK 2

PERFECTING PATIENCE

BLOW HOLE BOYS, BOOK 1.5

I BACKED AWAY FROM HIS mouth, expecting to continue to watch him sleep, but he followed me up with his eyes still closed and started to kiss me. Again, he moaned when I allowed him access and he slipped his tongue into my mouth. Flipping me onto my back, his naked body covered mine. His hand worked its way up my side and brushed against my breast before he rested it against the side of my neck. His fingers dug into the hair on the back of my neck as he invaded my mouth with Zeke sweetness.

Pulling away, he gazed down at me with sleepy eyes.

"You woke us up," he said with a lazy grin.

I wrapped my arms around his neck. "Us?"

Looking down between our bodies, he looked back up at me with a smile as he pressed his hips into mine. I couldn't miss the hard heat that pushed into my thigh.

“Yes, us. I’m okay in the morning, but the prick down-stairs will take a jab at you if you wake him up.

FINDING FAITH

BLOW HOLE BOYS, BOOK 2
FINN'S STORY

A LITTLE FAITH CAN GET you through...

One night. That's all Finn had with the only girl he ever loved. Years later, all he has left of that night is a silver cross, a broken give a damn, and the unrelenting desire to drink her memory away. As the lead singer of Blow Hole, Finn has his pick of women, but none are able to squash the need he still carries around for Faith. To hate her offers some relief, but when Finn sees her again after so many years, it's hard to despise her. Especially when every reason he had to hate her, turn out to be lies.

As the daughter of a strict Baptist preacher, Faith Warren lived sheltered from all things sinful. When she met Jimmy Finn, the epitome of all seven deadly sins, she found out exactly what she was missing. After being forced to choose between her soul and the only person in the world who made her feel alive, Faith walked away from Finn and dove head first into her father's preferred life. But now Finn's back and he's getting payback by wreaking havoc on her emotions. Except sometimes bad things feel good, and Faith has to decide once again if she wants to stay in her gilded cage or fly free with the dark angel of lust himself.

"SNOWFLAKES IN HELL"

BY BLOW HOLE

Lost in the dark, I stopped fighting it.
This is my world; this is my home.
Loss of air, wishing to forget,
It breaks me down, crushing bone.
There's no breeze; there's no sun,
Just this need to escape.
There's no end to what I've begun.
Too far gone, it's too late.
I'll drag you down, hold your breath.
With me, you're going under.
Escape my desired death.
Save yourself from dangerous hunger.

Chorus:

Can you see the broken parts of me?
They breed in my dark place, then leave without a trace.
There's a hole within my shadowed soul.
It's on your fingertips and dances on your lips.
In my depths, I already know.
I should never feel your glow.
A selfish thing to tell.
I want snowflakes in my hell.

I'll scar your perfect skin,
With black traces of my need,
Engulf you fully with my sin,
Make you wish that you were freed.
Dreams become nightmares,

Fueled by jealous rage,
Rocked by my careless cares,
Beg release from my black cage.
Dig deep inside your center,
Rot you from within.
A game without a winner,
No beginning gives no end.

Chorus:

Can you see the broken parts of me?
They breed in my dark place, then leave without a trace.
There's a hole within my shadowed soul.
It's on your fingertips and dances on your lips.
In my depths, I already know.
I should never feel your glow.
A selfish thing to tell,
I want snowflakes in my hell.

ACKNOWLEDGEMENTS

This is my third book, and still I have a hard time writing the acknowledgements. It's hard to thank the massive amount of people who have helped me when it comes to my writing. I have so many supportive people in my life and for that I am truly blessed.

First of all, I'd like to thank my girls—Melissa Andrea, Mary Smith, Jodie O'Brien, Amy Holmes McClung, Julia Hendrix, Kathryn Vanessa Spell Grimes, Shanora Williams, and Bree Foster High. All of you read *Playing Patience* before anyone else had their hands on it and I value your opinions so much. You girls and many others that I've met throughout this entire experience have become like sisters to me and I adore you all.

To Regina Wamba, my lovely cover designer and dear friend, you're amazing. There isn't much more I can write here that everyone doesn't already know, but I just want to say thank you for everything. I'm grateful to have met such an amazing woman and talented artist.

To my dear sweet editor, Cassie McCown, thank you for picking through my work and making it better. I look forward to working with you again in the future. I'm glad to say I have found an editor I trust—one that I can also call a friend. Thank you.

To my family, I love you. You look past the piles of laundry that need to be done and you rarely complain about the quick meals that replace the home cooking you're used to. I'm Mommy and Wife before anything else, but when I step into my office and I lose myself in my writing, you guys are still there waiting for me with a smile and hug and when I come out.

Matthew, I love you more than I could ever put into words, and words are kind of my thing. Ashlynn, my beautiful daughter, you're my breath, the reason I do anything. I can only pray that I make you two proud. <3

To my readers, YOU ROCK! Thank you for all of your kind words. I love you all!

PLEASE FEEL FREE TO CONTACT TABATHA AT THE FOLLOWING AVENUES.

WWW.FACEBOOK.COM/TABATHADVARGO

WWW.TWITTER.COM/TABATHAVARGO

WWW.TABATHAVARGO.BLOGSPOT.COM

THOUSANDS OF CHILDREN DEAL WITH ABUSIVE ENVIRONMENTS EVERY DAY. FOR MORE INFORMATION REGARDING SEXUAL MOLESTATION/CHILD ABUSE PLEASE VISIT THE AMERICAN HUMANE ASSOCIATION.

CPSIA information can be obtained
at www.ICGtesting.com
Printed in the USA
LVHW02s1951230118
563696LV00006B/1181/P